PROMISES TO KEEP

Claire Yezbak Fadden

ISBN: 978-0-9988645-6-3

Publisher: Brightwood Books

Disclaimer
This story is a work of fiction. Names, characters, and
incidents are either products of the author's imagination or
are used fictitiously. Any resemblance to actual events,
locales, organizations or persons, living or dead, is entirely
coincidental.

Dedication

Always for Nick. Shawn, Jake, Seth, Lisa, Rachel, Windley and Grace, my first and best fans.

Acknowledgments

My deepest appreciation goes to my critique partner Sharon C. Cooper.

A clink of a wine glass to my early readers Cathy Escobedo, Carol Schoenherr and Kim Yezbak. Your support, insight and not-always gentle nudges are irreplaceable to me.

Lastly, this novel is a work of fiction. Any errors, mistakes or missteps are solely my own.

Dear Reader,

In this second story from my *Begin Again* series, you'll meet Kate Wiley, the youngest of the Jameson sisters' trio. Being the baby of the family prepared Kate to overcome the desertion of her husband, mere days after their first child is born.

As the youngest member of my family, I relate to Kate's ability to reach beyond her years to make sense of the disasters befalling her. Ultimately, she relies on family, friends and prayer to unravel an endless mystery of deceit, lies and deadly consequences.

I hope you enjoyed Kate's story enough to want to meet her big sisters Julie Rafferty and Monica Morgan, each with her own unique story of inner strength, family bonds and deep faith.

Email me at claire@clairefadden.com for book discussion questions, to share your thoughts about Kate or just to say hi.

Happy reading!

Claire

Prologue

With one hand gripping his gun and the other adjusting his earpiece, Eric lingered, waiting for the team leader's signal. His partner, Trish, crouched on the other side of the hallway alongside local mercenaries, ready to take down their target—Anmar X.

The dangerous gunrunner was Eric's sole reason for leaving his pregnant wife two weeks before her due date. As a CIA special agent, he had made it his life's mission to ensure the man's demise, and he wouldn't rest until Anmar was wiped from the face of the earth.

His heart pounded triple time as he surveyed the dimly lit Mexican flophouse, verifying that entry points were secured. He hoped the informant got it right, but as he looked around this fleabag in the middle of Sonora, his doubts mounted.

According to their senior ops officer Ralph, several reliable sources pinpointed this aging hotel as a key depot for shipping arms from Mexico to the Middle East. Their snitch also reported that the operation was scheduled for shutdown soon, forcing the team to assemble quickly. A clandestine raid like this one couldn't employ US soldiers. So, Eric and his team were off the agency's radar.

Come on, come on. Let's do this.

Eric's patience was running thin as they stood at the ready.

His nose curled at the scent of last night's fast food and years of spilt cervezas wafting through the walls and up from the threadbare carpet. He enjoyed ice-cold Mexican beer as much as the next guy, but this pungent odor would have him ordering domestic beer once he returned home to Arizona. Nothing about this place matched Anmar X's modus operandi.

Eric stiffened. He gripped his gun tighter when Ralph spoke through the earpiece, telling them to get ready.

"Go! Go! Go!" Ralph's order vibrated in his ear.

Eric kicked, landing his foot solidly against the hollow-core door. Shards of wood flew as the barrier exploded off its hinges. His breath came in short spurts as the eight freelance military men entered behind him and Trish. Fanning out, they rushed into every room in the dilapidated space searching for weapons and more importantly, Anmar X.

"Clear!"

"Clear!"

Several team members yelled out seconds later.

"Nothing here, sir," a bearded soldier reported to Ralph the moment he entered the now-crowded space.

Eric clenched his teeth as anger and frustration clawed through his body while he holstered his gun. Unable to stop himself, he fisted his hand and punched the wall. "What a damn waste of time! *Again*."

"Stop your bellyaching and find something we can use," Ralph snapped.

With gloved hands, Eric and the others dug deeper, pulling open drawers, searching behind furniture, and throwing back blankets in search of anything that could give them clues on Anmar X's whereabouts. He was sick of riding this adrenaline roller coaster that sent spurts of hope to his brain only to ruthlessly yank them away.

I left my pregnant wife for another empty mission?

Eric hadn't wanted to leave Kate. He *never* wanted to leave her, but sometimes his undercover work required it, especially lately.

"We got the intel too late," Trish said, going through similar gyrations searching the bathroom. "They had time to clear out. How does that keep happening?"

"Beats the crap out of me," Eric grumbled, ignoring Ralph's excuses for why they didn't find a single clue as he droned on about spotty intel. Eric impatiently waited to hear one name–Anmar X.

After a series of unsuccessful careers, Eric had joined the CIA to track down this mastermind of death and destruction who, twenty years ago, irreparably ripped his life apart, taking from him everything he held dear. And if it was the last thing Eric did, he would hunt this guy down and make him pay.

Chapter One

Nine-month-pregnant Kate Wiley grunted and shifted her girth to avoid getting her belly bumped. Along with pressing deadlines at work and preparing for the birth of her first child, the third trimester offered little more than erratic, uncomfortable sleep, puffy feet and clothes that cinched where they shouldn't. The last thing she needed today was an urgent request from her boss to explain their architectural firm's sustainable design philosophy to a potential client.

Still, Kate wove her way through a sea of guests milling around the lobby of the Palm Coast Resort and Spa, past the elaborate floral displays and fountains, searching for the property manager.

She avoided bellhops as they crisscrossed the expansive entrance, pushing trolleys full of luggage while business folk chattered away. Must be some sort of convention in town, she thought, still unable to locate her contact. Instead, she spotted her husband, Eric, near the atrium.

Surprised and a bit mystified, Kate responded to his casual wave with one of her own. She shuffled toward him, taking in the refreshing scent of plumeria and sweet coconut filling the air. "Why didn't you call?" she asked, accepting his deep embrace. "I thought you were still in Mexico, buying sheets and towels."

"I got done early and hurried back. You look amazing." Eric cupped her face between his large hands and placed a lingering kiss against her lips. "I've missed you."

"I've missed you, too," she mumbled against his mouth and leaned into him, allowing his strength to course through her as though tapping into a replenishing elixir. The past week without him ground by slowly and she worried he wouldn't return home from his most recent buying trip in time for the birth of their child.

"Why don't you sit down," he suggested, directing her to a cushioned bench facing the koi pond.

"I can't. I'm supposed to be meeting a client... Wait. Why are you here?"

"Like I said, I missed you."

"And you guessed I'd be at the Palm Coast? I don't think so." Kate eyed him curiously, a smile tugging at her lips as excitement coursed through her veins. She was so glad to see him and knowing her husband was up to something sweet only added to her elation. "Okay, what did Harry tell you, and why are you really here?"

"Let's sit down." Eric pointed toward the bench again. "Your feet are swollen. The doctor said to watch out for that."

Kate took a seat. "I'm fine. Really, I am. Seems like every part of me is expanding, though." She patted her stomach before turning her gaze toward the ground. The tops of her feet puffed like small soufflés against the sides of her sensible pumps. She tugged off the right shoe and massaged her foot. "Thank goodness I won't have to wear these shoes again until after the baby's born."

"Today is your last day at work, right?" Eric said.

"Well, yes," Kate answered. About an hour ago, she finished final blueprints for a downtown Phoenix office complex and handed them to her new assistant, Mandy. Minutes later, Harry Mack, the architecture firm's managing partner, had summoned her into his office, insisting she call a taxi and meet a client within the hour. Confused and curious, she gathered her purse and headed to the Palm Coast. On the ride over, all she could think about was finishing the nursery in the next two weeks in hopes that baby Benjamin didn't come early.

"It's supposed to be my last day of work. So, I'm not sure why Harry insisted I come—"

Eric cut off the rest of her words with a sweet kiss on her lips. "It's also the first day of our babymoon."

"Our what?"

"I got us a suite for the weekend. We can relax, get that couples' massage you've always talked about us doing. Don't worry, I asked if they have maternity therapists and they do."

"How did you know I'd be here? I wasn't sure, myself. Only Mandy kept after me to…"

Eric grinned.

"You got Mandy *and* Harry into the act? I wondered why they pushed so hard to get everyone to sign off on the project by today. I don't have any clothes. I can't stay. I have a lot to do at home to get ready—"

"Not for the next four days, you don't. Monica and your nephews are at the house now, painting the nursery. I think she called it waterfall blue. I packed you a bag and if I missed anything, we'll buy it. Everything is taken care of." Eric kissed her hand.

"I… I don't believe—"

"That I'd plan our last vacation before we become parents. Well, believe it. I love you, Katherine Anne Jameson Wiley, mother of my son. And I always will."

A smile mixed with tenderness and appreciation teetered on Kate's lips. "I'm in love with you, Eric Simon Wiley, father of my son. And I always will be."

He dangled a key card. "Shall we?"

"We certainly shall." Kate removed her other shoe, and gave them both to Eric before extending her hand. "Yes, sir. We certainly shall," she agreed as they strolled toward the elevators.

***

Eric Wiley savored the beauty of his wife. Unfettered joy washed over him as he reflected on the serenity of the past three days. Growing up as an only child, he had been adopted in his teens by his deceased parents' friends. He craved the family ties many of his friends took for granted. Meeting and marrying Kate changed that desire into reality. Soon he would be a father and the life he wished for would truly begin.

He and Kate propped against two pillows, laid on the king-sized bed cherishing the last day of their getaway. From the panoramic tenth-floor view through floor-to-ceiling windows, they reveled in the majesty of Camelback Mountain and the valley expanding below. The hues of sunset barely visible, their babymoon was drawing to a close.

Eric bathed in the deep relaxation blanketing his body, a welcome peace leftover from their fifty-minute couples' massage ending an hour earlier. He'd only thought about the botched mission once during their stay at the hotel. One of these days, Anmar X wouldn't dominate so much of his thoughts.

"I didn't realize I had a cluster of knots in my neck," Kate said, rolling her head from side to side. "Sonia was amazing. Maybe a bit too amazing. I might need this kind of massage, weekly, for the rest of my life."

"That can be arranged. My masseuse was terrific, too. What was her name?"

"Celeste. How come you *never* remember anyone's name?" Kate chided.

"That's why I married you, beautiful, to remember names for me. And for a few other important qualities you possess. Don't know why I hadn't had a rubdown before. You introduce me to new worlds every day."

Kate rolled toward him, the sparkle in her eye–the one Eric knew he couldn't live without–sent spears of excitement through her heart. "Not a rubdown, babe," she corrected. "You got a deep-tissue massage. Stick with me. I'll take you places you've never dreamed of after I deliver this beach ball.

I look like a sack of oranges with the biggest ones collecting in the middle."

To Eric, she had never looked more ravishing. On the cusp of motherhood, her sexy, playful smile and the devilish twinkle in her deep hazel eyes enticed him beyond control. He placed his hand on her stomach and kissed her cheek.

"Your oranges are distributed perfectly, Mrs. Wiley." Eric's gaze traveled to her ample breasts. "I don't think I could handle any more perfection."

"Easy for you to joke. Your stomach hasn't been rearranged to accommodate the prize-winner from the pumpkin patch."

"True, but I'm still a fan of the arrangement."

"Ohh. Ohh." She rolled back and sighed. "Give me your hand," she ordered. "Here's one of those oranges I told you about."

Eric placed his hand on the side of Kate's stomach to feel the baby's movements. The thrill of what might be a tiny heel kicked against his palm, once again sending shivers down his spine. "He's definitely a mover."

"Boy, I'll say. If he's this busy now, I can only imagine what's in store once he breaks out." Kate worried about raising a child, but Eric had no doubts about her abilities. The woman had faced down much tougher obstacles. Motherhood suited her the way sunshine suited blossoming roses. She would be amazing.

Eric licked his lips, stalling for time. How could he tell her he might be leaving as soon as tomorrow? He hoped this latest sting operation would happen after the baby's birth, but hours ago he received a text from Trish. Their unit had been put on alert. He could be summoned to Mexico at any minute. Another chance to capture Anmar X.

Two facts were certain: He had to go, and Kate would blow a fuse.

Chapter Two

Kate placed the purplish-green stuffed dragon on the shelf next to the crib and stepped back to admire the nursery. With its pale blue walls, white-trimmed windows and storybook characters, the bright space appeared ready to welcome a newborn. And she couldn't wait.

"You did a great job painting," she said, turning to her sister, Monica. "Everything is exactly the way I hoped it would be."

"Well, Brady, Brian and Burke did most of the work. I kept them from painting each other."

Kate laughed at the image of her nephews chasing each other with brushes. "Glad I missed that. And how did you keep Eric's secret?"

"It wasn't easy. You are the suspicious type, but your husband was determined to have a surprise getaway with you, no matter what."

"That's true," Eric said, walking into the room. "And your fixation on redoing the nursery wasn't going to derail my plans."

Kate smiled, recalling the relaxation of the past few days. Just what every expectant mother needed.

Eric put his arm around her. "I'm curious. We have a cradle in our bedroom. When does the baby start sleeping in here?"

"Afraid Benjamin's crying will cut into your sleep?" Kate teased.

"Hey, it's a valid question."

"Don't worry," Monica replied. "Once the baby starts skipping those middle-of-the-night feedings, you can put him to bed in here. For my guys, that happened around four or five months. Seems like a long time, but it passes quickly."

Kate gulped. It would be months before the baby would sleep in his own room. Still, the warm nature and simple décor of the nursery comforted her.

Eric looked around the space. "Sure looks different than my bachelor days."

"Everyone has to make sacrifices," Kate said, pleased that Eric had surrendered his workout room. At Kate's urging and without much complaining, he donated the weight bench and most of the equipment to charity. What items were left got dumped in the guest-room closet down the hall, along with the stuff he relocated when Kate moved in a few months before their wedding. She had loved her condo, but Eric convinced her that this house with a backyard would better suit their future needs.

From the street view, the three-bedroom home looked larger than it appeared. Kate always seemed to be hunting for storage and stacking items in space-saving positions. There was no chance of parking either of their cars in the garage, now converted into a temporary storage unit and makeshift design center, with her drafting table shoved against the window. It was only a matter of time before they would begin hunting for a larger home.

They had been married nearly three years, spending the past two trying to start a family. A smile stretched across her lips thinking of their frequent baby-making sessions in practically every room in the house. She rubbed her belly, a warmth washing through her body, recalling the tender way

Eric had held her after each time until she fell asleep. For now, this home would be the site of their happily-ever-after. She was ready to begin.

"Mommy let me pick the dragon," six-year-old Bodie boasted, interrupting Kate's thoughts.

She turned to her nephew. "He's fierce looking. Your baby cousin will love playing with it."

"How can he reach it way up there?" Bodie asked.

"The baby won't be big enough to play with you or the dragon for a long time," Eric answered. "Do you understand?"

"I guess." Bodie turned to Kate, still unconvinced and pointed to her stomach. "When is he coming out?"

Kate's hands instinctively cradled underneath her protruding belly, now resembling a ripe watermelon about to burst. "Soon, I hope, and I know the two of you will be the best of friends."

"Enjoy these last few weeks, when you know exactly where your child is," Monica added. "The days fly by and you'll be like me, running from soccer games to guitar lessons without a moment to spare. Like right now. I need to pick Bella up from dance class."

Kate knew Monica was right. New pressures and stresses would soon close in from all sides. Still, she couldn't wait to be a mother; to cradle her son and tell him how much she already loved him.

"Thank you for your help in getting the nursery ready. Guess I thought once it was done, the baby would show up." She giggled. "You always said I'm impatient. It's really hard to be patient now."

"Waiting for what you want can be the hardest thing," Eric said.

Kate knew truer words had never been spoken. It had taken a long time to find Eric and what seemed even longer to bring a child into the world.

Chapter Three

"It's a boy!"

Kate heard Dr. Smith's voice, but her gaze locked onto Eric's deep brown eyes, brimming with a newly discovered pride.

"A beautiful boy, Katie. We have a handsome, healthy son." Eric kissed her hand. He had stayed in the labor and delivery room, constantly by her side during the eight-hour labor, always near when she needed him the most. And now they had a son. Benjamin Simon Wiley, named after Eric's dad, not Stuart, her deadbeat father.

"He's healthy? All his fingers and toes?" Kate asked, mustering what little strength still pulsed through her veins.

"See for yourself." Dr. Smith placed the infant on Kate's belly. Her hand immediately rested protectively on the boy's back, so small and fragile. *A son. My son.* With her other hand, she stroked his head, sparse with shocks of black hair like his father. Kate had read everything she could about the importance of skin-to-skin contact. She knew this technique kept her infant warm, beginning their lifelong bond.

A nurse covered the tiny body with a warm blanket and secured a knit cap on his head. After waiting a few minutes to allow extra blood flow from the placenta to the baby, Dr.

Smith clamped the umbilical cord in two places and showed Eric where to cut.

"What are you doing now?" Kate asked, relieved at her choice of birthing rooms. She and Eric wouldn't have to be relocated to another room for recovery.

Dr. Smith moved to where his nurse stood. "Just checking the baby's blood type."

At thirty-two, Kate questioned her ability to be a good mother. Eric, only two years older, seemed to have segued into his paternal role seamlessly, not displaying the insecurity and trepidation that permeated her. She stared at her son's angelic face, smiling as he wriggled in her arms.

Then she glanced at her husband. Eric was as stable and strong as a mountain, the backdrop of her life, the foundation to her security. Had it only been four years since she fell hard for this six-foot-tall son of her client? His muscular build, confident stance and broad shoulders, reminiscent of an athlete or firefighter, had caught her eye. Inexplicably, Kate knew this man with a blinding smile and unruly black hair would change her life.

She yearned for him to cut back on his purchasing trips to Mexico. Hopefully, now that he was a father, he would relinquish the daunting travel schedule to another employee and be at home with his new family.

"He's doing great." The doctor interrupted Kate's musing. "Heart rate, breathing, muscle tone, all normal. His reflexes and color are perfect." Dr. Smith snapped off his latex gloves. "Congratulations," he said, before exiting.

"Monica and my parents are waiting in the lobby. We need to give them the news," Eric said, his eyes glistening with emotion as he stared at their son.

Kate's breath thinned nearly to a stop, watching him blink back tears. "Are you happy?" she whispered, her own eyes misting. During their courtship and early years of marriage, Eric had never cried. Now having a son bound them together. Ecstasy flooded her every sense realizing his tears overflowed with love, tenderness, and delight.

"You three can hang out a little longer," the nurse, who Kate forgot was in the room, instructed. "Then we'll bring your family in two at a time to meet your baby. I'll pop out to let them know mother and son are doing fine."

Kate's sisters, protective mother hens in the best and worst of ways, were probably chomping at the bit to know that everything went well. But Kate wanted to savor this moment alone with her new family, before opening the doors for the world to enter. She needed this time with Eric and baby Benjamin, her family. Her life. She wanted to soak in these first-time-mommy emotions: happy, frightened, excited, fulfilled, anxious.

As soon as the nurse left, Kate looked up at Eric, his hand resting gently on Benjamin's back. "Having a child changes everything. You understand that, don't you?"

"Yeah, I know. Now we'll cheer for our own son at Little League games instead of Monica's. We'll wonder if some girl has broken his heart in eighth grade and then get to worry about how we'll pay for college," Eric teased.

"No, I don't mean those things."

"I know what you mean. We're parents now," Eric answered, swiping at an escaping tear.

In spite of the exhaustion fighting to claim Kate, she relished a new energy rising in her chest. A delightful surge ignited from the pride in her husband's voice. "There's that, but now you're not the only man in my life." She winked.

Eric kissed her forehead. "I've waited a long time to be a dad. I'll gladly share your attention with Bennie."

"You're giving him a nickname already?" she questioned.

"Do you prefer Ben-meister?"

"Ugh! I prefer Benjamin. He'll tell us if he wants a moniker."

The baby let out a wail. "I do believe you're right." Eric chuckled. "This little man will have no problem asking for what he wants."

"He's hungry," Kate said, not sure how to start the breastfeeding process. She had gathered dozens of books on the topic, all recommending to start within one hour of the birth. But now that she held this tiny bundle in her arms, their advice seemed meaningless.

"I'm so lucky I get to do this with you, Katie." Eric bent down and gently kissed her lips. "We're going to be terrific parents."

She smiled at him, her heart full of love for her gentle but complex man. "Yes, we will."

Seconds later, as if on cue, a lactation nurse pushed through the swinging door. "Let me help you. You'll get the hang of things pretty quickly."

They watched as Benjamin first licked and then latched on to Kate's nipple. As the baby suckled, the cramping intensified, increasing Kate's satisfaction in her first unselfish act as a mother. The responsibility overwhelmed and completed her, sending waves of love for her infant crashing through her like a tsunami.

Her son would never be left in tears while mean kids teased that he didn't have a daddy. Not on her watch. She'd made certain to marry a man committed to his family.

***

A son. I have a son.

Eric's pulse pounded in his ears as he stepped back, giving space for the nurse to tend to Kate, without taking his attention off of his wife and child. He had been in the birthing room for an eternity. He couldn't wait to show off the newest member of his family.

Never one to believe in miracles, today had forever changed Eric's hopes and dreams. Working undercover for the CIA had exposed him to the world's underbelly. Mission after mission left him jaded by mankind's inhumanity. Maybe there were happy endings for some people and maybe this time, he would be one of them.

Once Kate finished breastfeeding, the nurse left the room, allowing Eric a chance to reclaim his spot next to the bed. He gently stroked Benjamin's back as he slept against his mother's chest.

If only your grandpa were alive to see you. He'd tease me about all that black hair. He'd say something prophetic about how lots of hair means a wealthy life.

Eric could almost hear his father's laughter and wished his dad was in the waiting room, ready to share one of the many embellished anecdotes he was famous for telling.

Knowing his real parents would never hold their grandson drove a spike through Eric's heart. He had spent most of his CIA career committed to bringing their killer to justice. His obsession had cost him his first marriage. He wouldn't allow Anmar X to ruin this one, too.

"Can I hold him?" Eric asked.

Kate scooted to sit up on the bed, careful not to disturb the nest of tubes and wires monitoring her vitals. She placed the infant into Eric's outstretched arms, and he nestled the child against his pounding chest. Benjamin's heartbeat synced with his own. Awed by the compactness of this tiny bundle, Eric stared as though the universe pushed a pause button. His world had stopped to make room for Benjamin Simon.

"You are going to be a terrific dad. I knew that truth the night Bodie was born." Kate said recalling her youngest nephew's birth.

Eric grinned. With his free hand, he swiped a strand of auburn hair away from Kate's face. She had never looked more radiant, her skin smooth and flawless, her hazel eyes taking on a new gleam.

"That night stretched into early morning. And the hospital administrators didn't do anything extra to make visitors comfortable in their ratty, out-of-date waiting room. My back still hurts from where that plastic chair dug into me."

"Really?" Kate drew out the word and laughed. "You're complaining? That was more than five years ago. Anyway, Monica's boys will vouch for you with Bennie."

"Now he's Bennie?"

16

"I guess," Kate replied sheepishly. "Has a loving familiarity to it. But as I said, he'll tell us if he doesn't like the nickname."

Eric drew close and kissed Kate's lips again, lingering for a moment, soaking up their sweetness. "I can see where my place is going to be for the next eighteen years."

"We'll figure things out as we go along." She smiled. "Anyway, my nephews think you're terrific."

"Buy them ice cream for breakfast and they're fans forever." Eric chuckled just as his phone vibrated in his front pocket. The call had better not be from Ralph or Trish. His adoptive parents had been taking turns texting from the lobby. Hopefully, the message was from them, wondering when they could see their grandson and not orders from his operations officer, charging him with a new mission.

No matter who was on the other end of the message, they would have to wait. Nothing was more important than holding his son and committing to memory how beautiful his wife looked at this moment.

"I think we've kept the gang from this little man long enough." Kate adjusted her hospital gown and pushed back the matted hair gathered around her face. "We should let them meet him. I'll bet Colleen is pacing around with bags of baby stuff," she said of her best friend, a former cop who Eric had immediately liked the first time he met her.

"No doubt." He laughed. "She's been on the text message train with your sisters."

"Well?" Kate tilted her head. "Are you going to let them come in?"

"What's the rush? Let the whole gang sit in those luxurious chairs for another hour," Eric joked. "Seriously, give us a minute or two more. I'm not ready to share our family with the world yet."

Kate smiled. "Yeah, me either."

Still standing, Eric traced a finger down Benjamin's tiny nose, across his rosebud lips, all the while marveling at the crescent fringe of eyelashes gracing each lid. God didn't miss a detail.

Finally, he kissed the top of Benjamin's head before returning him to Kate, who swaddled him into her arms. Eric wanted to freeze this moment in his memory; the glint in her eyes, the slope of her mouth, the tenderness of their sleeping child.

Kate kissed Benjamin, her lips puckering in the same maternal way Eric's mother's had. How, as a little boy, he'd squirm and struggle to escape the kissing frenzy she'd unleash on his cheeks as he left for school or to play with friends. He still felt the smoothness of her lips as she smothered him with kisses. At seven, he couldn't understand the depths of her love. Now he understood.

His parents' friends, Ben and Adele Wiley, had adopted him. Eric, fourteen at the time, was grateful for their love. Still, the hole in his heart continued to grow. Benjamin's birth enlarged the ache, amplifying Eric's need to mend that growing abyss.

Eric vowed to himself to never let his career, or anything else, separate him from Benjamin. Someday soon, he'd quit and finally end the dangerous trips to foreign lands. When it was safe, he would tell Kate the whole story. He would divulge his true identity. That day couldn't come soon enough.

He squeezed Kate's hand and whispered a promise he planned to keep. "I will always be here for you and Benjamin, always."

Chapter Four

"I've never seen a more beautiful baby," Adele bragged. She wrapped Bennie tighter in his receiving blanket before handing him to his grandfather standing near Kate.

"You've said that for the past two weeks," Eric joked from his reclined position on the couch in his family room.

Eric's parents had visited almost every day since Benjamin's birth, helping with chores, showering them with meals and baby gifts and providing support Eric never suspected he would need. As he watched his wife, mother, and father fuss around his son, he witnessed how a newborn expanded the circles of familial love. There could be no stronger power.

"Well, it's true," Adele admonished, taking a seat across from Eric. "Look how tiny he is in Ben's arms."

Benjamin Wiley stood to his full six-foot-seven frame, his massive hands encompassing the infant in a gentleness Eric had never before observed.

"Guess we're going to have to call you Big Ben." Witnessing granddad bond with grandson sent a wave of pride only fathers knew racing through Eric's chest.

Benjamin's smile magnified the creases in his aging face as he peered into little Ben's eyes. "That's fine, but I'm fonder of another name. Poppa."

"Poppa it is," Eric agreed. "As for Nana," Eric continued, now directing his comments toward his mother, "dinner was delicious."

"Thank you. I'm more than happy to supply food, as long as it gets me extra time with this little fellow." Adele shifted her gaze to Kate hovering near Benjamin. Eric watched his wife assessing the baby's every movement.

Kate returned her mother-in-law's smile with a weariness that left Eric uneasy. Instead of guarding Bennie, he wished she'd sit down and relax.

During the first year of their marriage, he'd seen his wife put in thirteen-hour workdays to finish a construction project and then take her nephews and her new niece on a weekend campout to give her sister Monica and her husband Brad some time alone. Tired was not a word he ever thought he'd use in the same sentence when describing Kate. But nowadays, tired was all she seemed to be.

"How much longer is your maternity leave?" Adele asked.

"Another six weeks, but Harry says I can take on some projects from home," Kate replied, referring to her boss at Mack & Partners Architects. "I may delay my return a bit."

"That's wonderful," Adele continued. "You've definitely put your time in on our buildings. What is it? Six sites in four years. If anyone has earned a break, it's you."

Eric watched his father walk Bennie around the space, stopping only to point out the window at birds perched on a nearby tree, or to comment on the colors in the setting sun. Soon Bennie would be old enough to respond to the senior Ben's soothing babbles. The seeds of their lifelong friendship were being sown before Eric's eyes.

The same man Eric had witnessed take down a drug lord nearly single-handed during the brief time their CIA careers overlapped, now happily reduced to repeating nursery rhymes and singsong lyrics. Eric smiled at the irony.

"What is it, little man?" Benjamin asked as the baby began a sad yowl that grew louder. He bounced him a little faster, but to no avail.

"Dinner time?" Adele asked, explaining the baby's cries.

"It's always dinner time," Kate replied, extending her arms.

"Let me feed him," Adele suggested with a lilt to her voice. "It will give you a break."

Kate dismissed the offer. "I'm nursing,"

"Surely you have bot—"

"We're still experimenting," Eric said, rescuing Kate from Adele's disbelief.

Kate flashed a troubled look at Eric before excusing herself to the bedroom.

"I only meant—"

"I know, Mom. We're taking things slow. How about some dessert?" Eric said, changing the subject. He herded his folks into the kitchen while Kate began feeding Bennie.

"I didn't mean to offend Kate. I just wanted to help," Adele defended moments later.

"Adele, the woman wants to care for her own child. She'll let you know when she wants your help," Benjamin scolded.

"And how many babies have you given birth to?" she snapped.

"The same amount as you."

"Chocolate or vanilla?" Eric hoped to defuse the argument as he scooped chocolate ice cream from a carton for himself.

"Either," Adele answered, pulling out a chair and taking a spot at the kitchen table. "Honey, Kate looks exhausted. Is she sleeping at all?"

"Just bits here and there. She gets up every two hours to nurse. I'm on diaper-changing duty. She insists on being the only one to feed him," Eric complained. "She won't hear of buying formula or purchasing a breast-pumping machine. I don't know what else to do. It's almost like she wants to keep boundaries between me and the baby."

"I'm sure that's not it." Benjamin accepted a bowl of chocolate ice cream. "She's new at this and wants to be sure she's caring for her son perfectly. And the only way you can ensure perfection is to do everything yourself."

"He's probably right, as much as it pains me to tell him so." Adele smirked at her husband.

"But she's worn out. I'm worried," Eric said.

"Tell her how you feel. Not only are you concerned about her, but you're missing time with your baby," Adele said. "There's a reason why God gives a child two parents. It's almost like a tag team."

"You need to tag in," Ben said, "and somehow convince Kate that you won't let the team down."

"All of this is fairly common new mother behavior," Adele continued. "I'll bet every dad goes through this adjustment. The two of you have to find a happy medium. Kate needs sleep and you need time with Bennie. She'll see your side."

They finished their ice cream and Eric walked them to the door. They'd offered sage advice, but deep inside Eric suspected something more ominous than not sharing parenting tasks brewed inside of Kate. She wanted to be the best mom ever, but he worried that the scars of her past would threaten their future happiness.

**

Kate set the baby monitor down and tilted the screen for a better view. "Wow, I didn't think he'd ever go back to sleep." She joined Eric, already seated on the couch, feet up on the coffee table, channel surfing. She scooted into the crook of his arm, her eyelids as heavy as a metal roll-up garage door grinding closed. She leaned against his chest and sighed.

Benjamin was a good baby, as far as good goes when you're fourteen-days old and your world was sleeping, eating and pooping. The every-two-hour feeding schedule exhausted Kate. Still, she claimed this motherly duty for herself.

But being open like an all-night diner proved to be more than her body could handle. The weariness permeated her bones, and she feared she would never be the same again. Both Julie and Monica swore her energy and vitality would return as soon as Ben slept longer and eventually achieved the nirvana every parent hoped for—sleeping through the night.

"I put your dinner in the refrigerator," Eric said.

She yawned. "Thanks. I'll eat in a minute." Kate placed a nearby blanket over her legs and reclined her head.

"After your nap? Kate, this is ridiculous." Eric tossed the remote aside. "You have to let me take some of the late-night feedings. You need more than forty-five minutes of sleep."

"You're right. It's just that he's only going to be this little for a short time," she defended, opening her eyes. "I don't want to miss a second." That was true, but Kate's motivation involved more than missing moments. She treasured Bennie nuzzling into her breast and nursing. His tender body connected to her in the most basic of ways.

"You half-asleep through these first weeks isn't the best way to spend your time. I could take a feeding or two. I'm certain there's more to fatherhood than changing stinky diapers."

"What? You don't like your role as chief pooper-snooper?" She grinned, and he kissed her deeply. His warmth attached to her mouth, like jumper cables on a nearly dead battery, and sent a surge of energy through her spirit.

"Not fair influencing my decisions with your lips," she said once they finally broke apart.

"Hey, like Robin Hood, I'll use every arrow in my quiver." He kissed her again, more deeply.

His kiss exploded like a life-giving elixir, combatting the exhaustion that had ruled her life for several days. And when he pulled back, ending the kiss, she pouted, realizing she'd forgotten how good it felt to be a woman first.

"So, can I be promoted?"

Kate placed her palm against his, and intertwined her fingers. "Trying to be Super Mom isn't working out the way I expected."

"To Bennie, and me, you are Super Mom. That doesn't mean Sleepy Mom, too. Look at me," Eric tilted her face. "You don't have to do everything yourself to make certain Ben is okay. There will be times when things don't go according to the Book of Babies. But there will never be a time when I'm not as committed as you are to our son."

Kate pondered his words, a mounting anxiety building in her throat. Was she intentionally shutting him out of their son's life, as though he would be an absent father much like her own? No, her subconscious couldn't be working overtime, could it? She was like any other mother, convinced that the best for her child could only come through her. Now Kate had to realize that her love of Bennie denied Eric a chance to prove he was a capable parent. He didn't want to be number two.

"I'll get the pumping machine tomorrow. Will that be soon enough?" She bent toward him and kissed his lips quickly.

"What was that? A brotherly kiss? I get those from Trish," he laughed, referring to the woman Kate saw him with when they were dating.

"Trish better never kiss you again," Kate joked about Eric's business associate she once had mistaken as a romantic rival.

Eric wrapped his arms around her and kissed her properly. After coming up for air, he agreed. "No need, when I have your luscious lips. I am a lucky man."

Kate burrowed against her husband, allowing herself to become immersed in his love. In spite of their early history and her doubts, he deserved equal footing in parenting Benjamin. Still something niggled at her insides, urging her to not loosen her grip on their child. She had surrendered her heart to Eric, but that was hers to give. She would be more guarded in relinquishing Benjamin's.

Tomorrow would be soon enough to begin letting go, even a little, Kate thought, as sleep overtook her.

Tomorrow, I'll let go a little tomorrow.

Chapter Five

Eric snatched the vibrating phone from the nightstand and slipped quietly out of bed, hoping not to wake Kate. He closed the bedroom door and trailed down the hallway toward the living room, far away from where his wife peacefully slept.

"Yeah," he growled by way of greeting, knowing he wasn't going to like anything Ralph had to say.

"Anmar X has been sighted. We're wheels up in the morning." Ralph's gruff voice boomed through the phone line.

Eric cursed under his breath and rubbed his hands through his hair as he paced the room like a caged lion. There was no way he could leave Kate and the baby right now. She would kill him. But he had to go after Anmar X.

"How good is the intel?" he asked.

"Hell, the best we've had. Otherwise I wouldn't be calling you. Our new stoolie has fresh reconnaissance. Trust me. I've read it."

"Another inside guy, huh?" Eric questioned.

"He's good. I've read the report," Ralph snapped.

Spies, foreign emissaries and bogus informants sprang up everywhere. Eric didn't trust any of them. He barely trusted

Trish and or Ralph, and only because he had to. No way would he automatically put his faith in this unnamed source.

Ralph continued, "I'll text you the flight details. Be at the airport by ten." With that, the line went dead.

Disbelief and regret surged through Eric's every nerve. The same disbelief and regret he experienced hours earlier after he had excused himself from Kate as they cuddled on the couch. He anticipated this emergency communication from his handler. But that expectation didn't lessen his anguish. Even though he awaited this news, the orders couldn't have come at a worse time.

A growl boiled in Eric's chest, threatening to overflow.

Kate will never forgive me for leaving again.

The thought bounded angrily against the borders of his mind, warning him to avoid what he was about to do. He despised his fixation to capture Anmar X and how that obsession threatened his marriage, but he couldn't help it. He had to rid the world of this guy if he ever planned to have a normal life.

"Eric?" a sleepy voice interrupted the solace of his thoughts. "Are you up? Did you hear the baby?"

"No. No. Go back to sleep," he instructed.

Moments later, Kate padded to where he stood near the fireplace. "What's wrong?" she whispered.

"Nothing, honey. Nothing at all."

"Then why are you awake? Who were you talking to?" she asked, pointing to the phone he held in his hand.

Eric quickly slid the phone into the pocket of the basketball shorts that doubled as his pajamas.

"No one. I thought I heard a noise, that's all. Go back to sleep, honey. Bennie will be up soon anyway."

"You're leaving again, aren't you?"

Kate's words pelted him like darts, each one hitting its bull's-eye. She knew.

"Let's get some sleep. We'll talk about this in the morning," Eric said, piping in an artificial softness to his voice.

He reached for her hand, but she slapped it away.

"What's the excuse this time? Wait, don't tell me. I'm too tired to listen." She turned toward the bedroom and walked away.

Eric stood in the darkness for several minutes. Maybe he should tell Kate the truth. All of it. She was ready to hear it, but was he ready to bare his soul and reveal his true identity?

***

The next morning, Eric tossed a few shirts into his suitcase lying open on the bed before counting out a week's worth of socks and underwear.

"Please delay your trip until next week," Kate pleaded, holding Benjamin in her arms.

"You know I would if I could." Eric shoved a pair of jeans and a lightweight jacket into the case and zipped it shut.

Kate swayed and used her free hand to pat Benjamin's back. "Keep your voice low," she hissed, "or you'll frighten our son."

Eric raised his eyebrows. "We're not fighting about me having to work, are we? I thought we were discussing, the way married folks do." When Kate didn't respond to his attempt at humor, he stopped and took in her image.

Awash in the early morning light streaming across her face from a window, Kate's auburn highlights formed a halo around her head. *How can I continue to lie to this woman?*

The tiny lines that gathered around her lips when she was stressed magnified. Eric couldn't decide if she was frightened at the prospect of his leaving or fed up with his antics.

"Just one more week. You promised we'd have this time together." She wasn't pleading, simply stating facts.

He walked to where she stood and kissed her cheek before embracing his wife and son in a group hug. "I feel damn lucky this emergency didn't come up sooner."

He brushed her arm, noting the goosebumps prickling against his palm.

"If that call had come before Benjamin's birth, would you have left and missed seeing your son be born?" she asked.

How could he answer without adding more lies to the growing mountain of falsehoods he'd already fabricated? As far as she knew, he was committed to his profession as an importer for his parents' chain of discount stores. The success of his mission—and possibly his safety—depended on her believing that version.

"Of course not." Eric told her what she wanted to hear.

Smoke screens and twisting reality to suit his immediate goal had served him well, not just in his professional life, but in his married life, too. Sadly, he'd become pretty good at spinning the truth to where his story held little or no facts.

"Somehow, I don't believe you." Kate pulled away and walked to the other side of the bedroom, far from the light into a darkened corner.

"Don't be like that. I have to work," he snapped, overwhelmed at the pull of his conflicting responsibilities. She was right. He should be home, but he knew home would never be the sanctuary he sought until he completed this mission.

"What exactly am I being like?" Kate asked. "A woman who wants her family together? How unfair of me." Pain laced her words and broke his heart.

Eric's usual cover story—buying trips to Mexico's textile plants to purchase cases of cheap towels, knockoff handbags and other leather goods—had worked until today. Or had it? Perhaps she had been letting the inconsistencies in his myriad of excuses slide, hoping to maintain harmony. He pushed the limits. No man would miss the birth of his first child, or any of his children. Eric was grateful he didn't have to explain to Kate why he would have chosen work over his son.

"That's not what I meant. Anyway, all that doesn't matter." He deflected her question, at least for the moment. "The baby is here. Julie arrives later today and is staying for a week, right? I'll be back by then. You'll be fine. You're a fabulous mother, and an even more spectacular wife." He pulled her close and lowered his head to kiss her.

"So not the point." Kate turned away. Avoiding his lips, she broke their embrace and placed Benjamin in the bassinet nestled near her side of their king-sized bed. She covered him with a blue-and-white checked quilt Adele had made and stormed from the room, stopping herself from slamming the door.

His gaze shifted from the closed door to where their sleeping angel lay, oblivious that his parents were fighting. Eric ached, recalling his childhood, before he shifted toward his son.

"One more mission," he whispered into Benjamin's ear. "Once this is done, I'll never leave again. Your daddy will be here every day. I promise."

***

Kate plopped onto the couch and punched a pillow. Maybe it was the baby blues, but tears filled her eyes, competing with the mounting anger rising from her stomach.

He's leaving. Already.

She wondered if Eric's erratic work schedule contributed to the breakup of his first marriage. He never spoke about why he and Jenny had divorced after only being married six months.

Some weeks he was the happy husband, puttering around their garden and rearranging the garage. Then, the next week he would be on a plane headed for Juarez or Mexicali. Kate thought he would change after the baby was born. Obviously, she was wrong.

Four years ago, he had insisted they see a marriage counselor before setting a wedding date. They met regularly with Laura Ekker, the therapist who helped Monica and her husband rebuild their shattered marriage. After several sessions, Kate saw little change in their relationship, admitting to herself that she didn't know Eric any better after weeks of couples counseling. His actions tonight put an exclamation mark on that realization. If Eric could jump on a plane so soon after becoming a father, then he'd leave for any reason.

"Katie." Eric entered the room, interrupting her thoughts. "When you work for yourself, you can't take too much time off. And with this expansion, Mom and Dad are counting on me."

"Seriously? Whatever order you have to place or plant you need to inspect, can't it wait a few weeks?"

"Baby. Come here." Eric opened his arms and Kate fell into his embrace. They stood that way for several minutes. "If I didn't have to go, I wouldn't. But I'm not leaving you alone. Mom can take a shift so you and Julie can go shopping or relax at the movies. I'll be back in plenty of time before Julie leaves."

"But—"

"No buts. I want our son to grow up with a strong work ethic. What would he think if his old man goofed off from the beginning?"

"He'd think he meant more to his father than business growth."

"Don't go all 'Cat's in the Cradle' on me," he teased, referring to the Harry Chapin song about an absentee dad.

Kate pulled away and crossed her arms.

"Listen. I didn't want to bother you with my work troubles. One of our vendors fell through on our spring order. I have back-to-back meetings with secondary manufacturers to see if they can replace the products in time."

"And Big Ben can't go in your place. Just this once?" Kate pleaded, hating the whininess to her voice.

"He volunteered but I can't let him go. He's still on the medication for his irregular heartbeat. The stress of this trip would be too much for him."

"Where will you be? How can I get ahold of you if there's an emergency?"

"I'm not sure where my business associate made hotel arrangements," Eric answered.

"Would that be Trish?" Kate asked, with more snarkiness than she intended.

"Let's not go there again. As soon as I'm settled, I'll call. I will always be here for our son and for you. That's a guarantee."

Kate recalled overhearing a similar promise her father had made to her mother as he headed out the door one summer evening. He never came back. How could she prevent the same thing from happening to Benjamin?

Chapter Six

Eric spotted Trish Atwater, a fellow agent, seated inside the mostly empty aircraft. She stood and stepped into the aisle, allowing him to slide into the seat next to the window. Posing as American importers, they had to take a commercial flight from Phoenix, with two connections, before reaching their facility deep in Hidalgo, outside of Mexico City. A military transport, if one were available, would have gotten them there in an hour instead of seven hours.

Spending that much time on an aircraft would strain the patience of anyone, even a highly-trained operative like Eric. With their last mission ending badly, he and Trish had taken a forced hiatus, hoping time would improve their intelligence unit's focus and tighten the net around their target.

The leave suited Eric perfectly. Spending time with his new son and Kate made him feel normal, giving him a snapshot of what his life could be like if he left the CIA; if he didn't have to leave on missions at the spur of the moment. Knowing their task force was tracking Anmar X and closing in on his whereabouts, Eric savored in the panacea vacation that came to an abrupt halt.

He considered telling Kate where he was going, but decided that conversation would have to take place under different circumstances, at a time when he could prepare her for the dangers of his job. It wouldn't be fair to tell her half of the story. That would only increase her worry and do little to diminish his personal angst.

Her angry words as he had walked toward the waiting cab buffeted his thoughts.

You've got to make a choice, Eric. It's me and Bennie. Or the family business. I won't keep living this way.

Had he made the right choice by lying to her?

Trish's pitchy voice, as bothersome as a metronome counting out the beats of his next several days, interrupted his thoughts.

"Show me a picture, already," she snapped. "I've been waiting."

"You could have stopped by the house to see him," Eric bantered with his long-time partner.

"I'm not the stop-by-the-house type," Trish joshed. "Besides, Kate doesn't particularly care for me. She still sees me as the other woman. Boy, I can't wait until you tell her the truth."

"Why do you care? By then, I'll be out of the agency. You'll have a new partner and I'll be but a distant memory."

"Yeah, whatever. Stop giving me grief and show me a damn picture. I know you want to. You can thank me later."

"Thank you for what?" Eric reached into his front pocket for his wallet, pulled out a photo of Kate holding Ben and passed it to Trish. Soon he wouldn't have access to any of his personal belongings, including the cell phone he told Kate to text him on. Once they reached their destination, the agent-on-duty would seize all identifying possessions from him and Trish and store them in a locker until they returned.

Trish snorted, unladylike. "Thank me for making your happily-ever-after happen, that's what. If it wasn't for me, Kate wouldn't have ever gone out with you."

Eric smirked at the memory of her coming to his rescue, after Kate had witnessed a kiss Trish planted on him. She had hastily explained the brotherly kiss, crediting her Greek heritage for such displays of friendship.

"I think if your next child is a girl, you should name her after me," Trish continued. "Patricia Wiley. That sounds lovely."

Eric snatched the snapshot from Trish's grasp and carefully slid the photo inside a plastic sleeve and returned his wallet to his pocket. "Sounds more like something that will never happen. How's Delbert?"

"You really want to start this very long trip off with me pissy? I don't think so." Trish crossed her arms.

"What?"

"Dillon, his name is Dillon. And we broke up."

Eric stared at Trish for a moment, annoyed at himself for not recognizing the Trish-has-a-broken-heart signs present after her numerous boyfriend breakups. "I'm sorry?" he asked questioningly. "He wasn't the right man for you? Someone better will come along?"

"What are you doing, Wiley?"

"Trying to sound supportive, like one of your girlfriends. Isn't that what women say to one another?"

"God, you are so lame. Anyway, I broke it off with him. Thank you for caring," she said a softness now entering her voice. She grabbed her electronic tablet, jerked open the cover and place the device on her lap. "He truly wasn't Mr. Right."

"Someday your prince will come," Eric singsonged.

"Yeah, I know. Shall we?" Trish pointed to the screen. "Here's the most recent intel we have. A group of Anmar's men was spotted at a hookah lounge in downtown Hidalgo."

"That's why we got the code red for this trip? Some dudes sucking on a shisha." Eric referred to the water-pipe vessel used in smoking lounges to inhale tobacco through a hose.

"Peddis is hoping they'll lead us to Anmar."

Ralph Peddis, their team leader, was the point of the spear. Still, Eric's anger spiked, expecting more than an arbitrary social gathering to force him hundreds of miles away from his wife and newborn child.

He glanced around the airplane, grateful the nearest passenger was three rows back. "That's all we're going on? Someone's guess that they spotted some of Anmar's lieutenants? Good Lord, I hope there's more than this." He stared at Trish. Her returned stare cemented what he expected. The lead was weak at best.

"They wanted us back quickly because, odds are, these guys are moving on to a new location," Trish whispered. "Hanging out in a hookah is very temporary. You know that."

Trish's response didn't convince Eric that they were a smidgen closer to busting any crooks.

"What are we supposed to do, blend into the local nightlife until Anmar shows up? Eric questioned. "Pop in and out of hookah bars along Calle Fumar, hoping we get lucky and one of his Xers reveals Anmar's location after he's had too many hits on the pipe?"

Trish closed her tablet. "That's where we are as of right now. Wish I had better details, but I don't. Ralph will meet us at the airport. Maybe he'll know more."

"He damned well better," Eric snapped. He leaned against the chair back and huffed. He had told Kate he'd be back home in a week. Now he knew that it was improbable at best for him to keep that promise. Impossible was the more likely scenario.

Even with the weak tip, he had to stay all-in, follow up on tracking down this mastermind behind death and destruction, who continued to leave his horrifying scar on the world.

Using Ben and Adele's textile import business as a plausible cover for foreign travel, Eric willingly entered the CIA as a clandestine service officer. He climbed the ranks, biding his time, waiting to get assigned to this weapons-smuggling task force.

The promotion came through weeks after marrying Jenny. Without explaining to his first wife the importance and commitment he had to his job, Eric left on several extended missions to Pakistan, Saudi Arabia and Egypt. The operation eventually shifted to the Mexican states. By then, his short-lived romance with Jenny dissolved nearly as quickly as it had begun.

Eric wouldn't allow the same pitiful ending with Kate. As soon as he returned home, he'd confess everything and then beg for her understanding and forgiveness.

***

Seated comfortably in the family room, Kate tittered at the nineteen-sixties-something romantic comedy she and Julie watched. During the past hour and a half, they nibbled popcorn while Julie released raucous guffaws at the slapstick antics of the actors and actresses. Kate missed hearing her sister's laughter, a reassuring sound that everything in their world was okay. She had relied on the lightness and mirth during those years before Julie left for college and then married and moved to California. All before their mother died and she, Julie, and Monica had to grow up fast.

"How many times have you watched this movie?" Kate asked as the film's closing credits rolled. "You laughed as though this was the first time."

"At least five, but it doesn't matter. It's his accent and that crazy mustache that keeps me in stitches," Julie said, wiping a tear away before glancing at the watch on her wrist. "Hey, it's after eleven. We'd better get some sleep."

They stood, and hugged each other. Julie headed to the guestroom while Kate went to check on the baby.

The sun had set hours ago, but she understood that the demands of motherhood didn't punch a time clock. After feeding Benjamin, she carried him back to the master suite.

While Julie and Bennie slept, she peered out her bedroom window, spying the branches of a desert willow bend against a gentle night's breeze. The darkened sky provided the perfect backdrop for a mother and child to bond. With only a nightlight softly glowing through the doorway for illumination, Kate cherished this bewitching time. As she gently rocked her baby, her heart swelled with pride.

Up until a few weeks ago, designing the Ramble Hills Community College Learning Hub had been Kate's greatest accomplishment. When the building opened for students, she had reveled in a newfound sense of pride and identity.

Her sisters blazed their own trails to become independent women. Kate, without realizing it, used the dilemmas her mother and sisters had found themselves in as fuel to keep her on the path to success. Meeting and falling in love with Eric diverted her path significantly.

As she felt Benjamin's chest rise and fall against her hand, the words Eric spoke on their wedding day spiraled through her mind. His vows, borrowed from Kahlil Gibran's *The Prophet*, punctuated his marital pledge with words like space, alone, apart, shadow.

Kate crumbled at the thought of Eric flourishing without her, agonized that he could find her love to be limiting and suffocating. She didn't want to stand apart from him like the pillars of a temple. Why didn't he feel the same?

She kissed Benjamin's cheek and rose to lay him on his back in his bassinet. "Shhh. Shhh," she cooed, as he stirred for a moment before quieting.

She climbed into bed and exhaustion filled every corner of her body before her head met the pillow. She should have been fast asleep, but questions surrounding Eric's constant absences fought against nature, keeping her awake and restless.

Before meeting Eric, she purposefully lived her life as a protest to the childhood stolen from her. Her father's desertion had left a scar across the Jameson family, one that she hoped she'd healed by marrying Eric.

There was only one solution, she thought, as she punched her pillow and rolled over to her side. He had to change his work life if their marriage would survive. She'd help him understand that. Just as soon as he returned.

Chapter Seven

Eric watched as the Boeing 777 began its descent, the aqua blue ocean vanishing as the plane invaded the margins of the dusty brown, flat terrain. The site reminded Eric of a jigsaw puzzle in need of completion. The picture wouldn't become clear until the last piece was in place.

Eric stretched in preparation of an additional drive before he and Trish would arrive in Hidalgo.

Trish punched his arm. "Hey, when we land, you want to grab a cup of coffee or something? We're stuck here until we get picked up."

"Yeah," he replied, absently rubbing his forearm. "But first I want to call Kate and see how things are going with Benjamin."

"Your pride and joy. And to think I could have stood between you and true love." She chuckled. "You are one lucky dude."

"I know. Believe me, I know."

Eric winked and turned back to the bird's-eye view. How many times had he taken in this panorama from an airplane window? The first time was months after joining the agency. He had been a mixture of anxiety and calm, if that was possible.

From his earliest recollection, he wanted to be like his biological dad, serving his country in the most meaningful ways, playing a part to insure peace on the world stage. His adoptive father, Ben, understood what drove his obsession. After several careers that failed to launch, Ben had pulled some strings to get him an interview with the Directorate of Operations. Ben knew the DO under its former name, Clandestine Service, and maintained a friendship with its deputy director long after Ben had retired.

At work, Eric kept his head down, working to build trust with his superiors by recruiting assets and effectively capturing high-value targets. When reliable intelligence from agents in the counterterrorism center surfaced about Anmar X, he, Ben and Adele relocated to Arizona. He resumed the interests of his textile-merchant parents, allowing him the freedom to travel in circles the CIA had previously found difficult to infiltrate.

With the assignment Eric had waited for finally within reach, he made a difficult decision. Regardless of the mission's outcome, he would resign his position as soon as he returned to the States.

***

"Hey precious boy, give Daddy a smile," Eric cooed, his face in full-screen view on the video stream. The quality was spotty, still better than not being able to see her husband who had been gone for three days.

Kate smiled at the way Eric's eyebrows arched in his hopeless attempts to get Benjamin's attention. For the past twenty minutes, she held their son in an awkward posture in front of her desktop computer camera, coaxing a somewhat sleeping baby to greet his father. Up until a few seconds ago, their son displayed little interest. She knew the squirming had more to do with hunger than his eagerness to interact with his dad.

Kate had waited all day for Eric to call. She needed to see his face, stubbled with a five-o'clock shadow, even if it was through her computer screen. She shifted Benjamin to her other arm. *This must be how military families with one parent deployed feel.*

This wasn't the marriage she signed up for. Twenty minutes over a video call couldn't substitute for his presence.

It could be exhaustion or not getting regular sleep, but she wondered if the man she married was more like her father in ways she hadn't anticipated. Eric wasn't an alcoholic, a wife beater or a deadbeat. But neither was Monica's husband, Brad. Kate had witnessed how her brother-in-law's sins nearly ripped the soul of their family apart.

There were all sorts of ways to abandon your wife and desert your family. Just because she was most familiar with the ones her father implemented, didn't mean that she and her sisters wouldn't suffer from other approaches. Separated by hundreds of miles without knowing when he would return qualified as desertion of a type. At least in Kate's mind.

"I'm sorry. It's nearly feeding time and your son doesn't like to be delayed." Kate hoped to placate Eric's hurt feelings. In spite of his actions, she believed he wanted to be home with them, holding Bennie, sharing in his care.

"I meant to call earlier, but things here are hectic. This is the first time I had a chance to sit down."

"What is going on that's so chaotic?" Kate asked, puzzled by all the cloak-and-dagger references every time Eric left on a buying trip. Surely placing orders at one of the many textile mills in Juarez, or wherever he was this time, couldn't be all that complicated. He acted like he was a soldier under orders, sent to a foreign land to fight, without any recourse or ability to refuse the assignment.

Kate's resentment of Adele and Ben grew. How could they insist that their son leave his family and miss this precious time? What kind of parents did that?

"Just a lot of craziness, but I don't want to talk about that now. I want to hear what new things Bennie is doing." Eric put a finger up to the screen and Kate did the same, meeting in a virtual touch. "I miss you, Katie, my love."

She blinked. Unable to prevent the torrent building, a flood of tears streamed down her cheeks.

"Don't cry because I love you." Eric's lips twisted apologetically.

Kate's sobs started in force and she shook her head as though trying to whisk the tears away. "I miss you, baby. I miss you so much. I need you home. Bennie needs you here."

"Don't you think I want to be there, too?"

"Sometimes I wonder."

"Don't say that. Don't even think that." Eric pulled back from the screen, making his face harder to see.

Kate leaned in closer. "Don't move away." She gulped back tears. "Don't you want to be here?"

"Seriously, you're asking me that?" Eric snapped, running his fingers through his hair. "Look, I've talked to my parents and they agree. After this trip, I will be like a regular Joe, home every night, chasing you around the kitchen until I catch you."

Kate laughed despite the ache in her heart and swiped at an errant tear. She slid a pacifier into Benjamin's mouth, hoping the fake out would keep him quiet for another minute or two.

"Kate, you are my life, you and Benjamin. As soon as I complete this deal, I'm on a plane back into your waiting arms. That is, if Bennie will share."

"Oh, he'll share." Kate winked. "Besides, he has to sleep sometime."

"Can you lift him up a little, so I can see him better?"

She complied, her gaze shifting between Eric and Benjamin. Her two men, each stubbornly handsome. A gush of love welled inside. This joy was real, so real she wanted to capture the emotion and save it in a bottle, so she could drink it in longer.

"He's so perfect." Eric beamed with pride. "Look at his button nose. I love the gentleness to his breaths. He sucks the pacifier with rhythm."

"Really? R&B or Country?"

"Maybe both. Could be some classic overtones to his beat," Eric added. "Classic rock, that is."

Almost on cue, Benjamin spat out the pacifier and wailed. His cries reached their crescendo quickly.

"Guess I've overstayed my welcome," Eric said. "I'll text later, in case you're asleep, but if you're awake, call me. I love you, my Katie."

"I love you, too," Kate managed to say over the howling baby. "I love you," she repeated, but Eric had already ended their video chat. She unbuttoned her blouse, kissed Benjamin quickly on his sweet face, and guided him to his destination. The immediate peacefulness and extreme loneliness of the moment engulfed her, as though she wandered into a darkened cave and couldn't find the way out.

She secured her arms around Benjamin's tiny body, a mixture of deep love and unnamed anxiety blending in waves inside her stomach. "It will be all right." The words Julie had said in the days following their mother's death played in her head. "Everything will be all right. God will see to it," Julie had promised, much in the same way their mother would have done.

Five minutes later, Benjamin lay peacefully in his bassinet. Kate slipped into bed, grateful that Julie slept in the next room. Her sister, near enough to give solace, yet far enough away not to hear Kate's tortured sobs.

Chapter Eight

Eric stared at his blank computer screen, the image of his wife and son still freshly painting his memory. He hated lying to Kate. He hated waking up in an empty hotel room in sweltering Hidalgo. He hated the choices he had been forced to make. Mostly, he hated Anmar X.

Of the more than fifty countries covertly cooperating with the CIA's extraordinary rendition, Mexico was his least favorite. What his superiors euphemistically termed "off-the-book" extraditions often ended in torture and other abuses to yield usable results. No one wanted to talk openly about the work his unit, and others like it, performed.

A harsh thumping at his hotel door jarred Eric out of his haze, and he snatched his gun from the bedside table. His pulse amped up as he eased across the room.

"Yeah," he said, standing to the side of the closed door, his weapon cocked.

"It's me," a familiar voice boomed.

Blowing out a breath of relief, Eric shoved his gun into the back of his waistband before he opened the door. "Ralph? What are you doing here?" Normally his team leader didn't just drop by.

"Expecting someone else?" Ralph stepped inside.

"Usually you send Trish to round me up. Are we on our way to the site?"

"Yeah, in a minute. I wanted to talk to you first." He walked farther into the room. He repositioned a chair near the window, sat and pointed for Eric to do the same.

Eric took a seat on the edge of the unmade bed. "What is it now?" he asked, no longer worried about the exasperation coloring his words.

"Exactly that," Ralph barked. "What in the hell is going on with you? You're losing your edge, Wiley, and right now I can't afford anyone on this team who isn't performing at one-hundred percent. Your professional conduct is for shit."

Eric leaned back, shocked by his words. "Is it? Could it be that we've been chasing this rat bastard for far too long and every time we get close, he slithers away?"

"That's your excuse? Your job is too hard?" Ralph layered his speech in faux sympathy. "Man, this job *is* hard. It's supposed to be hard. You knew that coming in. That's what you signed up for. If I remember, you dogged your superiors relentlessly until you got assigned to this task force. Now that things aren't turning out seamlessly, you want to have a hissy fit?" Ralph stood, towering over Eric. "Not on my time. And not if you're risking the lives of my team. I won't take that chance. I don't give a damn what your personal jacket is on this case."

Eric had pulled a coup in getting assigned to the team investigating weapons smuggling and Anmar X. In the course of his rookie shenanigans, he managed to tick off a lot of fellow agents, angry that he received preferential treatment because of his adoptive father, Benjamin Wiley.

If only they knew the truth; that his connection to this case went deeper than superficial nepotism. Ben had done more than help Eric move up the ranks of the CIA. He and Adele took an orphaned, troubled teen and raised him into a responsible man. Eric would always be indebted to them. He would have wandered through life, struggling to put the pieces together, never truly coming to terms with the gnawing loneliness and pain that lived in his gut.

Eric rose slowly trying to rein in his anger at Ralph's accusation. "I would never, ever compromise anyone on this team. Ever."

"Is your head in the game or not? That's all I need to know. Trish and I are heading over to the site. A lot of time and work has been put into this operation. This weapons buy has to go down without a hitch. Understand?"

"Yeah, I understand and my head is in the game. I'm just sick of how many times Ops has sent us down a rabbit hole," he complained, his tone louder.

"This time is different. New agent. New intel," Ralph said.

Eric grunted. "Heard that before. This is my last mission, Ralph. No matter what. If we capture Anmar X in this deal, great. I'll put the murders and everything else he did to rest. If not, I'll live with the knowledge that I didn't get the job done. Either way, I'm going to be home with my wife and son. Not taking off at a moment's notice for some rag-tag tip that leads nowhere."

Ralph squeezed Eric's shoulder with force. "I get it. Don't you think I'm sick of this assignment, too?"

Eric shrugged. "We're always a day short, a clue away from completion. It's the mission that will never end. Almost like someone on our side is feeding their faction our next move."

"We can't give up, though. What good would that do? Your family wasn't the only one destroyed by these guys. I understand you want revenge, but there are other people who have suffered. Hell, there are folks suffering now and if we stop, more will be terrorized."

"I get that. I'm here to even the score not just for myself, but for all the families he's destroyed."

"Then act like it. I need you fully engaged."

"I'm all in."

"Good. We've invested too much manpower to turn the case over to another task force."

"Fine, but understand...after this mission, whether we catch him or not, I'm not giving that asshole another minute."

Chapter Nine

"Everything was delicious." Kate complimented Monica before leaving the dining table and moving into an overstuffed rocker-recliner in the adjoining family room. Operating on erratic sleep, she pulled the lever on the side of the chair to elevate her feet. She let her head drop against the faux suede fabric, allowing the cushiony softness to engulf her. From where she sat, Kate watched Monica put away the Chinese takeout and wash a few dishes. Julie wiped the granite countertops before carrying a wine bottle and two glasses into the family room where Kate relaxed.

"Benjamin's been sleeping nearly two hours," Julie said, setting the bottle and glasses on the coffee table. She took a spot on the couch facing Kate. "Soon those two hours will stretch to three and then four."

"That would be too wonderful to imagine," Kate said, tilting her head toward her ringing cell phone laying on the counter. Her heart leaped at the possibility of Eric calling. She jutted forward, using her momentum to sit upright and push the footrest in place.

"I'll get it for you," Monica said, glancing at the screen before handing the phone to Kate. "Colleen."

"Terrific." Kate's heart sank a little. She was happy to hear from her best friend and yogi, even though she wished Eric's voice would be on the other end of the call.

"Hello."

"Just checking in on the new momma," Colleen McCool said with an infused happiness. "Hope I'm not interrupting. I don't know the best time to call."

"This is perfect. I just finished dinner with my sisters and Bennie is still asleep, at least for the next few minutes."

"I wondered if I could stop by, maybe tomorrow. See you, Eric and the baby, and share this new-mother yoga practice I've designed for you."

"That sounds heavenly. Tomorrow would be great. Maybe after your early class. Julie will still be here, but Eric's out of town." Kate squirmed at the silence on the other end of the line.

Colleen never passed judgment. Still, Kate wondered if her friend was disappointed in her decision to marry Eric. During the beginning of their romance, Kate had confided her concerns and misgivings about Eric's constant traveling. Colleen had listened lovingly and dried a few tears during those distressing times and had been surprised when Kate decided to move forward in marrying him.

"I've got to go. I hear Benjamin rooting around in his bassinet. I'll see you tomorrow around ten, okay?" Colleen agreed, and Kate quickly clicked off.

"Auntie Julie to the rescue, huh, little man." Julie tenderly handed Benjamin to Kate who had already unbuttoned her blouse.

Monica, now finished tidying up the kitchen, poured Julie more white wine, not topping off her own.

Kate eyed their glasses. "Wish I could join you."

"You'll get there soon enough," Julie admonished. "Enjoy this precious time while he's so tiny and you are his world. Jason's now taller than me," she said of her teenage son, who was at home in California with her husband and their two daughters.

"No truer words ever spoken," Monica added. "Brady's already driving, and Brian is three years behind him. Seems like yesterday I prayed for those boys to sleep through the night. Now, I'm in bed before they are."

"Cheers," Julie clinked her glass against Monica's.

Monica took a seat on the couch. "You're really getting the hang of this, sis."

"There's not too much time to learn." Kate cinched her bra strap back into place as Benjamin lay on her lap, contented. "I had to be a quick study." During their first week home, she had almost turned to formula, complaining to Eric that she felt inadequate, concerned their infant wasn't receiving enough nourishment.

Eric assured her that if Benjamin wasn't full, she'd be the first to know. How she wished her husband was home now. Their video chat from yesterday left her restless.

Maybe I'll call him later tonight.

Twenty minutes later, Julie scooped her sleeping nephew into her arms.

"He fell asleep before he burped, and his diaper is probably pretty ripe," Kate warned.

"I'm going to miss you so much, little man." Julie swayed from side to side and planted a kiss on Benjamin's cheek. "Were Jason, Nicole, and Emily ever this little?" she asked, reflecting on her own children.

"Well, I know none of my boys were," Monica cracked with a chuckle. "Even Bodie weighed nearly nine pounds when he was born."

Kate loved being with her sisters, and she marveled at their endless support, encouragement and soothing demeanor. Still a rookie in Julie and Monica's eyes, both women seemed pleased that their protégé was progressing nicely.

"Why don't you lay down for a bit," Monica prodded. "Julie and I can take care of this little fellow. Between the two of us, we've been where you are seven times."

"Eight counting Bella," Julie corrected.

"No need to pad your numbers. I can't imagine doing this twice, much less compete with your records." Kate turned to Monica. "I've been so wrapped up in my own life that I haven't asked. How are things going with Brad? And Bella?"

Monica stood as though her answer needed movement. "Some days I think everything will work out perfectly, like a storybook ending. Then there are times when this rushing pain from Brad's dishonesty crashes against my brain and I can't stand the sight of him. How he–"

"It's not normal for you to accept all of this in a few weeks or even a few months," Julie whispered, still swaying the sleeping Benjamin.

"You've taken on a lot," Kate continued, "and it's really only been, what, five or six months, and you're still helping Bodie recover from his surgery."

"I'm grateful my son is healthy again. He's back in school. His teacher made certain he didn't fall behind. And he loves not being the baby of the family." She laughed.

"Everyone wants to be a big brother or big sister, don't you know." Julie puffed her chest a bit. "I'm going to change Bennie and lay him in his bassinet," she added heading toward the bedroom.

"Okay, but if he wakes up, it's on you," Kate said.

"Mission accomplished," Julie bragged, returning minutes later.

"More wine?" Monica lifted the bottle toward Julie walking into the room.

"I haven't finished what you poured me earlier." Julie grimaced. "Maybe you should spend the night. We'll have a Jameson girls' pajama party!"

"Naw, I can't. Kids have school tomorrow and I'm sure someone hasn't done their homework yet. Don't worry. I stopped drinking an hour ago. Just water, see." Monica held up her glass.

A heavy silence settled on the room, interrupted occasionally by the whir of the dishwasher changing cycles in the kitchen.

Monica blinked back a tear.

"Time will have all the answers," Julie said. "You have to be patient, mostly with yourself."

"Patience seems to be something in very short supply right now." Monica gulped the last of her water and slammed the glass on to the coffee table. "Sorry. It's just that everything makes me angry."

Kate unfolded her legs and placed her feet on the floor. She walked to where Monica stood and gently put her arm around her. "I think we all feel the same way. Nothing is for certain and most things don't turn out the way you convinced yourself they would."

"You haven't heard from Eric today?" Monica asked.

"Not yet, but it's still early. Did I make a mistake? Do you think he's leaving me and Bennie?" Kate choked on the words.

"What? What are you talking about? That man is crazy about you. I've known that from the first time he came home covered in mustard after Burke dumped his corndog in his lap."

Kate chuckled at the memory. "He enjoys your kids. Always has, but that's different than being responsible for your own."

Julie grabbed Kate by the shoulders and turned to face her. "Now you're talking crazy. I know what you're thinking."

"What's that?" Kate swiped a tear lingering on her eyelashes.

"That you married a man like Dad. And I'm here to tell you that you definitely did not. None of us did. Life has ups and downs. There are good surprises and challenging ones. Believe me, I know."

"I'm sorry," Kate choked out an apology. "You have enough worries."

"I'm here for you. This thing with Eric—whatever it is—will work itself out. Don't be looking for troubles that aren't there. Trouble will find you all on its own. I'm the poster child for that."

"Your job right now is to be the best mommy you can be to your son. Everything else comes in a distant second," Monica said.

Julie grabbed Kate's hand. "Being married is hard. Being a mother is harder. Both are worth every second you devote to them. But you'll always be struggling to catch up if you don't believe in yourself. That's how Mom raised us. We don't give up. We don't give in."

"We don't give a sh—"

"Monica! Mom never said that." Julie laughed. "Kate, what we're trying to say is, relax a little. And don't look for problems. I know you're disappointed that Eric isn't here right now, but I know him. Not as well as you do, of course. But there's nowhere he'd rather be. And he will be home as soon as he can."

"I want to believe that, but how can anything be more important than these first weeks with Benjamin?"

"I'll tell you how. When you own your own business, you can't slough off responsibilities to others. Things fall through the cracks because no one cares as much as you do. Some stuff goes by the wayside and doesn't get done. Other people don't have the same passion, accountability and connection to your enterprise," Julie added, her voice louder. "Before you know it, you don't have a business."

"Um...are we still talking about Eric or you? Is something going on with FunWorks?" Monica asked cautiously of Julie's toy company.

"No, but it could if I wasn't vigilant. Trevor understands that, even though he complains that I'm away so much."

"Like now? Your extended visit with me?" Kate asked, suddenly feeling guilty for needing her sister, perhaps too much.

"No, not at all. He gets why I'm here. He and the kids would love to join us if they could." Julie shot a stare at Monica before turning back to Kate. "Trevor has no problem with me visiting family. He gets a little weird about all the sales trips and conventions. He also has an issue with Derek, my marketing manager."

"He's hot," Monica chimed.

"Stop. You're not helping," Julie scolded. "Trevor and I are working through some issues. The thing is, if I don't make these sacrifices now when the company is starting to take off, there won't be a company to worry about."

Julie wrapped her arms around both sisters. "We're all struggling with something, and we know things will work out."

"As Mom would say, 'Keep the faith,'" Monica added. "I've been doing that a lot lately."

Kate lingered in her sisters' embrace, drawing energy and power from them. Everyone on earth had a cross to bear. Was she manufacturing one of her own? Creating a problem where there wasn't one? Was Eric distancing himself from her or was she imagining a change in his behavior?

Chapter Ten

Eric recognized the driver as one of the soldiers from the failed Sonora operation as he and Trish climbed into the back row of a rusty white van parked outside their hotel. Ralph rode shotgun. Along with another soldier, the pair was shuttled to the outskirts of Hidalgo where the weapons buy was scheduled to go down. During the two-hour drive, Eric peppered Ralph for more details, but the team leader remained closed-lipped, goading his underling to be patient until they reached their destination.

"You'll learn everything you need to know along with the rest of the team, Wiley," Ralph said. "We're not risking any leaks this time."

If you think I'm a security risk, why am I here? Eric wanted to ask, but thought better of antagonizing his immediate superior so soon after their last altercation. Instead, he leaned against the headrest, closed his eyes and visualized Kate and Bennie. With any luck, they'd apprehend Anmar X and he'd be on his way home in a day or two.

"Whatcha grinning about?" Trish asked, poking Eric in the ribs with her elbow.

"What?"

"You have a smug grin on your face. What's so funny?"

"Nothing. Just wishful thinking, that's all."

Ralph turned around from the front seat. "That's your problem. All wishes and not much thinking."

"Just what's climbing up your ass, Peddis. You've been riding me this entire trip. And I think—"

"There you go again, thinking." Ralph smiled and turned back to face the road.

"Don't do it," Trish growled, pushing her hand against Eric's chest. "Sit back. He's not worth it."

Eric blew a frustrated breath between his teeth and settled into his seat. *A few more hours and all of this will be over.*

Eric grabbed two bulletproof vests from the pile strewn on the cement floor of the abandoned warehouse. He handed one to Trish before popping his head through the opening of the other and securing the Velcro straps in place. He slipped a dark windbreaker on and zipped it before joining the rest of the team, already forming a semicircle in front of Ralph and another man.

"All right, everyone. We're going over this once, so listen up. Old Willy here spotted the same gunrunner who dodged us in Sonora," Ralph said, pointing to a man Eric didn't recognize.

"That's Willy Rodriquez," Trish whispered.

Eric had heard of him, or at least his legend. For ten years, Willy had been working under deep cover at various sites throughout Mexico. As far as Eric knew, no one had ever seen him in person and he couldn't help but wonder if the jeans-clad, mustachioed bulldog of a man standing before him was a master of disguise or elusively lucky.

Either way, an inward sigh of relief floated through Eric's chest. They were closing in on their target. Otherwise, Willy Rodriquez wouldn't be involved.

"Word on the street is that Anmar X is behind this band of arms dealers. Took me a while to infiltrate them and gain their trust." Willy grinned. "But if we get these weapons off the streets, my time was well spent." He went on to briefly explain how he had posed as a leader of a Middle-Eastern terrorist group in need of sniper rifles, the kind that could pierce most light tanks. The arranged buy would go down in less than an hour, just after nightfall.

"We finally caught a break," Trish said, sending a side glance to Eric. He nodded, concealing his urge to high-five at their good fortune. Eradicating illegal weapons from the world's landscape might be the agency's prime goal, but snaring Anmar X was Eric's sole purpose. The anticipation kept him from overthinking the weapons-selling portion of the takedown and focusing on the players involved.

Eric stepped forward. "This guy gave us the slip in Sonora. How do we make certain that doesn't happen again?"

"No guarantees around here," Willy snipped, obviously surprised at the question. "Wanna guarantee, buy a toaster."

The group chuckled, but Eric continued, not allowing the sarcasm to deter him. "What are the chances Anmar shows up? That he believes this is a real transaction?"

Willy walked toward Eric and put his hand on his shoulder. "I'm giving you the best chance to throw a net on this guy, but this isn't a racetrack where odds are posted. You've worked for the agency long enough to know nothing's for sure."

"Well, at least this place smells better than the last one," Trish said, offering small comfort to Eric.

"All right." Ralph sent a glare in Eric's direction. "Anyone else needing reassurances from their mammas? No? Terrific. You have your assignments. Let's make this one count."

Understanding their roles, each team member moved quickly into position, awaiting the arrival of the truck laden with weapons. Eric took point near the open roll-up door. From where he crouched, he had a clear view of the monitor feed from the surveillance cameras mounted around the perimeter of the facility. He would know the moment the dealers drove onto the property. Other than Willy standing near the same beat-up white van that had transported them earlier, the screens revealed no movement in or out of the area.

With his goal so close he could touch it, thoughts of Kate swirled in his mind. It had been two days since they last spoke and three since he watched his baby son babble on a video call. He loved his wife and knew she'd be worried; still, he couldn't risk even a text to check in. Right now, capturing Anmar X was the only desire he sought to fulfill.

***

Kate brushed her hair and secured her auburn locks in a ponytail before searching her closet for a dressy blouse, loose and long enough to overlap her maternity jeans. Definitely too soon to squeeze into her regular clothes. With a quick swipe of mascara and a dusting of blush, Kate Wiley, the accomplished architect, magically appeared in the mirror.

She had welcomed the call from her boss, asking for advice on a new proposal and to answer a few questions about the downtown Phoenix office complex. He offered to stop by the house, but she decided to visit Harry at Mack & Partners, and show off Benjamin to coworkers.

Nearly four weeks ago, she had rushed from her corner office without a backward glance—her husband and son the only visions brightening her horizon. She hadn't worn makeup or matching clothes since.

Excitement bubbled in her stomach recalling Harry's telephone call. "If we are awarded the job, I'd like to assign it to you," he had proposed. "That's why I want your input now."

Smiling at the memory, Kate glanced at the small clock on the bathroom counter noting she had forty-five minutes to get to the meeting.

We better get going.

"Julie, are you ready?" she called out, dabbing a bit of perfume behind her ears. Panicked that she hadn't allowed enough time to load the car with baby gear, she quickly lifted Benjamin from his bed, and headed toward the front door.

Thirty minutes later, they pulled into the company's parking lot. Kate turned off the ignition and gulped in chunks of air. Everything that once was routine now felt foreign and unconnected. She opened the door and walked to the trunk to retrieve the stroller. A nervous surge pulsated through her as she struggled to unlatch, and tug open the frame.

"Ouch!" Kate screamed at pinching her finger in the hinge. "Why is this so hard?" She sucked the skin where a blood blister began forming.

"Take a breath, you'll be fine," Julie said. She held the stroller steady while Kate clicked the car seat containing her sleeping infant into the brackets.

"I see women with two and three children seamlessly going about their business," Kate lamented, wiping beads of sweat rolling down the sides of her face before grabbing her portfolio case and purse.

"That's called experience."

"Heh. I can't even put one child in a stroller by myself. Guess I'm going to have to get better at balancing."

"You'll get the hang of things," Julie soothed, "and be a pro in no time."

Kate directed the stroller toward the building. "Maybe. I didn't realize how time-consuming all this is. I should have started packing last night."

"You're not kidding. As much as I won't encourage you to hurry this stage along, you will be happy when going anywhere doesn't involve mountains of gear." Julie pointed to the bulging diaper bag slung over her shoulder.

Kate slid Julie a smile as the pair walked side by side. "Thanks for chaperoning our first outing. I'll eventually get used to packing up baby and equipment, otherwise, I'll be confined to the house."

"You, housebound? Never happen." Julie held open the glass door, making space for Kate to steer the stroller through the lobby. As she pushed the elevator button for the third floor, an odd sensation swept through her. The familiar workplace surroundings now registered unfamiliar. Was this where she still belonged?

Her maternity leave stretched for several more weeks; however, Harry had suggested working from home, at least for a few months. Maybe he was aware of something she'd yet to learn. She had toyed with the idea of using the garage as a temporary office. With her drafting table already in place, all she needed was a computer, some storage and shelves to hold blueprint tubes. Voilà—she'd be ready for business.

When she brought up the topic, Eric had listened attentively, fully supporting her decision. He also offered to arrange interviews with potential nannies should Kate change her mind and decide to return to the office.

That was becoming a strong possibility, since doubts about the stability of her marriage continue to swirl in her mind. She questioned the wisdom of riding the mommy track. The urge to secure her place at the firm, should she need to return, overwhelmed her. Visiting face-to-face with Harry Mack would prove that she was still in the game, vital, productive and eager.

"There's our new momma," Harry said as Kate and Julie exited the elevator. "We're so glad you stopped by so we could meet this young man." He and several employees gathered around the stroller, *ooohs* and *aaaahs* peppering the air.

Kate unbuckled Bennie from his carrier, lifted him and turned him to face everyone.

"He's magnificent," Mandy declared, hugging Kate. "Just like we knew he'd be."

After several minutes of compliments and updates, Julie took Bennie, allowing Kate time to talk alone with her boss.

"Thank you for agreeing to consult on the Parker project. I have the proposal in my office." Harry directed her down the hall.

As she passed her office, Kate spotted a stranger behind her desk, talking on the phone.

Harry acknowledge the man before whispering in Kate's ear that he was a temporary employee. "Your spot is safe until you're ready to return."

Kate waited until he closed the door before responding. "It's a little weird seeing someone else in my space. Eric and I are figuring out our game plan, but the way things look now, I'll be back here as scheduled." Kate sat in the visitor chair in front of Harry's desk.

"I'm relieved to hear that. If you're worried about your job, you don't need to be. We're muddling through, but missing your skills terribly. That's why I asked you to stop by today."

Kate nodded, then looked away, wondering if her visit was a favor to Harry, or really to secure her spot at Mack & Partners.

"Our HR director alerted me to some accommodations we may be able to offer you as an incentive to return, including more flexibility in your workday. Let me know when you're ready to discuss your options."

Kate smiled. If only it were that simple. Despite what she just said, she wouldn't make any decisions about her job until she knew where her marriage stood. Eric had to call, and soon. She couldn't hang onto this tether of uncertainty much longer.

Chapter Eleven

As he monitored the surveillance screen, a box truck with two men slowly approached. Eric's earpiece buzzed with the sound of gravel crunching under its tires. Judging from the cab size, enough weapons and ammo to supply a small war could be inside.

Itching to put his finger on the trigger and squeeze, Eric forced himself to breathe in anticipation of Willy's signal. He watched the truck slowly pull in alongside the van, pointing its front end away from where Eric and the team waited. He turned to view a surveillance screen. Two men, both wearing black ski masks, climbed out of the cab and ambled toward Willy. Eric couldn't tell for sure, but in his gut, he sensed one of them had to be Anmar.

A chilling thought swept through him and he scanned the hillside. Anmar could also be positioned in the hills, guarding the payload from a remote location.

Eric watched the taller man unlock the back of the truck and roll up the overhead door. The driver, a good foot shorter, stood nearby, his gun visible. No one waited inside the vehicle.

Eric counted three rows of wooden crates, stacked four high. He couldn't tell how far back the rows went. If there were twenty guns in each crate, this operation would remove hundreds of illegal weapons from the black market.

After exchanging cursory greetings, Willy gestured for a crate to be pried open. He then asked for a second crate from the back of the shipment to be brought out.

The taller man complained but eventually unloaded several crates to get to the ones in the very back. Satisfied, he handed a backpack to the tall man. The team's signal to close in.

"Hands in the air! Now!" Ralph's voice boomed, his rifle trained on the men. "Nobody moves."

The taller man followed instructions, but the shorter one, not understanding the command or not willing to be taken prisoner, scurried into the truck cab.

"You heard him," Eric shouted, leaving his position inside the warehouse. "Drop the gun and climb out of the truck with your hands in the air."

Instead of complying, the driver sent several shots whizzing past Eric, and crashing against the warehouse's metal siding. Using the truck as cover, Eric edged along the side. When he heard the engine come to life, he took his chance, firing two shots through the window.

With his gun trained on the vehicle, Eric approached and yanked the door open, finding the motionless driver slumped over the steering wheel. He reached inside and checked for a pulse.

"Is he dead?" Ralph shouted from where he stood, cuffing the taller man.

"Yes." Eric ripped the mask off and jerked the man's head back. Blue eyes. Dirty blond hair. Tattoos of a nineties rock band on his forearm. He wasn't Anmar.

Eric jogged to where Ralph stood, surrounded by the rest of the team, except for Willy, who had left the scene unnoticed. Eric stepped closer for a good look at the man who had ruined his life.

We finally caught you.

Ralph turned the suspect around.

"Who the hell is this?" Eric shouted, realizing the young man was not the aging criminal he sought.

The painful truth burned like acid against his rib cage, causing his chest to seize. This couldn't be happening. Not again.

"Maher Beshiff," Ralph grumbled, yanking the guy toward their van. "He sure as hell isn't Anmar X, but I'm sure we can get him to tell us where he is."

"What can you tell me about the weapons you were transporting?

"Who was the driver? How do you know him?"

"Who supplied the guns?"

For over an hour, Eric and Trish took turns yelling questions at an unwashed detainee. They received no meaningful answers. Seated in the center of an eight-by-eight-foot cell, slightly larger than an average prison lockup, the curly-haired bearded man kept his head down. With his manacles hitched together and secured to a table, the prisoner had limited hand movement. He mumbled empty responses and avoided all eye contact.

Maher Beshiff, twenty-nine, married, one son, and a pregnant wife. Eric scratched his head, exasperated about what now passed for a complete dossier. The profiles were so scant, they left little for any agent to work with. If the negligible bits that were provided were true, the guy could have been him. A husband and father, eking out a living.

Eric committed select facts to his memory the same way an anteater chooses termites for nourishment. Beshiff spoke several languages, including English, Spanish and one of the many Arabic dialects. Convinced that the now-dead driver was a local kid looking for a few extra bucks, Eric turned his full attention to Maher.

What interested him most was his supposed connection to Anmar X and how they could exploit that. Consistently, the guy had denied knowing the man. Said he didn't know the name of the *jefe* behind the sale. Eric had to figure out how to refresh his memory.

The detention facility, swathed in gray and olive-green hues, with accents of drab and dull, provided the necessary desolate backdrop to a hopeless, forsaken situation. The air conditioning, probably installed last century, spat out a lukewarm breeze almost strong enough to flutter toilet paper. Beads of sweat poured down his face, causing additional strain on what little patience he had left. Eric slammed his fist on the table's surface, causing the man to jump. He shifted to within an inch of the prisoner's face. "Maher, you have to know who provided the weapons."

Eric smelled fear and angst surge through Maher's pores; still, the guy remained silent.

"Things will go easier on you if you tell us the truth," Trish added.

Maher turned toward her voice and Eric yanked him back. He had to crack this guy and quick.

If there wasn't a breakthrough soon, Ralph, who sat in the adjoining room in front of a two-way mirror, would replace Eric with another agent. He couldn't let that happen. He had to be the one to capture Anmar.

He had begun the interrogation portraying a tough agent, but now it was time to change gears. Time to extend a helping hand to this hapless pawn of a gang of gutless gun-smugglers. Trish, still vacillating between tough cop and understanding seeker of the truth, would catch on quickly to his revised tactics.

"Look, Maher, we all get in over our heads at times. From what I know, you have a wife and a family. You're a good man. It's easy to see that your coworker may have taken advantage of you." Eric glanced at Trish. She shrugged as if to say, go for it.

"I'll bet you didn't even know there were weapons in the back of the truck, did you?"

Maher nodded.

Eric infused a tiny bit of enthusiasm in his voice. "I thought so. Listen, help us find the guy behind all this. Get everything on the table, then we'll know how involved you are and what we're dealing with. Then we'll be able to help you return to your pregnant wife and son."

Maher nodded again, but remained stone silent. Eric had planted the seeds for a confession. He knew the prisoner was considering the offer, but wasn't quite ready to give up his employer.

This schmuck had better offer up some real information soon, or good-guy agent Eric would turn into his worst nightmare.

Eric would lock him in the cold room with instructions to the guards for regular, frequent watering. He predicted an hour, two at the most, in the freezer-like setting, before the man cracked. He'd seen it before. Much more seasoned combatants—ones who withstood hours of physical abuse—couldn't bear the freezing temperature.

As if on cue, Eric's phone vibrated, the phone he wasn't supposed to have on him. He quickly placed his hand on his front pants pocket to quell the pulsation, surprised that civilian communication penetrated the site's two-feet-thick concrete walls. He left his hand against his thigh, not bothering to check the call's originator. He knew. Kate.

God, he wanted to talk to her, but now wasn't the time. He had to keep his focus on Maher and what information the team could extricate from him.

***

Kate should be asleep, but she couldn't shut her mind off, waiting to hear from Eric. She had phoned him as soon as Julie went to bed. Her call dropped immediately to voice mail. She tried again and again, but each time her appeal went straight to recording as though he had turned his phone off. *Why won't he answer?*

An ache, more powerful than any Kate had endured, jumbled her thinking. That link, her only connection to her husband hundreds of miles away, rendered useless. She fought the panic surging through her by phoning Adele to get some answers.

"Hi, Mom. It's Kate."

"Kate, honey. Is everything all right? It's past ten. Is the baby sick?"

"No, Benjamin is fine and I'm sorry for calling so late. I was wondering if you'd spoken to Eric recently?" Kate hated exposing the cracks in her marriage to her mother-in-law, but her pride took a back seat to her mounting anxiety.

"Uh, no. I don't think so," Adele answered, a tentative lilt painting her voice. "I wasn't expecting to, though. Has something happened to him?"

Kate immediately regretted placing the call. In attempting to quell her own concerns, she had planted the same seeds of worry in Eric's mother's mind.

"No, I don't think so. I've tried calling, but he doesn't answer. I thought he might have checked in with you or Dad about the progress of his trip. Do you know where he is or how I can get ahold of him?"

Adele paused as though searching for a plausible excuse for her son's elusiveness. "Let me wake up Ben and ask if he's spoken to Eric. Hold on a second, dear."

"Kate, Ben is sound asleep," Adele said, returning to the call several minutes later, "but I'm certain Eric is fine. I'm sure by the morning you will have probably heard from him. I'll have Ben call you anyway."

"But—"

"Try to get some sleep." Adele signed off, a sweetness in her tone that had been missing moments earlier dripped from her words.

Kate suspected that Ben was awake and for some reason, refused to talk to her. Surely Eric would have contacted his parents during a company buying trip. If, in fact, he was in Mexico on family business. What wasn't Adele and Ben telling her? Unless they were deliberately covering for Eric.

Kate set her phone down on her nightstand, accepting a new reality. Adele and Ben were buying time for him to come up with an exit plan. She spent the next several minutes formulating other excuses for why Eric hadn't returned her calls. Each possibility circled back to the answer she didn't want to believe. He didn't love her anymore. How could she have misread the signs so completely?

She didn't dare say those words out loud, or tell Colleen or her sisters. They would attribute her dramatics to postpartum depression, dismissing the seriousness of her concerns. Some of her emotions could be chemically related to changes in her body, but that didn't alter the facts. Eric was in a foreign country and she had no way to reach him.

Her hair still in the day's sloppy ponytail, Kate sat quietly in the glider. From inside the shadowy darkness of her bedroom, a nightlight cast a soft glow on the carpet. She took comfort listening to Benjamin's rhythmic breathing emanating from the bassinet near her bed.

She willed herself to remain positive. *Think happy thoughts. Remember the joyful moments.* An image of a delightful grin spreading across Eric's face the first time he held their son materialized in her mind's eye.

That's the picture she fought to visualize minutes later when she closed her eyes and attempted a few minutes of sleep. Not the disturbing vision of her happily-ever-after slowly slipping away.

Chapter Twelve

Eric and Trish's good-guy/bad-guy roleplay failed. Miserably. The suspect, unresponsive to cajoling, threats or bribery, practically laughed in their faces at the idea of providing any information on the men he sold arms to.

"Maybe it's time to increase the pressure," Eric said, turning to Trish. After eight hours with this smug sucker, Eric was ready to start the cold treatment. Maher knew a lot more than he was willing to disclose. But just as he was about to suggest shaking things up, Trish shot him an odd look, eerie enough to make Eric keep his notion to himself, at least for the time being.

Minutes later, Ralph entered the room. "Let's take a break." He unlocked Maher from the table, keeping the manacles on his wrists in place.

"Take him to the bathroom," Ralph ordered a guard, "and bring him some water on your way back."

Eric and Trish, taken aback by their team leader's unorthodox directives, remained silent, incredulous at the delays he ordered. Neither had ever seen a time-out called during an inquisition. Ever.

Several minutes later, the guard returned Maher to the interrogation room and secured him to the table. Ralph shooed Eric and Trish out, and the trio regrouped in the observation room next door. From their perspective on the other side of the two-way mirror, they observed Maher struggle to keep his paper cup from tipping as he drank.

"Why'd you take a break? We were just getting somewhere," Eric said, surprised Ralph hadn't removed Maher's shackles, to guarantee their prisoner maximum comfort.

Ralph took a sip from his travel coffee cup and set it on the table. "You weren't getting anywhere. I had to do something to change the rhythm."

"Change the rhythm?" Eric thought the words would explode through his chest. "If you hadn't interrupted us like this place is some sort of vacation resort, we could have intensified our approach. It's time to start the deep freeze."

"Think so?" Ralph snorted.

"Think you could do better?" Eric snapped.

"Anybody could do better than getting nowhere." Ralph frowned and took another gulp of coffee.

Perspiration dripped down Eric's face and on to his chest, leaving noticeable wet spots on his T-shirt. "Can't they fix the air conditioning, at least?" he hollered. "We're not the people who should be sweating."

"Calm down, Wiley. You're the one who blew this, walking in like you knew the guy. Old college pal, rah. Rah. Damn, after all these years, you still don't know nothing."

"Is that so?" Eric grabbed Ralph's metal coffee cup and hurled it at the wall. "If you'd let us actually apply some pressure to the man, we'd be farther along. Honest to hell, it's like you want to drag this session out! Maybe we should call for pizza. I think Maher likes pepperoni and mushrooms."

Trish handed Eric a soda. "Here, cool off with this."

He wrapped his hands around the can. "Crap, this ain't cold."

"Didn't say it was, but you have to mellow if we're going to get this guy talking. We're almost there. I can feel he's getting close to breaking," Trish added, taking the seat across the table from Eric.

"Yeah, until Ralph called recess. What the hell was that about?" Eric yelled, louder this time.

"I want him to squirm a bit. Think about why he's here."

Eric slammed his hand on top of the table. "He knows why he's here!"

"Sit down and shut up," Ralph ordered. "We've already gone through all this. Once we're done, I'll recommend you for reassignment. You've had enough of this task force, and we've had a bucket load of you!"

"Stop with the testosterone-driven jabs." Trish crossed her arms as though reprimanding two kindergarteners fighting over finger paints. "We have a job to do. Maybe a break was a good idea. Not for Maher, but for us."

Eric looked at his watch. "Excuse me for a minute. I need to take a leak," he said to Ralph.

"And make a phone call?"

"Yes, make a phone call. What business is it of yours?"

"Get the hell out of here," Ralph blustered. "Ten minutes, no more."

***

Kate nearly tripped over the leg of the coffee table reaching for her ringing phone. "Hello," she answered, relief pulsing through her.

"Babe. I can't talk for but a minute, but I saw several missed calls. Is everything all right?" Eric's clipped words, so detached and measured, left Kate uneasy.

Their phone connection was strong; still, he clearly sounded distant, bother and burden in his voice. The realization that he had called out of obligation, not his unending love for her, weighed on Kate's heart like a kettlebell laying on her chest.

The harried man at the other end of this call was not the same Eric who had googled "best first dates" before asking her out or the man who waited all night in a hospital lobby while she was in the labor room with Monica. This Eric was not the man she had committed her life to. The hardness in his voice convinced her of that truth.

"We're fine," she snapped, an icy surge added to her words that moments before would have been warm and welcoming.

"Oh, thank God. I miss you," he said, sounding softer. "I'll be home soon."

"You're still coming home?"

"What is that supposed to mean?"

"Just tell me, Eric. I'm a big girl. I can handle it."

"Handle what? That I'm madly in love with you and the sooner I can leave this miserable place and be with you, the happier I'll be."

Kate thought about his words. About how his speech went from harsh to harmonious. He sounded sincere, but she'd been fooled before.

"Are you still there?" he asked.

"Yes, I'm here. We're both here. And you're not."

"Not because I don't want to be. It's this job—"

"Stop it. I can't take this anymore. If you want out of this marriage, say so. You don't have to pretend that you're urgently needed to get away from me."

"Wait. What? You think I'm on this trip to get away from you? Where did you get that crazy idea?"

"I don't know. Maybe because you left when our son was just weeks old to go on a shopping trip. With Trish."

"Oh, so that's where this is coming from. Trish and I work together, that's all. There's never been anything romantic between us. You know that." That edginess from earlier returned to his voice, forcing Kate to question his sincerity.

"No. I don't know that. I don't know where you are and why I can't reach you. I don't understand why you're not here, if that's really where you want to be."

"Look, Katie," his voice deepened to a velvety timbre. "I love you. I need you and I want only you. The aftereffects of having a baby are messing up your thinking."

"Seriously? You're going to go there?" she exploded. "Don't blame what's happening between us on postpartum or whatever you think you know about women who have just had a baby. I felt this way before Bennie arrived. Only now it's more obvious that you don't want to be here."

"I stepped out of a meeting because I wanted to talk with you. I have to get back, but listen to me. I am not leaving you or Benjamin. You are my life."

"What meetings are going on at eleven o'clock at night? Tell me what you're really doing, Eric, because I can no longer believe the bull you've been shoveling about buying textiles. I'm a college graduate, I know how to use the internet to find out things."

"I promise you, when I get home I'll answer every question you have. Right now, I have to get back."

"Are you doing something illegal?" Kate threw out another theory. Maybe something more sinister was happening.

"What?" he yelled.

"That's the only other explanation I can come up with that makes any sense. If you are committed to me, then what else could drag you so far away, especially now. Tell me the truth. What are you doing in Mexico?"

"I don't expect you to understand. How can you really?" Eric asked. "Sweetheart, you have to trust me, though. As soon as I get home the day after tomorrow, I will explain everything. I'll answer every question. Trust me, Kate, because I trust you."

Kate didn't answer immediately, sensing Eric's urgency to end their call. "Are you breaking the law?" she questioned again.

"No. Never. Now I really have to go. I love you and I need you. Only you. Kiss our Ben-meister for me. I'll call tomorrow."

Kate didn't know how long she stared at the phone after Eric disconnected. Bennie's whimpers emanating from the bedroom jolted her into the present. "Coming, baby," she cooed. "Mommy's coming."

She dashed to her bedroom and lifted her son from his bassinet. She smothered him with kisses before clutching his tiny body against hers. "Daddy's coming home soon," she soothed, gently circling his tiny back with the palm of her hand. "He misses us and loves us," she said, wondering if her words were meant for Benjamin or simply an effort to convince herself of what she wanted to be true.

Chapter Thirteen

Eric nodded at Trish standing on a wooden porch about a football field away, frantically waving. Behind her stood the doorway leading into the detention site, beckoning his return. Obviously, Ralph had ended their short break, but all Eric could think about was how his call to Kate had ended.

As he headed back to the detention site, he regretted the way his choices affected his family in such a negative, piercingly painful way. Their lives should remain untouched by the horrors, inhumanity and harsh realities his career imposed. He had to convince Kate of his commitment to her and Benjamin, but how could he put her mind at rest while he was so far away?

"Ralph's on a rant," Trish said when he got closer. "Get in here."

"Yeah. Yeah," he answered, his boots crunching against the gravel as he walked across the parking lot. There was a small copse of palm trees providing minimal shade to what looked like a dove swooping into its boughs. He grunted at the irony of seeing a symbol of peace while such a torrent of rage exploded inside him.

What made the hairs on his skin stand on end were the kinds of deviations set in motion and where he sensed they would take this investigation. Behind the scenes, the true goals of their mission had altered recently without any input from the task force in the field. On the fly, rules were being misused, broken and dismantled.

An outside source was making changes, but who and why?

A sick feeling swelled in his gut at the thought that Ralph was stalling. He, and maybe even Trish, was holding something back.

Apprehension gnawed at Eric's brain like when a person's name was on the tip of his tongue, but he couldn't quite retrieve it. What clue, what tidbit was he overlooking? He was certain the information was there, if only he could uncover the signs.

In his dozen years as a CIA operative, Eric never needed to look over his shoulder, until today.

"Talked to Kate?" Trish asked once Eric reached her on the porch.

He shrugged. "What's Ralph's deal?"

She hesitated, probably sensing he didn't want to discuss his wife with her.

"He wants to get back at it. Wants you to—and I quote—get your head out of your butt hole and crack this guy."

"We've been at this all day," he snapped. "Can't we resume the interrogation tomorrow?"

"Ralph's not having it. He's paranoid that someone will get to Maher before we do."

Eric remained silent. Maybe Ralph was onto something. Either way, a long night stretched ahead. He held the door for Trish and trailed down the darkened hallway behind her.

An odd vibe followed him to where Ralph waited, just outside the interrogation room. Were the two people Eric trusted most sabotaging this mission? Had they, somewhere along the line, changed their allegiances, or at least their priorities?

More importantly, how could Eric convince Kate that he hadn't changed his?

***

Eric entered the small, coffin-like interrogation room and immediately took offense at the dense, heavy air assaulting his nostrils. The smell of garlic and sweat, a horrible mixture of Ralph's lunch and the lack of air-conditioning, made him gag.

While he had been talking to Kate, the guards relocated Maher into a tighter chamber. The lower ceiling, dim lighting and drab color palette of dark, darker and darkest green completed the dismal ambiance. Eric had hoped for the ice treatment, but being trapped in claustrophobic conditions could also turn Maher into a songbird.

The metal table, where Maher sat in the center of what wasn't much more than a walk-in closet, engulfed most of the area, leaving what amounted to a catwalk perimeter.

Eric nodded to Ralph, standing with his arms clasped behind his back. He would have been performing his signature pacing routine, had there been room. Eric glanced at the two-way mirror, where Trish loitered on the other side of the glass.

She must be thrilled not to be mashed inside this simmering stink hole.

"Hey Maher," Eric opened the conversation, his face less than an inch from the prisoner's, "how do you like this new suite?"

The man issued a barely discernable nod, letting Eric know he was listening before lowering his head.

"Know how we found you?" he continued. "One of your pals tipped us off."

Maher stared at his cuffed hands and didn't reply.

"Yeah, that's right. Somebody close to you is richer today because they sold you out, isn't that right, Ralph?"

"Cash for crooks," Ralph added, leaning against the wall.

"Maybe your wife cashed your ass in. What do you think you're worth? A hundred bucks? A thousand? Maybe a million? Is that what illegal gun suppliers are being ransomed for these days?" Eric poked Maher in the chest. "Answer me!

How much do you think you're worth to the US Department of State?"

Maher shifted his stare to a wall.

"Look me in the eye, you son of a bitch," Eric yelled, grabbing a hank of greasy matted hair, and yanking Maher's head to face him. "Tell me, what is the going rate for a high-explosive anti-tank warhead?"

Maher remained silent.

"Aren't you familiar with your price list? What other inventory do you peddle?" Eric asked, releasing his grasp, causing Maher's head to snap forward.

"Let's try this again," he said, staring down at the prisoner. "Tell us what you know about Anmar X and you can go back to your family. Don't you want to be home instead of here, wondering what's coming next? I guarantee things aren't going to get easier."

"Water." Maher finally spoke.

"Thirsty? That's why you've been tight-lipped? We can give you all the water you want, perhaps not in the way you'd like, though." Eric felt Ralph's heavy stare at the veiled reference at waterboarding. Both agents knew this technique was forbidden, but did Maher?

"I don't know Anmar X," Maher answered, unable to wipe the sweat forming rivulets on his brows because of the shackles immobilizing his hands. "I don't know who that man is. This sale was my first. Never done this before."

"We can do this all day," Eric said. "And move you to a cell so tiny, you'll think this room was a palatial mansion."

"I don't know anything, I swear," Maher said, continuing his denial dance, taking one mental step back each time Eric pressed him about his connections.

Ralph relinquished his position against the wall to remove a short stack of papers about the size of index cards from his back pocket and handed them to Eric. He shuffled through the photographs chronicling Maher's movements over a period of several weeks. A panic surged through his chest as he stared at Ralph.

Where the hell did you get these and why didn't I know they existed?

Masking his surprise, Eric slid a photo in front of the prisoner. "Look familiar?" he barked, observing Maher's posture instantly change from mistreated innocent to alarmed perpetrator. "We knew this wasn't your first rodeo."

In the photo, a smiling Maher preened for the camera, displaying one of the machine guns from the dozens of wooden cases stacked in front of a cinder block wall.

"You're smuggling guns from the United States through Mexico into Iraq. Hell, man, you're up to your armpits in trouble!" Eric barked.

With each snapshot Eric displayed, Maher's claim of innocence evaporated like steam through a whistling teakettle. Realizing his tall tale was collapsing like a folding chair, Maher visibly paled. His eyes searched the room for a nonexistent exit and he licked his chapped lips, avoiding eye contact with both agents.

It wouldn't be long now before the negotiations would begin. Maher was about to make a deal; he just didn't realize it yet.

Chapter Fourteen

"I can't believe you're leaving already," Kate whispered to Julie the next day. "Do you really have to go home?" The sisters stood outside of Kate's master bedroom, peeking in at Benjamin asleep in his bassinet.

"Uh, yes. My husband and kids miss me too, you know." Julie raised her eyebrows. "Don't give me that panicked look. Eric's on his way home."

Kate made a pouty face, the same one she used as a child to guilt Julie into taking her to the mall. Julie wasn't biting. "You'll be fine. Besides, Monica is minutes away, your mother-in-law is around the corner and you got this mommy thing down pat."

"Yeah, I'm a master."

Julie rolled her luggage toward the living room and leaned the case toward the wall. "He's an angel, Kate."

"He is, isn't he. His eyes are Eric's chocolate brown, but that's the Jameson nose." Kate beamed. "I never knew how much I'd love being a mother."

Julie's brow furrowed. "Really? I always thought you'd be an amazing mom because you're an amazing auntie."

"That's not what I mean. The caring and nurturing part came easy. I learned all that from watching you, Monica and Mom, while she was alive. What kept me awake at night was the overwhelming worry parents must feel. I didn't think I could handle that. I can design an office complex to maximize the northern light, but raising a child…that's grown-up work."

Julie chuckled. "Every mom worries if she'll be good enough."

"How do you calm that growing fear inside when the baby cries or the terror of not knowing what to do when they look to you for answers?"

"You just do what makes sense. And once in a while, you ask a big sister for advice." Julie winked.

"Oh, I'll be calling for advice. I'm overwhelmed by how my feelings changed once I saw and held him."

"I had that feeling with Jason, and then again with Nicole, and three years later with Emily. Gloriously, you never get used to the miracle."

"You understand what I mean about mothering. With your kids, or Monica's, I could always hand them back. But with Benjamin, I don't want to ever hand him off, ever, unless it's to Eric."

"His flight lands tomorrow?"

"Around six. His folks are coming to watch the baby while I pick him up at Sky Harbor. He'll be surprised at how much Bennie has changed since he left," she said, not mentioning Eric's call from the night before.

"They do that and rather quickly," Julie agreed. "When he rolls over for the first time, you'll cheer. And then, before you know it, you and Eric will be putting everything you own out of his reach."

Kate picked up a receiving blanket and tossed it onto the couch near a pile of clean laundry in need of folding. "A mom in my Lamaze class told me, 'The days are long, but the years are short.' I now know what she meant."

"No kidding." Julie looked at her wristwatch. "I wish Eric's return hadn't been delayed. I hoped he'd be home before I left. Sort of tag me out. But I'm glad the two of you will have some alone time."

"Me too." Kate smiled. "Even if it's just the twenty-minute drive from the airport." Eric had offered to catch a ride home, but Kate insisted on picking him up. This would be the perfect opportunity to talk without anyone overhearing their conversation.

First thing that morning, she had dialed Adele and asked about a babysitting date for tomorrow. Adele eagerly accepted, offering to come early in the day, so Kate could nap. Neither woman mentioned Kate's ten p.m. call from the night before.

"Still, I'd feel better if he were here," Julie lamented.

"I'll be fine. Colleen is headed over with her new-mommy yoga routine, guaranteed to un-hunch my achy back." Kate attempted to mollify Julie's concerns while rolling her shoulders back and down. "Breastfeeding stoops me forward like a vulture."

Julie's phone dinged. "My ride is here." She hugged her sister, grabbed her suitcase and disappeared through the front door.

Kate wandered back into her bedroom and stood for minutes watching Benjamin's measured breaths lift his chest in small, barely discernable puffs. She laid her palm on his tummy, already rounding, and patted gently.

"Daddy will be home soon, Bennie," she whispered, realizing how easily his nickname slipped through her lips. Tomorrow would be a day of reckoning. Kate wondered how she could prepare for whatever the outcome.

***

Reveling that the irksome pain radiating across her lower back lessened for a moment, Kate exhaled harder than she meant to. Colleen had arrived about an hour after Julie left and immediately began the yoga practice. Kate was grateful for Colleen's yogi skills almost as much as she appreciated her friendship.

"Namaste," she replied as they ended their yoga session.

"New mommies deserve a special pampering," Colleen said, "including an extraordinary kind of yoga."

"New mother or not, those poses were…" Kate paused, searching for the right word.

"Relaxing?" Colleen supplied.

"Oh, more than relaxing. I've relaxed in your class lots of times, almost to the point of falling asleep. These poses were rejuvenating. I feel as though energy is being infused into my system."

"Excellent. That's the end result I was shooting for."

Kate dawdled, sitting cross-legged on her living room rug, leaving her eyes closed. She wasn't in a rush to rejoin Colleen and the rest of the chaotic world. She bowed her head and rolled it from side to side, eliciting a cacophony of creaks, pops and snaps, each sound a celebration of release from the knots of worry clustered in her neck and emanating through her shoulders.

A moment for myself, Kate thought as Benjamin slept, hopefully for another thirty minutes or more. With Julie gone and Eric not yet home, she felt blessed to have her dear friend's company. She didn't like being alone.

"I don't understand how time can crawl along like an endless DMV line, and simultaneously whiz by like the excitement of opening presents on Christmas morning," Kate said, more to herself than to Colleen.

"You're caught between an eternity without Eric and a nanosecond with Benjamin. I'm not surprised you feel this way. I've never had kids, but I expect lots of moms feel the same."

"If only pregnancy passed as quickly," Kate joked, her head still bent forward. She blinked her eyes open, ending her brief meditation. "I didn't realize I was holding in so much tension," she said, using a nearby end table to hoist herself to standing. "Since Benjamin's birth, I've become a human filling station, with everything flowing away. It's sorta like having the life sucked out, pun totally intended." She laughed. "Not much time to replenish."

Kate walked to where Colleen stood and hugged her tightly. "Boy, I've missed you," she said, releasing her friend.

"Not just your healing powers, but your innate sense of right and wrong."

Colleen grinned. "Oh boy, that sounds like a conversation starter."

"Yeah, I guess it is, and me without a glass of chardonnay in my hand. Will you still recognize me?"

Colleen shifted to a nearby couch and patted the cushion, indicating for Kate to sit. "What's going on?"

"Everything and nothing." Kate took a seat and tucked her legs underneath her. "I have everything I've ever wanted, right?"

"As far as I know," Colleen replied. "You're not worried about Eric again, are you? There's no way he's cheating on you. He's not the type."

"Everyone is the type under the right circumstances." Kate thought of her brother-in-law, Brad, and the struggles he and Monica overcame to save their marriage.

"What are you saying? You're the one who's cheating?"

"Oh, good heavens, no." Kate rolled her eyes and pointed to the chaos that bloomed in every home where an infant was found. Diapers and baby equipment, unwashed dishes and undusted tables. The very last thing on Kate's mind was another man. Any other man.

If she was to have an affair, it would be with her pillow. Her deepest, most sensual desires recently were for more than three hours of uninterrupted sleep, deep and delicious sleep. The kind of shut-eye that when you wake up leaves you wondering if your dreams were real. The kind of dreams she used to have about her mother.

Surprisingly, she hadn't dreamed of Bridget Jameson in months, long before Benjamin was born. In fact, her recurring dreams had stopped about the time she married Eric. Once Kate became Mrs. Wiley, perhaps her mother knew her daughter would be well cared for and stopped visiting her from the other side.

"When would I have time to cheat? And I certainly wouldn't want to, even if I could. I love Eric. With all my heart." The words swelled in Kate's throat like a dry sponge, now wet and fully expanded, choking off her airway. "I love him."

Colleen scooted closer and reached for Kate's hand. "He comes home tomorrow, right? That's what you told me. So why so blue. Oops, I mean glum."

"Not you too," Kate huffed. "Everyone thinks I have the baby blues. Maybe I do, I don't know. I've never been a mother before. But I know this uneasiness wedged in the middle of my chest isn't from hormones. It's because…"

Kate stopped and screamed in frustration. For the moment, she wasn't thinking about waking the baby or looking crazy.

Colleen didn't speak or move.

"I'm so sick of all of this. I feel like he's left us." The words scraped against her throat, like something vile that had to be expelled from the inside.

"I know, but he's coming back," Colleen whispered.

"No. You don't understand. I don't think he is." Kate refused to let tears fall, but one and then another slipped through.

"Come here." Colleen opened her arms.

Kate fell into the embrace and allowed herself a good cry, releasing every emotion she had bottled up. Speaking her darkest truth, even to Colleen, left her agonized as though stripped to her base, exposed for the impostor she was becoming.

"What did Eric do to make you think he doesn't love you?" Colleen asked.

For the next fifteen minutes, Kate shared the conversations she'd had with Eric and his adamant denial of her accusations. "He's hiding something from me. I don't know what it is, but I'll tell you this; as soon as I pick him up at the airport, I'm going to find out."

"You're talking crazy. If I learned anything from my years as a police detective, it is not to jump to conclusions."

"I'm not doing that." Kate folded her arms tightly across her chest.

"Where are your facts? You're already in divorce court, but you don't know what, if anything, Eric did to deserve this."

"He's not here, is he," Kate answered, loudly. "And I don't believe his half-baked version of the reason why. I won't live with a man who lies to me."

"Eric is lying to you? About what?"

"Where he is and why he's there." Kate stiffened. "I won't linger for years, like my mother did, while he deceives me with one story after another, only to eventually leave."

"Haven't we had this discussion before? Kate, you're not your mother and Eric isn't your dad. Hanging on to your past is ruining your present. And you have a lovely present to enjoy. I think I hear Bennie calling now." Colleen tilted her head toward the bedroom door where soft, slow squeals emanated from Benjamin.

"If you're really worried, I can do some checking," Colleen continued as they headed to the bedroom. "I still have a few sources from my days on the force who might owe me a favor or two. I'll wait until you give me the go-ahead, though, before I start asking around."

"What would I do without you?" Kate asked, truly amazed at the depth of the friendship she and Colleen had forged during the past five years.

"Don't need to find out. I'm here for you. Feed Bennie while I whip up a snack for us. We'll talk about this later, okay?"

Kate hugged Colleen a bit tighter before heading toward the bassinet. "Don't cry, little man. Mommy's here," she whispered, picking up her son. Without turning on a light, she slipped into the glider, and snuggled him closer.

I'm going to figure this out, she swore more to herself than to Ben. Something is wrong, and I can't pretend it's not. I'll convince Eric to tell me the truth. Even if it turns out that his truth is a reality I don't want to accept.

Chapter Fifteen

Photos of Maher engaged in weapons trading littered the interrogation room's table. In spite of being angry for not getting advanced notice, Eric fingered each photo as though framed in gold before gingerly placing it in full view.

He shuffled through each snapshot, sizing up Maher's appearance in a variety of locations through Mexico and the Middle East. When he reached the last two photos in the stack, his gaze shifted from Maher's silhouette to the man standing next to him, brandishing an assault rifle hanging from a strap slung over his shoulder.

Eric's insides turned cold as though shards of ice pierced his torso. He recognized the face, the overgrown beard, the mottled teeth piercing through a defiant smile. Did the face staring back belong to Anmar X? Or did Eric need it to be? Coal-black eyes, same ones that turned his childhood dreams into nightmarish terror, seemed to reach off the paper with a haunting signal.

Eric would never forget anything about the second man in the photo. How could he? He had spent his adult life hunting him, like a hound tenaciously searching for a missing bone. Pursuing him had been Eric's singular quest. And capturing him might be within reach.

The interrogation had limped through the wee hours of the night. Without glancing at his watch, Eric guessed that it was close to four in the morning. There had been little reason to get excited until now. His heart beat faster at the prospect that their investigation finally hit a tipping point. Things were about to fall in one direction or the other. He pressed harder to ensure that the result tipped in his favor.

"And this snapshot." Eric slapped a second photo on the table. "Who's the man standing next to you?"

"I don't know."

"You don't know?" Eric yelled "How could you not know him? That's you in these pictures, right?"

"Well…I…um. All I know…his name is Hondo." Sweat dripped from the man's forehead, and his eyes were wild with worry.

Eric snatched the guy by his collar, lifting Maher momentarily off his seat. Only the length of chain anchoring him to the table held the man in place.

"Don't give me that crap. This is Anmar X. You know who he is! We all know." Eric slapped his hand against the table, his patience stripped. Judging from the terrified look on Maher's face, he had passed frightened and was on a bullet train to petrified.

Ralph squeezed his bulky body next to Eric's, causing both men to form a human wall. "Your wife knows. Your mamma knows. Damn, man, don't insult us by continuing to pretend," Ralph bellowed.

Maher shook his head as though dusting the question away. "He's Hondo. I know him as Hondo."

Eric leaned forward, his body shaking at the possibility of being an eyelash away from ending his nightmare. "I'll make this very simple for you," he finally said in slow deliberation. "I want the man who is standing next to you in this picture and you're going to help me find him."

"I don't know Anmar. That man is Hondo."

Eric tossed a police sketch matching the features of the surly-looking behemoth, who appeared to be some three inches taller than Maher. "He's a dead ringer for Anmar X. You've heard of him, haven't you?"

Maher shook his head violently. "No. Only from you. He's not anyone I know. I swear."

"Maybe you know him better as Anmar Xanthos."

"I keep telling you I don't know this man!"

"But you two took such a nice photo, as though you were on vacation together. Do you want me to believe that you posed together in front of all those weapons, like you were at a theme park taking snapshots with a walk-around character? Not buying your BS. Not this time."

"That man is Hondo, I told you. I don't know no Anmar."

Eric shoved another print into Maher's face. "Where was this photo taken?"

"I don't remember."

"Don't remember or won't remember?" Eric screamed, yanking Maher toward him. He shook the man with such force that fresh abrasions blossomed red where the bindings encircled the prisoner's wrists. "You're going to tell me where these photos were taken. And you're going to tell me where Anmar X, or as you call him, Hondo is, or—"

"What the agent is suggesting," Ralph interrupted, "is that your cooperation will result in great benefit to you. Isn't that what you meant, agent?"

Eric regained his composure enough to release Maher from his grasp. He walked to the other side of the room, which amounted to two steps away from Ralph. "Yeah."

"Might be a good time to take a little break." Ralph signaled at the two-way mirror and directed Eric out into the hallway and pushed him toward the room where Trish stood waiting.

"What in the world are you doing? Do you want to blow this investigation?" she asked.

"He needs a little more pressure."

"Not from you," Ralph snapped. "Go cool off for a bit. Watch from behind the mirror. I'll bring Trish in your place."

"Don't. Ralph. Really. I want to crack this guy." *I need to crack this guy.*

"Where'd you get the photos?"

"What?" Ralph snapped.

"The photos. Where did they come from? And why didn't I know they existed before now?"

Ralph waved off the question as insignificant.

Eric didn't let the topic rest. "You should have told me about them, so I could have researched the shots to see if there were any other clues besides the machinery and weapons pictured."

"They were handed to me while you were playing telephone tag with your wife."

"While I was what?" Eric closed the space between him and Ralph, spittle punctuating his words.

"Stop, you two." Trish wedged herself between the men. "Step back, Eric. Fighting amongst ourselves isn't helping."

"I'm busting my ass trying to get a break in this case, and when one finally comes, it's the size of the Grand Canyon. You don't even tell me about it. I find out in the middle of questioning."

"Sure, that guy in the photo looks like the artist's rendering of Anmar, but we're not sure it's him, Eric," Trish cautioned.

Eric huffed. "I'm not buying this crap you're both selling! What's really going on?" he asked, infusing an artificial casualness into his tone.

Ralph scrunched his face, as though deciding what version of the truth he should share. "You've been acting whack recently," he finally said. "So, we decided to play a hunch and spring the photos on you at the same time we flashed them around Maher."

"Play a hunch!" Anger and disbelief burst through Eric's every nerve, his rage returning with a vengeance. "You thought I'd be caught off guard? What would that have done?"

"Don't know," Trish reluctantly confessed.

"So now it's you two against me? I'm the odd man out and you expect me not to be pissed?"

Trish looked away, but Ralph held his ground. "Your head's not in the game, Eric. We thought we had a better chance of popping Maher if the information was fresh to both of you. There have been too many screwups with this case. Too many fumbles with evidence. We have to tighten up our protocols."

"You both think I'm the leak? I'm the one sabotaging this case? I don't friggin' believe this is happening!" Eric roared, all pretense of appropriate behavior released like a helium balloon inescapably rocketing toward the clouds.

Trish laid her hand on Eric's forearm and he jerked away. "We don't know where the problem is coming from. That's why we're trying to shake things up a bit. Think outside the box, as you always like to say."

"I've virtually put my life on hold. Now you're telling me we're trying a new tactic, but I'm not included in planning the strategy?"

"We made a mistake." Trish inched closer, but Eric took a step back. "Thing is, we need to get our stuff together right now. Maher is about to pee his pants that we have pictures of him with the smuggled goods. And you bouncing off the walls isn't helping. You've got to calm down."

Eric paced around the room. *Don't blow this.*

"Okay. I'm calm. Fill me in now on who brought the photos in."

Ralph stepped toward him. "We will, but after we finish questioning Maher. He's ripe for picking. I don't want to give him any time to think. Eric, you man the post behind the mirror. If anything strikes you odd or you have a suggestion, use the buzzer."

"But…"

"No buts. Not today. Here's a duplicate set of the photos. Examine them all you want, make notes. Use a magnifying glass, for all I care. We'll regroup after we—"

"Sir." A guard clad in fatigues approached. "There's a call for you in the office."

"Meet me in five minutes in front of the room." Ralph dismissed Eric with a nod and followed the soldier to the command center.

"Listen." Trish leaned toward Eric's ear. "Something weird is happening. The order to not show you the photos came from way up the chain of command. You better watch your back."

"What?"

"Rumors are flying that you may be the reason why Anmar X has never been found. Why we get close, but he always slips away."

"That's crazy. Why would anyone think that?"

"Speculation is that you're keeping the investigation at bay, channeling information that isn't pertinent, sending folks on wild goose chases."

"That's a bunch of bull—"

"I know. I've worked with you. I know your passion for this. Still, someone has the director's ear. They're watching you. And that's never a good thing."

"The field director thinks I'm a traitor?"

"She's not sure. I probably shouldn't have told you this much, but I owe you, Wiley, and I believe you. Just know that I'm following other leads. If something breaks—"

"Let me help," Eric pleaded, his thoughts whirling inside his brain like a runaway rollercoaster. "If there's a double agent, I'll track his ass down."

"For now, just stay focused. Don't give them a reason to fire you. They'll realize it's not you, and then you can launch into action like some superhero." Trish grinned.

Eric raked his hands down his face. "This isn't happening. Not when we've nearly caught the bastard."

"I gotta go. See you on the other side." Trish patted Eric's shoulder, glanced at the two-way mirror, and exited.

Eric stood in the middle of the room, stunned at Trish's disclosure. How could anyone in the CIA think he'd sabotage this mission? He lived for the day when Anmar X would be put behind bars. He had no reason to obstruct that goal and every reason to expedite its completion.

Chapter Sixteen

Kate appreciated Colleen staying to help clean the kitchen, but as soon as her friend drove away, she grabbed the baby monitor and hurried to her drafting table in the garage. Ideas for the Parker project had been bouncing around in her mind. She had to get them on paper before they evaporated from her memory.

Kate clicked on the overhead light, and exhaled deeply at the familiarity of her trade; her L-square and mechanical pencils right where she had left them the day she had set up the workspace. After securing a section of tracing paper in place, she pulled the cap from her favorite pen and began sketching design concepts. A wave of possibility swept through her as she performed the work she loved.

An hour later, Kate stepped back to review her drawings. Although rough in nature, the strong vision she held for this new project pleased her.

Harry might be right, maybe I can work from home after all.

She glanced at the screen and spied Bennie, still asleep. She knew that wouldn't last long. Exhausted and content at stealing a sliver of time for herself, she turned off the light and padded to her bedroom.

The next morning Kate woke up on her unmade bed. Benjamin's gentle whimpers providing the perfect soundtrack to this sleepy start of the day.

Eric's coming home today.

She allowed herself a moment to soak in the realization. Soon, they would be face-to-face and he couldn't dodge her questions. No more speculating what she thought was happening. He promised to tell her the truth.

She rapidly blinked her eyes to focus her vision on the bedside table clock. She wiped dried kernels of sleep gathered in the corners of her eyes and yawned.

Seven-twenty-eight.

She recalled laying on her bed for just a second after Bennie's five o'clock feeding, where she fell asleep, not bothering to change into pajamas. She raised her hand and sniffed under her armpit.

Yuck.

She headed toward the bathroom, thrilled that her son was still sleeping. The downside, though, had her hustling to wash her face. That extra hour meant Bennie's tummy would be empty and his crying would escalate accordingly.

She found herself looking forward to Adele and Ben's visit in a few hours. She'd wait until then to shower and put on fresh clothes. The stench emitted from the outfit she'd worn for more than twenty-four hours permeated her breathing. A flash of embarrassment swept through.

Why didn't Colleen comment on the smell?

Refusing to reclaim the maternity pants stuffed in a nearby bag, Kate dug through her old clothes, hoping her jelly-shaped stomach would cooperate enough for her to fit into one of her regular outfits. Nothing with zippers or buttons would do.

She would talk to Adele and Ben that morning about reducing Eric's travel. And then afterward, she'd run to the store to buy a few pairs of relaxed-fit jeans to get her through these next few weeks. The more relaxed, the better.

But what to wear now? I can't welcome Eric home in these frumpy clothes.

Kate recalled Eric squirreling some of their items in the guest room closet. There had to be something inside those discarded boxes suitable for a quick jaunt to the department store. She slipped her robe on, adjusted the already-tucked blanket around Benjamin's pear-shaped body and waited a moment to hear his measured breaths before heading down the hall.

She slid open the mirrored wardrobe closet door and eyed several boxes, stacked untouched in the same spot where she watched Eric unload them from the dolly cart.

This might take a while.

One at a time, she pulled three cartons marked "ERIC" from the pile and shoved them across the carpet. Lined up, side-by-side, Kate knelt in front of the farthest one and sliced open the packing tape with a closed pair of scissors.

Inside was a mishmash of trophies, uniform jerseys and high school yearbooks. From their appearance, Eric must have been in a real hurry when he dumped these things into the box. The items clustered together haphazardly, displaying a lack of care from their owner.

She unfurled a red velvet sash emblazoned with "Junior Homecoming Prince." Her hubby had been one of the popular kids in school. No surprise there. Eric was both handsome and charismatic. A killer blend to hormone-infused adolescent girls. Predictably, that same combination had won her heart some sixteen years later.

Now more interested in getting a peek into her husband's childhood than finding a pair of sweats, Kate combed through the yearbooks until she found the one corresponding to Eric's junior year. Getting cleaned and dressed no longer seemed important. She craved insight into the man who stole her heart and–she feared–was about to break it.

Sitting cross-legged, she made herself comfortable on the carpet, hefted the book onto her lap, and scanned the pages until she found the homecoming court layout. The two-page spread highlighted the chosen few members of high school royalty, the cheerleaders and team captains.

There, in the middle of the page, smiled teenaged Eric. Her knight in shining armor, decked out in a black tuxedo, exuded confidence far beyond his youthful years. Holding tightly to his arm, the junior homecoming princess tilted her head slightly, displaying her crown.

Although Kate had many friends in high school, she would never have considered herself popular in the way teenagers were depicted in movies and on television. High school was a means to an end for her, not the end itself. She did well in her art classes, but spent most of her free time away from extracurricular activities. She didn't join drill team or the drama club. In fact, had it not been for her best friend Daisy digging up a date for her, Kate wouldn't have gone to the senior prom. She wasn't a princess or a queen, although marrying Eric made her feel that way.

Kate couldn't recall Eric talking about his high school exploits, but after ferreting through these boxes, she had uncovered a few plaques, one touting him the MVP for the varsity soccer team and another honoring him as the varsity football team's academic team captain. Handsome and smart.

Kate removed Eric's letterman's jacket, buried in the bottom of the second box and spread it on the bed to take a better look. She smiled reading *Wiley* embroidered on the back before turning the jacket over to see *Eric* written in a cursive script on the front. Underneath, his coveted varsity letter dominated in the school colors, maroon trimmed in gold felt. She ran her fingertips across the oversized chenille C touting Claremore High, Eric's alma mater.

She opened the third box to find more of the same souvenirs. Kate continued unpacking and making stacks of her discoveries. Missing were the typical ribbon awards and certificates every elementary school kid received. She thought it odd not to find any school photos or trophies for Eric before the age of fourteen. His history seemed to start in ninth grade.

Surrounded by piles representing his schoolboy life–at least his life after freshman year–Kate cleared a space sufficient enough to stretch out on. She folded her hands behind her head to make a pillow and reclined to the carpet for a brief rest. Puzzled by the gap in her husband's past, she closed her eyes to think.

Where are the mementos from his elementary school years? When Adele gets here, I'll ask if she still has any of Eric's childhood stuff taking up space in her home.

Kate opened her eyes and grimaced. From her new vantage point, she spied cobwebs collecting on the ceiling fan. Not having the energy to tackle another a cleaning project, she sat up and diverted her stare to inside the closet. Her gaze landed on a rectangular-shaped container not much larger than a shoe box lurking in the shadows of the top shelf that was previously hidden from view.

Kate wrenched herself up and stood on her tiptoes to retrieve what appeared to be a metal safety chest partially obstructed by the bend of the closet corner. Carrying the box by its handle, she moved to sit on the bed and review its contents. Relieved that the latch was closed, but not locked, she opened the lid and reached inside to find a collection of passports, and other official-looking documents.

All the items, including a marriage certificate, belonged to Simon Erol Khory and Leah Haddan. As she sifted through the pile of papers, a few black and white snapshots slipped from inside the folds and fell to the floor. Kate bent to retrieve them, studying the square-shaped photos with scalloped edges. Along the white borders, she read the dates.

The photos were from the late fifties and early sixties, well before Eric was born. Kate marveled at the resemblance and wondered if the Khorys might be family members. Considering how much the two women in the photographs looked alike, it was possible that Leah and Adele were sisters.

She dismissed this idea since Adele's maiden name was Thomas, not Haddan. Still, the resemblance was uncanny.

Another mystery to unravel. She'd ask Eric and his mom about the people in these photos, too. Or should she? Would Eric be angry that she snooped through his things? Had she broken some unwritten trust by riffling through his belongings, even belongings he'd long since abandoned? And the metal box? Was it purposely hidden or simply set on the shelf to be out of sight and out of mind?

Kate slipped the photos and two of the passports into her robe pocket and reached for a folded manila envelope wedged in the bottom of the box. Just then a knock on the front door broke her concentration. She glanced at the digital clock on the nightstand. *Nine fourteen.*

She hurriedly tossed the items back in the strongbox and returned it to its clandestine corner in the closet. Shoving the other boxes to the side, she closed the bedroom door.

No time to put everything back. I'll tidy up before I pick Eric up from the airport.

Chapter Seventeen

Eric peered through the streaked, faded two-way mirror separating him from the adjoining interrogation room. Fingerprints, scratches, and nicks peppered the reflective coating, compromising the glass's transparency. He suspected the window was installed long before he was born.

Eric stood and turned the wooden chair around to straddle the seat, hoping this movement would break the monotony of the past several minutes and send fresh blood flow to his numb backside. Bored or not, he had to pay attention to possible clues, look for a crack in Maher's demeanor, ferret out any sign that he was about to break. There was no evidence that the prisoner was wearing down. But as Eric leaned over the low-back desk chair to get a better view of Ralph wiping sweat from his brow, he realized there was a good chance one of his partners might be on the verge of snapping.

He shifted his gaze to observe the stream of perspiration building on the prisoner's olive skin and collecting in his mustache. Maher swiped at his coarse hairs before resting his wrists near the center of the army-green aluminum table that most likely predated the two-way mirror. He was nervous, just not nervous enough to be their Judas.

Eric struggled to stay focused on what amounted to an inquisition going nowhere. His mind continued to drift off, eager to process the accusations about him.

Who is behind this frame-up? Some other agent is doing what I'm being accused of, but who?

The idea sent a shudder down his back and he swallowed hard.

Who has that much juice to shift suspicion onto a coworker?

Framing a fellow agent required a special kind of unfettered daring. That kind of treachery took big balls. Not only was it illegal, it was immoral to break the agency's code of brotherhood. The worst offense imaginable was to take down one of your own.

A final thought ricocheted through Eric's mind.

Who could possibly want Anmar X to go free?

"Get in here, Wiley!" Ralph commanded, waking Eric out of his daydream. He blinked, trying to make sense of the changed image now displayed on the other side of the mirror. Maher's limb body, still chained to the desk, slumped against Ralph.

He watched in disbelief as Trish frantically searched for the keys to unlock the handcuffs, while Ralph lifted the prisoner's head, desperately seeking any signs of life.

"Now!" Ralph bellowed again, with heightened urgency.

Eric scurried out of the room leaving his notes behind. "What the hell happened?" He asked, entering the room, but not touching the prisoner.

"Don't you damn know?" Ralph retorted, placing his fingers on Maher's neck to detect a heartbeat. "Weren't you watching when he collapsed?"

Eric sliced his gaze to Trish, who shrugged and returned her attention to unshackling Maher.

"Yeah, he was sitting there with his hands on the table. Seemed like the whole interrogation was going nowhere."

Ralph stepped aside for a medic barreling through the door. The extreme tightness of the space forced the other two emergency crewmembers to stay in the hallway.

"Is he dead?" Eric asked.

"No, but he might be soon. Help me get him through the doorway and onto the stretcher," the older medic declared, motioning for Eric to move out of the way.

Ralph, Trish and Eric stood in a cluster and watched the medical team roll the gurney toward the compound hospital.

"We'll do what we can," the senior medic acknowledged, not giving much hope of revival for their potential informant.

Eric cursed and slammed his hand against the wall. "If we lose Maher, we lose this investigation. We'll lose everything. All the time we've put in. We'll never get this close again if he croaks."

"Then you shoulda been paying better attention, huh?" Ralph spit the words. "You had the best view. Why didn't you warn us?"

Because I didn't see anything, Eric thought but knew he couldn't reveal what amounted to insubordination. "Maybe he had a heart attack?"

"At his young age? Hardly," Ralph said. "Could he have smuggled in a drug?

"Even if he had drugs, he couldn't have taken them," Trish said. "His hands wouldn't reach his mouth."

Ralph, standing with his arms folded, turned back to Eric. "Unless someone helped him take it while Trish and I weren't looking."

"What are you accusing me of? That I somehow signaled Maher? Ralph, that's BS and you know it."

"Is it? All I know is the guy is close to dead."

"But, you can't think—"

"Wiley, you're off this team. And quite frankly, if my recommendation holds any weight, you'll be out of here by the end of the day."

Eric stepped aside to clear a path for Ralph. His team leader would have no trouble making a case for dereliction of duty, so there was no point in defending himself, at least not at this moment.

"He's just pissed," Trish said, as she followed Ralph out of the room.

Eric nodded, appreciating her support, fully aware that everything Ralph accused him of was true and indefensible. He prayed that their prisoner had a weak heart; otherwise, he was in a load of trouble.

Chapter Eighteen

Kate hurried to open the door. Her in-laws had a key, but Kate knew they'd never use it when she was home.

"Good morning," Adele's voice announced with exaggerated happiness, reaching to hug Kate.

"Didn't want to ring the bell and wake the baby," Ben said, heading toward the kitchen, a large pastry box cradled in his hands.

"We brought breakfast," Adele volunteered, following her husband.

Kate trailed behind, inhaling the scent. A heavenly mixture of cinnamon and over-the-top sweetness floated to her nostrils. She hugged Ben and Adele before peeking into the donut container and retrieved her favorite. "You always remember." She grinned and took a bite.

"Adele taught me a long time ago, it's the little things that hold lasting joy." Ben winked at his wife. "Putting the cap back on the toothpaste. Not leaving an empty ice cream container in the freezer. But the most important one is knowing your wife and daughter-in-law's donut preferences."

Adele let out a snort.

"Jelly-filled for my bride," he continued unfazed, pointing to Kate, "and an apple fritter for you, my dear. I'm a Boston cream man myself, in case you were wondering." He fished a chocolate-icing-topped pastry from the dozen or so lined up in three columns. "What do you think little Bennie's favorite will be?"

"Oh, something with sprinkles," Adele answered with finality, ending all donut-related discussion, before turning to face Kate. "How are you feeling this morning? Did you and the baby sleep well?"

"Well enough, I suppose. He's stretching his naps to three hours in between meals, so I guess that's progress. Thanks for agreeing to babysit tonight while I drive to the airport. Uh, I was wondering if you'd mind me taking off for an hour or so this morning. I need to go shopping for some clothes that fit me better." Kate tugged at the waistband of her maternity jeans to emphasize her point.

"Sure, we can stay, but what do we do if Bennie gets hungry while you're gone?"

"I have you covered. The bottles are in the fridge," Kate replied, referring to the two she filled yesterday, planning for Eric to be the one feeding their child that night.

Adele raised her eyebrows. "Oh."

Kate recognized that grimace. She had first witnessed Adele's dismissive facial contortions five years ago while working on the blueprints for the Wiley shopping mall. Kate and her boss, Harry Mack, had to tell Adele and Ben that the permits for their project would be delayed at least two weeks, pushing back the grand opening by a month and possibly missing the Black Friday shopping rush.

That news had caused Adele's eyebrows to arch in such severity, that Kate worried they might not return to their natural shape. This woman didn't like surprises. She preferred having everything unfold according to plan. Her plan.

"Eric wants to take the middle-of-the-night feedings once he gets home. At first, I was against the idea, but sleep deprivation is a powerful convincer." Kate reflected on her words. Perhaps she had more in common with her mother-in-law than she realized, when it came to getting things her way.

Ben put a hand on Kate's shoulder. "You don't have to cover every base by yourself. There's a lot of folks to give you a breather now and then."

Adele nodded but didn't add her opinion.

"I get it, now. I had first-time-mom jitters," Kate confessed. "I thought no one could care for Benjamin the way I do."

"And that's true," Ben said. "Nothing replaces a mother's love. Nothing."

Kate thought she saw Adele send Ben a fiery stare, so she didn't reply, waiting for her mother-in-law to say something. Instead, Ben continued.

"What I mean is…some things you can't understand until you've lived through them," Ben added. "You'll always be number one to that little boy, but the rest of us can pitch in here and there to give you a break."

Kate smiled. "I want to take a shower. Hopefully, by the time I'm done, Bennie will be awake and ready for me to feed him. You'll be able to bottle -feed him while I'm out, so I should have plenty of time to get my errands done and find a few outfits to tide me over until this baby bulge recedes."

"You're already in better shape than I ever was," Adele observed, breaking her brief silence.

"How did you recover after Eric was born? I don't recall you talking about him as an infant or even as a toddler," Kate said, aware that she had never seen a photo of Adele holding Eric as a baby. There were very few photos of her husband as a child and each one was of him alone, not with either parent.

"Oh honey, I wasn't in shape before Eric was born."

Kate licked sugar glaze from her fingertips. "Seriously, I want to hear all about your first few weeks as a mother. I'm curious about what kind of baby Eric was."

"He was a good baby, a very good baby," Benjamin interrupted, as though rescuing Adele from discussing an uncomfortable subject. They weren't debating tax cuts or global warming, so why did he need to save her from this conversation?

Every woman relished sharing stories from her life as a mother. Everything from labor pains to stretch marks to diaper rash cream seemed to be topics of interest to her sisters and girlfriends.

Adele, who usually had an opinion about everything, wasn't eager to share hers on the topic of motherhood. And unless Kate was completely misreading their interaction, Ben was helping her steer the conversation far away from newborn Eric.

Ben moved to the other side of the table and reached for a napkin. "Anyway, we'll talk about all that later. Go take your shower. Make it long and hot. We'll distract Benjamin if he wakes up before you're done."

"That sounds wonderful," Kate said. "When I get back from the store, maybe we can talk about Eric. You see, I was going through some of his old things and—"

"Right on cue," Adele cut Kate off in mid-sentence. Kate turned her head to the recognizable whining of her son.

"A hot, relaxing shower *after* nursing Benjamin will work just as well," Ben said.

"I guess so," Kate said, heading in the direction of the cries, but the nagging feeling that Ben and Adele were hiding something followed her to the bedroom.

***

Eric crossed his arms and stood in the doorway of the empty interrogation cell. The answer had to be inside the closet-sized room, and he had maybe five minutes to uncover the solution. No doubt Ralph would be returning soon with a couple of guards to escort him off the compound and out of the CIA. That is unless Eric could uncover what really happened.

He switched on the lone light, casting a haziness equal to the foggy confusion seeping into his brain. He blinked, allowing his eyes a chance to focus inside the dim illumination and scratched his head.

What am I missing?

He paced the perimeter, which amounted to four small steps in each direction before kicking the leg of the chair Maher sat on less than an hour ago. Frustrated by this unforeseen and unwelcome development, Eric dropped onto the hard aluminum seat.

Sure, he could live without being in the CIA. He planned to quit anyway, but he wanted to leave on his terms, with his head held high, and with Anmar X behind bars. The way things were going, he would be the one incarcerated if he didn't think fast.

Reenacting the scene might provide some insight, so he leaned forward and placed his hands on either side of the protruding steel ring where the prisoner had been yoked. Eric wanted to see what Maher saw. Maybe somehow experience what the detainee endured.

Aside from the table and chair, the room held nothing. The walls were bare. The light fixture bolted inside a metal cage on the low ceiling only added to the dark mystery.

Eric turned to the right and heard the joints in his neck release a series of stress-infested pops, loud enough to cause him to jump. He closed his eyes and shook his head back and forth, allowing the symphony of cracking, grinding and popping to finish before massaging the tops of his shoulders the way Celeste had done during his couple's massage with Kate. Mimicking the therapist's movements, he kneaded his granite-hard muscles for a few seconds, but the action failed to garner the relief he sought, so he gave up.

He opened his eyes and glanced into the two-way mirror on the wall about a foot away. He aimed his gaze to where he had sat on the other side. The humorless reflection of a haggard, soon-to-be-ex-CIA agent greeted him.

You really screwed up this time, Wiley.

With the pads of his forefingers and thumbs, he rubbed the bags forming under his eyes.

Two hours of sleep and allowing a key informant to nearly die on your watch will do that to you.

But Eric hadn't done anything to allow this cluster of trouble to evolve. Sure, he was a bit distracted by the photos Ralph had sprung on him and the combative attitude their team leader exhibited recently. None of that would have blinded Eric to see what had happened to Maher. Would it?

Eric leaned against the table again and placed his hands as though they were shackled to the metal ring anchored in the center.

"Ouch," he hollered and rubbed the side of his wrist where something had poked his skin. "What the...?" he leaned closer to see two drops of blood, each about the size of a pinhead and what appeared to be a needle-like spike ascending from the desk, like a thorn.

That answered the how, but not the what, the why and the who.

The facts—at least what Eric believed were the facts—didn't add up. He needed to tell his theory to someone other than Ralph and Trish. He needed a mentor-agent with experience, insight and an unbiased ability to weigh the information.

Eric glanced at his watch. *Eleven.*

A few seconds later, he raised his phone to his ear and listened as it connected.

"Hello."

"Ben? It's Eric. Can you talk?"

Chapter Nineteen

Relief pulsed through Eric at the sound of Ben's voice. His biological father's best friend, now his adopted dad, would know what to do. In his time, Ben had been on more missions and turned more informants than any of his colleagues. His ability to come up with last-minute intel at the right moment made him a bit of a legend in CIA history.

According to Ben, the President had personally asked him to delay his retirement some five years earlier. "This job takes more out of you than you could ever possibly reclaim," had been his response to the commander-in-chief. Instead of a presidential handshake, Ben received the traditional gold watch and flag pin, and never regretted his decision.

He and Adele began a new life as entrepreneurs, but Ben still enjoyed being a resource for the young agents. From time to time, he would attend various conferences and classes, so that his wealth of knowledge and experience could be imparted to the up-and-coming force. He always made time to answer a question, give a perspective, review a plan.

Eric was grateful he answered.

"What's up?" Ben asked.

"Can you talk?"

"Well, yes. We're babysitting, but—"

"You're at my house?"

"Yes. We're giving Kate a break. What's wrong? You sound panicked. Wait. Hold on a sec and let me step outside for some privacy."

Eric wanted to ask how Kate and the baby were, but he didn't have time. He needed answers. He heard Ben's steps and the screen door slam.

"Okay, talk to me," Ben said.

"I need to get your advice on something."

"Things not going well with Maher?"

"No, they're not," Eric responded, momentarily taken aback that Ben knew the name of the prisoner under interrogation. He blew it off, thinking that maybe he had mentioned the guy's name the last time they talked.

"Tell me what happened."

Eric heaved, recalling the trauma of the last thirty minutes. "During questioning, the prisoner became unresponsive."

"What do you mean, unresponsive? For Chrissake, just tell me what happened."

For the next ten minutes, Eric briefed Ben about the developments, including the thorn-like spike and the drops of blood on the table. Ben didn't interrupt, except to interject an occasional "Hmm." or "I see."

"He went down during our interrogation. And the team leader thinks I had something to do with it. He's trying to get me suspended and sent home."

"Calm down a second. Who's in charge?" Ben asked.

"Ralph Peddis."

"Oh, I remember that slick dick. He doesn't have the juice. He's trying to cover his own ass. Forget about him."

"He's going to throw me out of the CIA. I don't see any way to prevent it. I don't mind leaving. It's just that, I've always..."

"I know, Erol," Ben used his birth name. Erol Khory, the name Simon and Leah, his birth parents, had given him. "This has been a long-held goal for you. I want that bastard brought to justice, too. But listen, how long have you been at this? One marriage already destroyed. Your obsession is damaging your future with Kate."

Eric listened as Ben recapped the reality. His fixation with capturing Anmar X had ripped his world to shreds, ruined his childhood and continued to destroy his life. Chasing his parents' murderer had produced a bounty of distrust, cynicism and anger. He yearned to exchange those entrenched reactions for faith, delight and joy, the emotions Kate brought to their marriage.

"Perhaps it's time to let this go." Ben's voice interrupted Eric's thoughts, snapping him back to the present. "Take over the family business. Enjoy your wife and son. You've given enough."

"That's always been my plan. But now, to leave this hanging, when I know we're close. Those photos have to mean something. And how did they get here?"

"Listen, son—"

"I can't!" Eric snapped. He sucked in a deep breath to rein in his anger. "How could someone have embedded a poison needle into this table? That's definitely an inside job."

"Eric," Ben shouted, an obvious attempt to end the pity party. "It's time to stop. Time to move on."

"I want to, but I can't. I've put too much of myself into this to walk away." Eric swiped at the sweat trailing down his face. "May not matter anyway. They're going to force me out. You and Adele were right. You never wanted me to join the CIA in the first place."

"We didn't think it was a healthy choice for you. But it was your choice and we've supported it, frankly longer than we thought we would," Ben groused. "Turn in your resignation before that Peddis punk has a chance to make more of this than is warranted."

Eric licked his suddenly parched lips, and wiped more sweat from his forehead. Ben spoke sense. He should listen, and he would. Just not yet.

"Someone is impeding this investigation," he protested. "I know they're working from the inside."

"Could be, but that doesn't change your circumstance. You asked my advice. I'm giving it to you." Ben's voice turned soft. "No matter what you do, it won't bring Simon and Leah back. Don't let Anmar X have this much control of your life. Kate's life. The SOB isn't worth one more second of your time. Believe me, I know."

Eric couldn't disagree; still, the urge to finish what he started claimed power over his soul. "I hear voices in the hallway. I gotta go. Peddis is coming back."

"All right, Eric. Think seriously about everything I said."

"I will. I had planned to be flying home in a few hours, but the way things look…will you smooth things over for me with Kate after I tell her I'm delayed? She's asking a lot of questions and I don't want her worrying."

"I'll cover for you, but you need to tell your wife the truth. And soon," Ben admonished.

"I'll straighten everything out as soon as I get home," Eric vowed before ending the call.

"Sit down," Ralph commanded, moments later. "We need to talk."

Chapter Twenty

Kate paid for her iced coffee and scurried to claim an outdoor bistro table facing the sidewalk on the nearly full patio. She placed her bags on one metal chair and tilted another into position for a better view of the passersby. Grateful that Colleen had agreed to meet, Kate happily waited for her friend to arrive. She watched folks scurry along the sidewalks of downtown Avondale. The same street where Eric, with his soulful brown eyes and engaging smile, had asked her for a date.

Kate thought back on that day. She and Colleen had exited the coffee shop and a minute or so later, Kate spotted Eric several feet away. A silly grin teetered on her mouth, recalling the way his eyebrows had furrowed after he approached them, and she questioned him about the woman he was kissing moments before.

In what she now knew as his deliberate, unhurried style, Eric took his time to compose a reply. She wondered if he had been formulating a lie. But before he could spurt out an answer, the leggy woman approached. Trish Atwater introduced herself as a clothing designer and companionable co-worker. Kate later learned that Trish traveled with Eric on virtually all of his foreign buying trips, like the one he was currently on.

Kate sipped her frappuccino and pushed the last thought to the back of her mind. Instead, she decided to savor these few stolen hours, courtesy of her in-laws, to shop for clothes and spend time with her girlfriend. Everything in her life had been turned on its ear; nothing seemed to make sense anymore. Especially Eric. Marriage and motherhood were definitely not unfolding the way she had envisioned.

"There's the mother of the year."

Kate turned her head in the direction of a familiar voice. She stood and leaned over the waist-high railing to embrace her friend. "I'm so glad you could come."

"I would never miss time with you, even a last-minute invite." Colleen pulled back from the hug. "How long do you have?"

"Eric's folks said to take my time." Kate laughed. "I probably can hang out for an hour or so. That's about as long as I can stay away from Bennie.

"Understood. Let me grab a coffee and I'll be right back."

A nervous wave roiled in Kate's belly as Colleen strolled away. She dismissed the queasiness as stemming from not eating a proper lunch, but something menacing sprouted in the recesses of her mind, that had little to do with her diet. This mounting anxiety was grounded in something more than an unbalanced meal.

Things with Eric were getting stranger by the minute. She worried that the man she married and the one she was married to was not the same. Kate flashed back to a made-for-TV movie about a woman who discovered that her husband led a double life. He was married to a woman in a foreign country and had children with her. Could Eric be a party to the same duplicity?

Kate shook her head, attempting to release the melodramatic thought as ludicrous. Too many late-night flicks were falsely coloring her reality. Still, she knew she had called Colleen, not to have coffee and chat, but to tap into her knowledge and experience as a former police detective.

Kate craned her neck to see Colleen still standing in line. Minutes later, her friend placed a pastry nestled inside a sheet of bakery paper on the table in front of Kate. "Golden currant is your favorite, as I recall."

Kate moved her shopping bags from the other chair and set them on the ground, making room for Colleen. "You remember everything."

After a few minutes of small talk, Kate shifted forward and whispered. "I have something I need to talk with you about."

"You don't need to whisper, and I'm not offended."

Kate knitted her eyebrows and stared at her friend. "Did I do something to offend you? Oh, Colleen, I'm so sorry if I did. Things have been a bit crazy and—"

"You haven't offended me at all. I thought…"

"Thought what?"

"Now I'm embarrassed. Guess I jumped to a conclusion. I thought you wanted to have coffee today to tell me that you picked Monica or Julie to be Bennie's godmother. I understand that your sisters would come first. I'll still be Auntie Colleen, and spoil him unmercifully."

Kate blinked rapidly as though the movement would somehow aid her in processing the words. She hadn't spent a moment thinking about Benjamin's baptism, much less considering who his godparents would be. In her sleep-deprived stupor, her full attention had been riveted to her son's care and her husband's mysterious whereabouts. Those worries left no energy or brain power to focus on normal life concerns.

Kate pursed her lips, mentally slapping herself for her inability to keep her life together. Colleen was right. She should be planning a christening, not wondering if her husband has a girlfriend in a foreign country.

Colleen leaned forward, apparently realizing the inaccuracy of her assumption. "That's not what this little get-together is about, is it? What's wrong, and how can I help?"

"Look at these," Kate said, after fishing a smattering of photos from her purse. She hadn't planned to share the pictures, but as soon as she handed them to her friend, a relief washed over her. Now she knew why she had slipped them into her purse instead of returning them to the strongbox where she'd found them. Colleen had to see them, review them and give her a fresh perspective, some rational explanation for their existence. Kate prayed the result would be something more plausible than her theory of Eric leading a double life.

Colleen would be calm, methodical, unemotional. She'd caution Kate to stop allowing her imagination to spin such crazy tales. Her dear friend would help her get her life back on track, assume that Wonder Woman stance she had been famous for.

"These are old. Where did you find them?" Colleen shuffled through the snapshots, turning them over in her hand.

"In our extra bedroom closet. Tucked on the corner shelf, out of view," Kate hurried to add.

"Who are these people? Do you know them?"

"No, but I think Eric does."

"Judging from the date imprints, these were taken before Eric was born. Someone wrote 'honeymoon' on this one."

"I know. I found a marriage certificate and some other documents stashed in a metal strongbox. I didn't bring those." Kate waited for Colleen to give her a verdict, some declaration about the meaning of these pictures.

"What other documents did you stumble upon?"

Colleen's piercing stare caused Kate to shift in her chair, switching from one uncomfortable position to another. Kate cleared her suddenly parched throat and reached for her drink. She took a sip, returned the glass to the table and tried to push down the guilt she felt for going through Eric's personal things.

Reluctantly she slid two blue-covered booklets, each displaying the bald eagle centered on the gold seal, across the table.

"Passports for Simon Erol Khory and Leah Haddan Khory." Kate easily identified those as originating from the United States. She wished she had taken the time to look more closely at a rubber-banded bundle of faded green and maroon passports. What countries did they represent?

"Old photos, a marriage certificate, passports."

"It looks to me like you stumbled onto someone's safety deposit box. Maybe the family who lived in the house before you."

"No. These belong to Eric and he hid them from me." Kate's shaky voice squeaked the declaration.

"Hid them from you? That makes no sense."

"I know. That's why I asked you to meet me on such short notice." Kate waved her hand across the photos and passports splayed on the table. "I figured with your experience, you could give me a better scenario about all this than the one floating around in my mind."

"And your scenario is…?"

Kate averted her eyes just as a sparrow landed on the ground nearby and nipped at muffin crumbs left by earlier patrons. The patio had been crowded when she first arrived, but now only a couple of tables were occupied, mostly on the other side of the area. Kate was grateful for this unplanned privacy.

"Well?"

"That he's leading a double life," Kate answered without turning to face Colleen, embarrassed by the conclusion she'd drawn, and terrified to receive her friend's judgment or confirmation.

Colleen gasped. "Are you out of your ever-loving mind? Eric leading a double life?"

Kate moved closer hoping to lessen the shock and envelop them both in a make-believe cone of silence. She'd have to make her case fast. "Hear me out. There are a lot of reasons why this makes sense."

Kate had never witnessed such a severe eye roll from her friend. Even after listening to her yoga students' embellished complaints about their aches and pains, Colleen always appeared sympathetic, offering her brand of gentle, useful advice. Right now, Kate needed helpful Colleen, not critical Colleen, who, at any moment might look up the phone number for the local loony bin.

"When Eric and I started dating, you suggested an investigation into his strange behavior. I'm taking you up on your offer now."

She and Eric had dated for a few weeks before she sensed an uneasiness in his actions. Then and now, he had definitely been holding something back. At the time, with romantic possibilities on the horizon—and the relief that came when Eric saved her from her ex-boyfriend—Kate had pushed away her doubts about him. She declined Colleen's offer to "make a few phone calls."

That same apprehension Kate experienced early in their relationship was back and stronger than ever. It had invaded her system the moment Eric packed and left for the airport. Each day her husband remained away, the mounting anxiety grew with an unrelenting intensity.

She could no longer deny, dismiss or ignore the warnings pulsing through her heart.

"Back then, you were worried about him fooling around with Trish. On a lark, I offered to play detective. You were just dating, no big deal. Now you have a life together; a child. Kate, I hope you know what you're getting into; what you're asking me to become a part of."

"I have to find out if the man I married is who he claims to be. The pieces don't fit. Everything is a patchwork of misinformation. And I think his folks are in on the ruse. They have to know where he is and what he's doing. He's not buying sheets and towels, I can guarantee you that."

Colleen patted Kate's forearm. "You need to calm down. You can't go home to your baby all wired up like this."

Kate blew out a heavy sigh, attempting to subdue the drum-like pounding emanating from her chest. "Everything is crumbling. My marriage… Everything I believed in, strived for…" Kate's words caught in her throat. An image of Benjamin growing up without a father at home appeared in her mind. The last thing she ever wanted—the one thing she swore she would never do—was to raise a child without a dad.

Colleen handed Kate a glass of water. "Take a sip and then tell me what's really bothering you."

Kate swiped at tears pooling in her eyes. "I never believed there was something going on between Eric and Trish. That's why I didn't take you up on your offer when you suggested investigating them. And I dismissed Eric's secretive behavior as residue from a bad breakup with his ex-wife. You know—once burned, twice shy. I felt that way myself after the drama with Ross," she said referring to the lunatic ex-boyfriend who had tried killing her a few years ago.

Colleen nodded for Kate to continue.

"But after we married, my suspicions grew. He was guarded about so many things, leaving me out in the cold. I knew his odd actions stemmed from more than the aftermath of a hurtful marriage. An alarm rings in my head when he leaves at a moment's notice on these random business trips. The details are always sketchy and the time frame nonexistent. Like now. Eric packed and rushed out the door, leaving Bennie behind." Kate stuttered a bit, contemplating the grim possibilities. "What could be so important that he'd leave our newborn son…and me?"

"Maybe he's working hard making money to keep you and Benjamin safe and secure."

Kate smiled at Colleen's attempt to assuage her fears. "If only that were the simple answer. I'd welcome a husband who provides for his family. My dad never did."

Kate noticed a mother and son sitting at a table behind Colleen. The boy, maybe five, licked the whipped cream piled at least three inches high on what Kate guessed was a glass of chocolate milk.

"What are you staring at?" Colleen turned to take in the sight engaging Kate's attention.

The woman smiled. "On a date with my main man," she replied, pointing to the young boy. "My nephew is really into whipped cream. Say hello, Nathan."

Nathan nodded without taking attention off of his drink, a white peak of foam dotting his nose.

Kate smiled. "Enjoy," she said before returning her gaze to Colleen. "He's so cute. I thought for a moment that—"

"I know what you were thinking. You have fast-forwarded your life, projecting the worst. One thing I know for certain is to get the facts before making any decisions. You don't want permanent solutions to a temporary problem."

Kate knew Colleen referred to her own decision to quit the Pittsburgh Police Department in hopes of saving her marriage. She had found out the hard way that the problem rested with her ex-husband, not her career.

"Don't get me wrong," Kate continued, "Eric makes certain we have everything we need. Everything except him. I complain to Adele, but she shrugs off my questions and offers to bring me dinner or do my laundry. Big Ben flashes his bright smile and returns to reading the newspaper."

"You call Eric's dad Big Ben, like the clock in England."

Kate snickered, grateful for a glimmer of levity in this sober conversation. "We had to differentiate between the Bens somehow. Anyway, I have a feeling they know where Eric is and what he's doing while he's gone. They just won't tell me."

"He works for them, right?"

"Yes, but I suspect his job is a cover for something else."

"And that something else is another family? Do you really believe his parents would be involved? That Eric has two wives?"

Kate considered the point and agreed that Adele wouldn't support that type of masquerade. "Still, there has to be a reason. He's either leading a double life or doing something illegal and clandestine. The last time we talked, I asked him if he wanted a divorce."

"And he said...?"

"That I was crazy. That he loved me. Then I asked if he was involved in something illegal. He blew his cool, yelling that he didn't expect me to understand. But that he did expect me to trust him. That he'd explain everything when he got home tonight."

Kate saw patient indifference in her friend's eyes and wondered how many criminals had witnessed this stoic poker face during an interrogation. Kate couldn't discern if Colleen's seemingly sympathetic, professional demeanor pointed to a willingness to help or not.

Kate continued, emptying out her innermost fears, praying Colleen recognized the depths of her panic.

Colleen moved the straw around in her glass and took a sip. "You make him sound like a robot, conditioned like a mercenary soldier, or worse."

"I never considered that before, but his behavior does have a military tenor. Like a call to arms or something. Remember when we were first dating, and Eric wouldn't give me a phone number?"

"Yes."

"Now I have a number, but he hardly ever answers. What other reason could there be? I mean, honestly. He avoids me...and now his son, too." Kate glanced at her watch. She needed to leave soon, but not until Colleen agreed to check into Eric's background. She hated asking for this favor and exposing the failings in her marriage. She would do the investigative legwork herself if she knew how.

Colleen tugged at an ebony curl dangling along the side of her face as though contemplating her next move. "Guess I could phone some people and turn over a few rocks. Are you sure you want to go down this road? You might not like what I uncover."

"I have no choice. I need to find out what's going on and the sooner, the better."

A mixture of relief and tension spread through Kate. Was she strong enough to handle whatever the investigation turned up? Could she live with this decision to spy on her husband and the consequences that came with it?

"Then I'll see what I can do. I don't promise anything. We may find out that Eric is a workaholic. Then you'll have to deal with that. But if he learns what we're up to, he may not react very kindly to being investigated. You might be setting yourself up for bigger issues."

"I have to know the truth. I'm willing to accept the fallout." Kate straightened, and pulled her shoulders back as though fortifying her decision. "I need to get home." She reached for her purse and automatically retrieved her phone. She glanced at the screen, her throat tightening as she opened a text message.

Delayed another day. Miss you love you home soon.

Kate blew out a disappointed sigh. *What else should I expect?* What little faith and patience she held for Eric suffered an irreparable blow. For a moment, she considered dialing his number, but she couldn't face the probability of her call being sent to his voicemail in front of Colleen.

"What's wrong?" Colleen asked.

Kate returned the phone to her purse and gathered her bags. "Eric's not coming home tonight. Says he's been delayed again."

Colleen frowned, but remained quiet.

"Are you available tomorrow morning?" Kate asked, deciding to pursue the answers she desperately needed instead of being immobilized by Eric's broken promises. "I want to show you the rest of what I found in the closet."

"Yeah, I can do that. I only have my morning class at seven to teach."

Kate kissed Colleen's cheek. "You are a fairy godmother. Mine. This means the world to me."

"You're welcome. I'll stop by around nine," Colleen said, patting Kate's hand. "And listen, there's no shame in changing your mind in the meantime."

"After reading that text, there's not much of a chance I'll feel differently. If anything, I'm more committed than ever to finding out what's going on."

Kate scurried through the café's patio gate and headed toward the parking lot. Her mind swirled with fresh doubts about her husband's behavior. How could she prepare for what Colleen would discover? How would she handle the truth that would definitively alter her future? And Bennie's?

**

On the short drive home from the cafe, Kate's thoughts vacillated between relief and dread. Colleen had agreed to help, but Kate knew her actions would show Eric that she didn't trust him. Maybe she never had.

She parked in her driveway, turned off the ignition but remained in the car. She hated agonizing over the unknown. The uncertainty pressed against her skull, cutting off all circulation, like a ski cap three sizes too small. Even though she knew the outcome, she dialed Eric. As soon as she heard his recorded greeting, she disconnected.

Just as I suspected.

With outrage coursing through her nerves, she wanted to hurl the phone at the windshield. Instead, she texted.

What delay? Call me!
WHEN WILL YOU BE HOME????

Kate gathered her belongings and headed toward her front door.

"Looks like a successful shopping spree," Ben said, meeting her in the entryway with outstretched arms. "Let me carry those for you."

"Thank you." Kate allowed him to remove the bags from her hands. "How's the baby?"

"Sleeping like an angel," Adele said, now standing alongside Ben.

"Thank you both for watching him. I really needed a few hours to myself."

"We were happy to help." Adele beamed. "There's nothing we love more than spending time with our grandson. We're planning to stay until after you pick up Eric."

Kate didn't respond. Instead, she began unloading her packages.

"You look a little down. Is everything okay?" Adele asked.

"Not really. Eric isn't coming home tonight."

"Oh?" Adele moved to stand closer to Kate.

"Something about a delay. I'm not sure when he'll be home."

"He'll be home tomorrow," Ben said.

"How do you know? Did you talk to Eric?"

"Well, yes."

"You talked to Eric?" Adele asked. "Why didn't you tell me?"

"I didn't have a chance." Ben sounded vague, as though he was putting words together on the fly. "Said he tried to call you, but the call wouldn't connect, so he phoned me instead. Maybe poor cell phone reception."

Kate looked at the screen. The meter showed five solid bars.

"I have a full signal," Kate replied, a spidery quiver crept up her spine. Ben was lying to her and she wondered why.

"I don't know, then. Maybe there's a problem with his connection. Anyway, he was on limited time, so he called me. He figured you'd worry if you didn't hear from him."

Kate stepped closer toward Ben and fixed her stare on him. "If my phone wasn't working, then why did I receive this text? You're not making sense."

"That is odd," Ben continued, evading the question. "Anyway, Eric said to tell you he misses you and Benjamin. He'll try to call as soon as his meetings wrap up."

"When will that be? Why won't he answer his phone now? I'm really worried." Kate pushed her fingers through a thatch of hair hanging in her eyes.

Something is wrong. Someone is not telling me the truth.

Ben laughed nervously and glanced at his wife. "Now you sound like Adele, always worried about anything connected to her son's well-being. Doesn't matter how old Eric is and that he's married and has a child of his own."

"I need to talk to him," Kate said, fighting to keep indignation out of her voice.

"Eric is fine. This project is taking him longer than we thought. That's all."

"And what project is that?" Kate baited, fully realizing the chances of Ben telling her the truth were nil.

Adele stepped between them. "We can come back tomorrow and give you another break. Let me know what time you want us here once you get Eric's flight plans."

Kate nodded absently.

"I can bring dinner," Adele continued. "I'll make stuffed bell peppers. Eric's favorite."

"No need. You've already packed my fridge with meals for the next week. Thanks again for minding Bennie today." She walked toward the door and waited for Adele and Ben to follow.

Kate's phone rang in her hand, and her heart leaped as she glanced at the unfamiliar number on the screen, praying it was Eric.

"Hello," she said on a breath.

"Hi, Kate. I'm calling from work."

"Julie," Kate replied, the hope of hearing Eric's voice snuffed out like a doused candle.

Adele and Ben waved their goodbyes and left.

"Sorry I forgot to text when I got home yesterday," Julie said. "The kids kept me busy and then my phone died. This is the first chance I've had to call. How's my newest nephew?"

They chatted for a few minutes, the entire time Kate fumed. Her phone was working fine for everyone but her husband.

Chapter Twenty-One

A prickle of doubt surged through Eric as Ralph stepped further into the room. With his arms crossed, the team leader shot a dismissive glare his way. Eric diverted his gaze.

"I said, sit down." His boss slammed the interrogation room door shut, as though this sudden action would intimidate his junior agent.

In spite of Ralph's directive, Eric remained standing. "How's Maher?" he asked, rubbing the spot on his wrist where the hair-like needle grazed him minutes earlier.

Since he hadn't experienced any ill effects, Eric reasoned that Maher absorbed the full dose, luckily leaving little residue to enter Eric's system and cause him harm. He wondered if the medical staff noticed Maher's wound when they evaluated him?

"Looks like he'll recover, but no thanks to you. How'd you do it, Wiley? And why?" Disdain rang from each word.

This guy really thinks I poisoned our only lead.

"Do what, Ralph? Interrogate a suspect until he poked himself with a poisoned needle someone implanted in the table?" Eric pointed to where the tiny spike, still protruding from the surface, could be found. "Oh, wait. That's right. I wasn't the one interrogating him at the time," he added sarcastically.

"Holy damn," Ralph yelled after running his hand across the table and discovering the thorny barb. "How did this get here?"

"Damn if I know, but I'm certain someone on this base, possibly someone on this team, put it there."

A frown formed on Ralph's lips. "I'm supposed to believe you stumbled on this accidentally?"

"Nothing accidental about it," Eric said, happy to boast about his discovery. "I reenacted those last few minutes with Maher."

"Then wouldn't you be near death, too?"

"I thought about that. Guess there was just the right dosage on the needle to accomplish their goal."

"What a crock of... Let me get Atwater." Ralph shifted toward the door.

Eric tilted his head toward the two-way mirror. "Ralph wants you in here, Trish," he said before returning his focus to his boss. "Yeah, I know the drill. She's been monitoring our entire conversation. Do you think I'm that stupid, really? I'm a trained operative, too."

"Calm down," Trish said, entering the room. "When did you find the needle?"

"While you two were out playing 'get rid of Eric.'" He lifted his arm, exposing the tiny puncture on his skin. "You should direct the medical team to examine Maher's wrists. That needle must have been dipped in some toxin, enough to knock him out long enough so we would give up interrogating him."

Trish squatted to examine the spot where the needle jutted from the table. "So that's how he did it," she said, amazement coloring her words.

"You knew?" Eric asked.

"After ruling out the obvious—heart attack, heat stroke, stuff like that—Dr. Miller spotted the puncture mark on Maher's wrist. He couldn't speculate on how the prisoner was injected, but he believes the toxin got into the bloodstream through the puncture. Now we know, thanks to you."

Eric sent a slender grin in Trish's direction.

"Why didn't you fill me in, Ralph, if you already knew Maher was pricked with a needle?" Eric waited, but Ralph didn't answer.

"Guess you wanted to hear my theory, which seems to match the good doctor's."

Trish glanced at Ralph, as though waiting for his okay to continue. Ralph's face, now a bright shade of crimson, the vessels in his neck engorged, nodded noncommittally. He stood with his hands on his hips, obviously mystified that Eric had arrived at the same conclusion as the medical team and, as a bonus, found the barb.

Trish recited the remainder of the update without emotion. "They're taking every precaution and working quickly to learn which poison. Should have preliminary blood tests back from the lab as soon as possible. Dr. Miller said, from what he'd seen so far, Maher is very lucky to be alive."

Eric blinked, pondering the fragility between critical and lethal. Too much toxin ingested, and their prisoner would have died where he sat. Who taught Maher exactly how far to allow the needle to penetrate his skin before its results would be permanent?

Eric grimaced, realizing that the perspiration pooling on the gunrunner's forehead might have been caused by the anxiety of over-injecting himself, not from the pressure of their inquisition.

Trish stood and leaned over the table, careful not to snag her skin on the spur. "Ingenious. How'd you even find it?"

"I positioned myself the way Maher had right before he slumped over and looked to God for an answer. He poked me, in a sense." Eric briefly explained his process, leaving out the parts about his frustration.

"You're a bloody genius," Ralph said, sarcasm seeping through every word.

"Stop trying to bust Eric's balls. He's given us a big break in this case. And now we know for sure that Maher's cohort is on the inside. We better prepare for what they try next."

Ralph flicked his gaze between Eric and Trish, as though assessing his options. "Yeah," he finally said, switching from a tough cop bark to a professorial tone. "This needle is so thin it blended in with the woodgrain. We would have never seen it. Good work, Wiley."

Eric nodded. "But Maher must have known it was there. A sort of Plan B if we were getting close. Who furnished him with this escape?"

"That's what we have to figure out," Trish agreed. "If you had left the room when we did, I suspect someone would have stopped by to remove the needle. We'd never uncover how Maher was poisoned. We got lucky."

"All things considered, I'd rather be lucky," Eric said, reciting a quote he'd heard numerous times from Ben as a teen.

"True that," Ralph added. "I'll call the forensics team to come in and check this out. Maybe there will be some prints they can lift."

"Definitely ours will be on the table and the manacles, but we can hope." Eric released a huff, as though his credibility had been reinstated, at least temporarily.

He looked at Ralph and Trish. Were they still thinking he was the traitor? Who was putting those doubts about him in their minds? His front pants pocket vibrated, and he reached for his personal cell phone. A crooked smile spread across his face as he recognized the name on the screen.

Sweet Kate.

Even though he expected to see his wife's name pop up on the display, a warm surge at the realization spread across his chest. To his workmates and parents, this phone didn't exist. Only Kate knew the number.

The image of her smile swept through his mind, accelerating his urge to wrap up this investigation, return to her and begin to rebuild their relationship.

No time to talk now. Reluctantly, he let her call go to voicemail, again, powered off his phone and returned his attention to Trish and Ralph. His partners, moments ago willing to believe the worst of him, now seemed baffled at this new development that absolved Eric of their mistrust.

Or were they the culprits, casting large shadows in Eric's direction to divert suspicion from themselves? Eric sincerely hoped that wasn't true. He had worked with these two, entrusted his life and his safety to them. If his instincts were that wrong, he would have to reevaluate every major decision and judgment he'd made recently.

***

Eric walked across the compound to his makeshift desk, awkwardly tucked in the back corner of the detention facility's headquarters. The short distance from interrogation room to office space left Eric dripping from sweat. Even though evening descended an hour or so earlier, the heat remained.

Temperatures inside the US government's quartet of trailers stifled oxygen movement, making breathing difficult. Fighting the one stuck caster that refused to roll in the same direction as the other four, Eric pulled his chair across the faded linoleum. He dropped into the seat, leaned back and extended his legs. He kicked his shoes up onto the two planks of board serving as a desktop, causing them to teeter against stacked milk cartons.

Eric righted himself, and returned his feet to the ground, safeguarding against everything crashing to the floor. Not able to stay still, he swayed back and forth, embracing the *creak, creak, creak* of his battered chair, desperately in need of oiling.

Eric assessed the simulated wood paneling–a visual reminder of the mid-seventies when this trailer rolled off the assembly line, brand spanking new–impressed at how well the decorative façade endured the area's elements for decades. If the designers had selected wallpaper to grace the insides of this rusted excuse for an operations center, the steam from the humidity would have peeled off the layers years ago.

He chuckled at how he never thought of those details before he fell in love with Kate. Someone made those decisions. How big the windows should be; how many bathrooms on a floor; the parking space ratio for the tenants. Kate, his Kate, made all those choices. She considered every alternative before submitting her plans to her clients.

He retrieved his personal cell phone from his pocket and read Kate's text. She was angry. What else did he expect? He hoped Ben had been convincing in his fake explanation.

Eric looked at his watch. Half-past nine. He folded his arms against the boards and dropped his head onto this makeshift pillow. He'd close his eyes for a few minutes and then call home.

He had spent the past few hours waiting for word from their forensics team. He prayed the prints they lifted would point to a defector. And he prayed that Ralph and Trish weren't involved.

Still, the facts were the facts. Someone with access to that room planted the poisoned spike. As far as Eric knew, only four of them could have done it. Ruling out Maher and himself left Ralph and Trish. If Eric was a betting man, he'd guess Ralph, in some twisted claim of patriotism, had been the one to plant the needle. Maybe he was trying to kill Maher and guessed wrong at the dosage. It could be Trish, though, but why? As his mind attempted to unscramble that riddle, sleep overtook him.

"Wake up, Wiley," Trish's voice seeped into his dreams. "Wake up!"

Eric bolted upright, blinking to gain focus before glancing at the time. Twenty-five minutes had passed. Long enough for his power nap. He rubbed the sleep gathering in his eyes and watched Ralph and Trish head to their ragtag desks. Trish's setup mirrored Eric's, except that her milk cartons were a matching blue. Ralph, the team leader, sat on the edge of his puke-green metal desk, complete with drawers. Rank did have its privileges.

"Well? Don't keep me in suspense," Eric joked. Ralph's deadpan glare forced Eric to swallow hard. Nothing funny happening here, he realized, sliding his gaze to Trish and being met with an inquisitive frown.

Ralph kept his stare on Eric and kneaded his hands together as though stalling for time. "In addition to Maher's, there was one set," he finally announced.

"And?" Eric waited. When Ralph didn't respond, he continued, "Don't tell me. My prints are the only ones they were able to identify."

"Bingo." Ralph exaggeratingly pointed a finger at Eric. "You win the prize. So, either you're a double agent or you erased any of the other prints when you decided to do your Sam Spade routine."

"I'm a fan of Dashiell Hammett's, but I'd never claim to have detecting abilities on par with Spade's."

"Now you're a comedian, too?"

"Okay, you two. Eric's not the traitor, so let go of that," Trish admonished Ralph. "Still, why aren't there any other prints?"

"How the hell should I know. Maybe that was part of Maher's job; jab himself and muddy up any other prints. Or maybe the inside man wiped everything clean before he left."

"Both of those explanations make sense," Trish said, turning to Ralph.

"Oh, yeah. Young Wiley always makes sense, sounds reasonable, rational and out-and-out righteous in every explanation he fabricates. Trouble is—facts stay the same. We still don't have any information from Maher. We're no closer to capturing Simon and Leah Khory's killer. And shit. He was our last, best chance."

Eric walked to where his boss now stood, positioning his face inches away from Ralph's. "Don't lecture me. Nobody wants to capture that murderer more than I do." Eric's chest expanded with a deep inhale. He exhaled slowly. "Nobody. Do you understand?"

"Well then, you better do what you do best and come up with a plausible excuse for this cluster or it's all our asses," Ralph yelled, his voice spiraling toward panic. "You talk to this guy. I've had it with him," he said to Trish, before storming out and slamming the door, shaking the trailer as he exited.

Trish put her hand on Eric's shoulder. "Let me buy you a drink."

"Nah, I'm all right."

"Look, it's too early to go to sleep. Not that either of us would," Trish said. "We might as well get something to eat, in air-conditioned comfort. Let's head downtown and find a restaurant."

"Not hungry," Eric grumbled.

"Doesn't matter. Let's get out of this roasting hellhole. Maybe we'll get a new perspective. We're missing something. Some connection. Some small detail."

Yeah, some small detail that led to my parents' death twenty years ago. If Benjamin didn't uncover it then, there's no way we'll figure it out now.

Ben had spent the waning years of his career pursuing the same criminal. Anmar X had eluded them for two decades. It was unlikely that Eric would miraculously track him down and prosecute him.

"Whadda you say?" Trish cajoled. "Take a few minutes and let's clear our minds."

"All right. I need to check in with Kate first." Dread dripped from those last few words. Eric could count on one hand the times he held Bennie.

He was putting an end to this nightmare. He'd tender his resignation in the morning, that is, if Ralph didn't have him fired first.

Either way, he'd be on a flight home tomorrow, just like he had promised Kate he would.

Chapter Twenty-Two

Perturbed at tossing and turning for over forty-five minutes, Kate punched her pillow with more aggression than she meant. It wasn't her bedding's fault that the sandman skipped over her tonight. Without Eric's warm body alongside, sharing their king-sized bed, Kate's loneliness and frustration magnified to a higher level. How she wished she could stop her anxious thoughts from invading, if only for a short while. Soon Benjamin would be ready for his ten-p.m. feeding and her efforts to catch up on her sleep would be unfilled.

Still no call or text from Eric.

So much for the adage, sleep when the baby sleeps.

Conceding defeat to her whirring mind, Kate threw off the thin sheet covering her, pushed her palms against the mattress and propelled herself to seated. She remained in that position in the darkened room, listening to Benjamin's soft, rhythmic breathing. His sweet sounds, so comforting and reaffirming.

Kate chided herself for focusing on Eric's absence, instead of on the joyous miracle asleep a few feet away. She closed her eyes and asked God for comfort and wisdom. She prayed for her husband to return home safely. Inexplicably, she knew he was in danger; some threat Kate couldn't comprehend had whisked him away at a moment's notice.

Instinctively she reached for her drawing pad and pen she had left on the nearby nightstand and sat in the rocker. Bathed in a ribbon of moonlight, she began illustrating rough concepts for the Parker project. Perhaps working would help relax her enough to fall asleep.

As a child, sketching had always gotten her through stressful times. She had turned to art as an escape after her parents split up. The magic of watching lines and shading turn into an illustration carried her away from any worries clouding her thoughts.

Now as an accomplished architect, Kate relied on her artistic skills not only to make a living but also as a therapy of sorts. Unlike her marriage, her career relied on plans, order and structure. Drawing calmed her down and helped her think clearly. Every building she designed began with a blueprint she carefully crafted after discussing the client's goals, dreams and desires. If only she could design a blueprint for her life.

This time though, the stakes were higher. Her personal happiness required more than sketches on a piece of paper, clearing city permits and hiring the right contractors.

Kate first had to search her soul. Outline her dreams and goals for her life and her marriage. How else could she uncover what was going on with Eric without first acknowledging her motives?

Was there another woman? Or was this peril more threatening; a demon Eric couldn't control? Kate couldn't rest until she learned what influence pulled him away from her and their newborn son. She drew for a few minutes more, but the respite that usually accompanied her sketching refused to soothe her apprehensions. No easy answers appeared on the paper.

Kate's heart struck a deep thud. Wherever Eric was, he wasn't safe. She sighed. Somehow acknowledging her deepest fear provided a small amount of relief.

She pulled a tissue from a box on her nightstand and swiped away the dampness gathering between her breasts and dripping down her chest. Too young to be going through the change of life, Kate attributed her sweating to the anxiety spreading through her body. She closed the cover of her drawing pad, tiptoed to the bassinet and gently laid her hand on her son's tummy, enjoying the movement of his expanding breaths against her palm.

Then, as though drawn by a magnet, she crept to the guest room. If she was lucky, Bennie would sleep another thirty minutes, long enough for Kate to sift through more boxes. Any shred of information that would mollify the drilling agony deep inside would be worth the lost sleep.

As she ferreted through papers and memorabilia, Kate realized she neglected to talk to Ben and Adele about the missing keepsakes from Eric's childhood. Also, she had wondered if they knew the people in the old photos. Had she merely forgotten to ask, or was there a more ominous reason keeping her from questioning her in-laws?

***

"Hi Katie," Eric forced a smile into his voice, hoping to remove all trace of tension in his words. "I miss you."

"Eric! Where are you?"

He jumped at Kate's bullet-like response.

"On my way home to you." *If only that were true.* "Am I calling too late?"

"No. I'm feeding Bennie."

A smile teetered on Eric's lips. "How is our son?"

"He's fine, although I practically dropped him grabbing for the phone. I've been trying to reach you for what seems like days. Why didn't you return my calls, at least with a text so I know you're all right?"

"Honey, how can I be anything but all right when I have you."

"I'm serious. Ben said you couldn't get through on my phone, but everyone else could. Why are you delayed again?"

"It's a short delay. I'm booked on the same six p.m. flight tomorrow," Eric said quickly, hoping to assuage Kate's concerns.

"How come you didn't video-call? That way you could see us and we could see you."

"It's not private where I am." Eric frowned, gazing around the deserted office. "I'm heading into a meeting, but didn't want to wait until morning to call."

"A nighttime meeting? It's almost eleven," Kate sniped, her verbal bullets flying again. "Are you going out with Trish?"

"No, baby, nothing like that. I've already told you, Trish and I work together. That's all," Eric defended, realizing the half-truth. He was catching a bite with Trish, but not for romantic reasons. He needed to discuss the case, find out what she knew and if Ralph was being straight with him. He wanted Trish to confirm his assessment—there was nothing left to be done on this mission. He could return home to his wife and son with his head held high, satisfied he had done everything possible to capture Anmar X.

"I can't imagine what kind of meeting takes place after-hours, unless—"

"Kate Jameson Wiley, I'm in love with you. I'm married to you," he raised his inflection to emphasize *you*.

"Wait a second. Let me put Benjamin in his cradle. Okay," she huffed a few seconds later. "Tell me what's going on. Really, Eric. I'm worried."

"About what? You know I do these purchasing deals all the time. We're nearly finished. I have a few loose ends. Will you still pick me up at the airport?"

"Of course, but you were supposed to be home today!"

Eric continued, not acknowledging her outburst. "I will text you when I board the plane."

"So, your job is done?"

"You don't sound thrilled at the prospect of me coming home," he joked.

Kate paused. "It's been really hard without you being here."

Eric heard sobs swell inside her words. "I know a newborn is a lot of work and I'm—"

"It's not taking care of our son," Kate said. "I'm loving every moment. He's growing so fast already. You should see him smile. I can't wait until he's old enough to giggle."

"I'm missing so much not being home with you both. That's why I'm changing my role in the company. I'm done going on these trips." There, he planted the seed, so when he was fully out of the agency, Kate wouldn't be surprised when he took on a new role with the family business.

"That's the best news. It's what I've been hoping for." Lightness infused into her voice. This was what she'd been pleading with him to do, at least cut back on the travel. But he couldn't let go of the mission. That was until now, when he realized the mission had let go of him.

"Hope you're reaching out for help until I get there."

"Yeah. Everyone's been great this past week. Your mom and Monica have popped over a couple of times. Colleen's coming in the morning for a visit. I'm not alone in that way. I miss you. I miss us."

"I'll be there before you know it," Eric said.

"How can you wrap things up so quickly?" Kate asked, sounding suspicious of Eric's transformation. "Before, you said—"

"I know what I said. My priorities changed. You changed them, Kate." He imagined her smile at his words. "Anyway, the products I came for are no longer available and I'm not going to wait around until another vendor can be found." Although speaking in code, Eric told the truth. Clues to Anmar X's whereabouts had dried up and there was no purpose in him hanging around hoping another lead would magically appear. He had to leave before Ralph or some of the senior agents forced him out.

During their last conversation, Ben called in Eric's promise to let go of capturing Anmar X before it ruined his life. "Time is up," he had said. And Eric had agreed.

"I have to tie up some loose ends. We'll discuss all this when I get home."

"But, Eric—"

"Gotta go, baby. I love you. Kiss Benjamin for me." Eric clicked off, terror welling inside. How could he keep the promise he made to himself without breaking his promise to Kate? There had to be a way.

Chapter Twenty-Three

Nearly midnight and humidity still hung in the air as Eric and Trish entered the Indulge Me Grill. A young hostess standing behind the podium greeted them. "Inside or out?" she asked in heavily accented English. "AC broken inside."

Eric inhaled the dense scent of burnt grease wafting through the local eatery. *I won't be ordering the fries.* "Guess outside it is. Too damn hot inside with no air conditioning," he replied, convinced of the wisdom of his outdoor request.

"Not much cooler outside," Trish said, "but at least we can look at the moon." The pair followed the hostess to a table on the rim of the open-air seating. A dozen or more diners, already enjoying limited relief from the overhead misters, barely noticed the pair taking seats near the railing.

Eric waited until the hostess left, then leaned over the bistro-size table. "Thank you for sticking up for me with Ralph."

Trish shrugged, continuing her perusal of the cocktail specials handed her by the hostess. "Didn't take much. He doesn't want to nail you as the bloodsucker. Just needed a reason to sell his theory to the higher-ups."

"He won't have to defend my honor much longer. I'm resigning as soon as I can tomorrow morning."

Trish folded her menu, placed it on the table in front of her and stared at Eric. "What the hell are you talking about? You're quitting?"

"Hell yes. I'm flying home and putting this crap behind me." Relief pulsed through his body at uttering the words out loud. Hearing them made his plan all the more real.

"You'll never let go. At least not until Anmar X's head hangs from your belt loop."

"I used to think that, too, but I have to end this. Now."

Trish shook her head. "Well I'm not giving up and when we capture the bastard, guess who's going to be my first call?"

Eric grimaced. "I'll be happy to answer the phone and listen to you gloat."

"Wanna order drinks?"

Eric glanced up to see a slender woman standing next to their table.

"Give me whatever beer you have on tap. Trish?"

"I'll have a vodka Collins and some jalapeño poppers."

"We have potato skins, too," the server added, proudly highlighting American fare on the menu.

"The poppers will be enough for now," Trish said.

As the woman turned to leave, Eric scooted his chair closer to Trish.

"I want you to understand where I'm coming from," Eric continued, knowing he might not get this chance again to explain himself. "Anmar X got what he wanted when he started his murdering rampage twenty years ago. None of the senior agents, including Ben, could catch him," Eric said, referring to his adopted father. "They never got close. Coming in as the hot-shot kid on the team, I fancied myself as a super sleuth who could trace his whereabouts, outsmart him and nab the rat bastard. Figured the seasoned guys were too old; they didn't understand new technology. But we never got any closer than they did, no matter how good our intelligence or how quickly we acted."

He stopped, allowing Trish to respond. Instead, she remained quiet, her poker face staring blankly at him, concealing any reaction.

The server delivered their drinks. "Your poppers will be up in a few minutes," she said, before turning on her heels and leaving.

Eric took a swig of the cold beer, grateful that the refrigeration was working even if the air conditioning had conked out.

Trish slid her cocktail closer, and inspected the contents. "Damn."

"Something wrong with your drink?"

She fidgeted with the garnish dangling across the rim. An orange slice, folded taco-style, encased a maraschino cherry. Both pieces of fruit carelessly impaled on a tiny plastic sword reminded Eric of a Caribbean cruise he and Kate had shared. Fruity drinks and paper umbrellas. Kate loved both of those.

Trish used the black straw to stir the ice cubes, banging them mercilessly against the glass. "Only one cherry," she grumbled, and took a gulp.

"Gee, you don't get that worked up about our failed missions. I'm sure I can get you more cherries."

"Naw. It's just that they're so chintzy. One cherry in this big glass." She lifted the tumbler to prove her point. "And hell, I do get that worked up about our job. I'm not the one hightailing it home."

"You have been listening."

"I always listen. A good skill to have when you're an investigator." She winked and swallowed another gulp. "You were saying…"

"It sickens me to admit that Anmar turned someone on the inside. Whoever is responsible for this chaos, they're stellar at covering their tracks. He or she is ruining our investigation and ruining my life."

"So, you quit? Game over. The bad guy wins. You can't mean that. You, more than any of us, have a vested interest."

"What are you trying to say?" Unease crept through Eric's body. Did she know his real reason for going after Anmar?

"Simon and Leah Khory were friends of your dad's. You grew up watching the way their deaths ate away at Ben. He vowed to bring Anmar X to justice. You assumed Ben's mantle of responsibility as soon as you could. We all know it. Finding this killer is personal."

Eric paused, relieved that Trish didn't know his full background. "Maybe that's why I'm not productive. I'm too close to the case. Running down one blind alley after another," he said reflecting on every promising clue that led to a disappointing dead end. "I finally accepted the truth."

"What would Ben say if he knew you were giving up."

"He's been after me to leave for months; maybe years."

"But Eric—"

He put his hand up. "Stop. It's decided. I won't be the walking dead for that murdering scum any longer."

Trish turned away in disgust, allowing Eric an unobstructed panorama of the road bordering the restaurant. He glimpsed a man getting out of a white van parked in front of an all-night liquor store.

That van looks very familiar, like the one Ralph picked us up in.

"What? What is it?" Trish asked, following his gaze.

"Why is that guy wearing a raincoat in this eighty-degree heat?" Eric asked, but stiffened as the man lingered by the van before moving toward the restaurant.

"Maybe his mother gave it to him," Trish snapped. "How the hell am I supposed to know? Stop changing the subject."

Eric nodded, keeping his gaze on the man unbuttoning his knee-length raincoat. "Not changing the subject. Maybe saving your life. Gun!" Eric shouted as a series of shots rang out.

"Get down!" he yelled to everyone in the area. He and Trish dived to the ground. Together they crawled behind a nearby wall and waited for the gunfire to cease.

Patrons, who moments before were enjoying their meal, began screaming as they ran inside the restaurant to safety.

"You cover me from here," he said to Trish, reaching for his weapon. He scooted on his belly guerilla-style across the cement pavement to where they sat moments earlier. Wedging his face in between the stakes of the metal railing, he shifted into a clear view of the shooter now jumping into the same van he emerged from. The man shouted something, and the driver sped off.

YBC-45-56, YBC-45-56, Eric recited the license plate number over and over in his head until he could write it down. The van might be stolen, but in case it wasn't, this could be the lead they were waiting for. Someone definitely wanted him and Trish gone, but who? No one knew they'd be there, unless they had been followed.

Eric quickly typed the license plate number into his cell phone notes before he stood. "Safe to say that was meant for us," he said to Trish, still hunkered between a wall and the water station. "What are..." His words trailed off. Fear clawed through his body at the red stain spreading out on the sleeve of her white shirt. He hurried to her side. "Damn, you're hit."

"But not dead," she said, grimacing. "They were probably aiming for you. Piss-poor marksman missed you and hit me."

"Jokes. You've got jokes at a time like this. How bad is it?" Eric asked as the buzzing sirens of police vehicles got louder. He ripped open the sleeve of her shirt and gently touched the wound before applying pressure. "Looks like he grazed you."

"Well, it hurts like hell, but I guess I'll live."

"Who knew we were coming here?" Eric asked quietly when a restaurant staffer headed their way and others who had taken cover started moving around.

"I—I didn't tell anyone. May—maybe we were t— tailed," Trish stuttered, her face contorting in pain. "Damn, this really does hurt, and that jerk ruined my new blouse, too."

Eric shook his head in relief. Even injured, she didn't lose her snarky sense of humor. "Help's on the way. Stay still."

"Hurt bad?" their server asked Eric, concern on her face as she nodded toward Trish.

"She's been sh—"

"Ambulancia is coming," she said, handing Eric several clean towels.

"Gracias."

Eric folded a towel into a small square and placed it over Trish's wound. He continued surveying the area as he considered Trish's assessment. They had been followed. Someone wanted them eliminated. Or at least injured enough to leave the country. But he was resigning tomorrow. They couldn't wait until then?

"Guess what, Wiley? Now you can't quit," she said, as if reading his mind. "You gotta find out who put a bullet in me. Find the gunslinger, hotshot," Trish teased. "But until then, can you get me another drink? I'm parched."

Chapter Twenty-Four

"I thought you'd never get here," Kate said, answering the front door around nine o'clock the next morning. With Benjamin propped against her shoulder, fresh from a feeding, Kate eyed Colleen's freshly scrubbed face, lightly applied makeup and perky hairstyle. Her hand immediately flew to her unbrushed tresses, where she imperceptibly scratched off flakes of dried milk, evidence of Benjamin's burps.

"Sor-ree." Colleen raised a paper bag. "I brought muffins."

"I'm never going to get my figure back with you around." Kate smiled and hugged her friend. "I'm really glad you're here. It's about time to put Bennie down for his nap."

"In that case, I'll trade you." Colleen set the white pastry sack on a nearby table and extended her arms. "Aww," she whispered, accepting the infant into an embrace. "He gets more handsome every time I see him."

"I can't disagree." Kate yawned. She opened the bag, slipped out a muffin and nibbled a cranberry surrounded by cake. "Hmmm. Thank you. I can put a pot of coffee on, or I can make tea."

"None for me. I ate earlier." Colleen followed Kate to the family room. "Want me to rock him or something? I'm not very practiced with this sort of thing, but he feels so incredible in my arms. Why do babies smell so good? You must be in awe of him."

Kate motioned Colleen toward the glider. "Yeah, sometimes I sit and examine his every little nuance. The shape of his lips, the dimple on his chin. His eyelashes and pinkie toenails."

"Pinkie toenails?"

Kate removed Bennie's sock. "Look. His toes are so tiny. How does God manage to fit toenails on them?"

"A miracle."

Kate took in the peaceful image of Colleen cuddling Bennie. "Yes, so many miracles. I need to remind myself to keep my eyes open for all the blessings showered on me. They abound if you take the time to notice." *And stop focusing on what might be.*

"Did you have a rough night?"

Kate secured the buttons of her blouse, and realized a plop of grape jelly had fallen off her morning toast and rambled down her front. The purple path marring the green fabric reminded her of an abstract painting she once admired at a Phoenix art gallery when she and Eric were dating. His call had only served to intensify her suspicions.

"Why do you ask? Do I look terrible?"

Colleen frowned. "It's not your appearance."

"I didn't have time to change this morning. Barely had time to eat breakfast." Kate half-grinned, pointing to the stain on her top.

"You look like you're supposed to. A new mommy getting the hang of things. Did you sleep?"

"Sorta. Not as much as I wanted to. I kept thinking about Eric. He's been gone a week and two days, not that I'm counting. I can't stop wondering why I don't hear from him regularly... And the forces that are changing him." Kate turned away, stopping herself from saying something that might dissuade Colleen from helping. She wouldn't mention Eric's late-night call. "Really, I'm fine."

"I'm worried about you. Maybe you should get a little sleep while I look after Benjamin."

"No!"

Colleen pulled back, obviously surprised at the intensity in Kate's voice.

"Sorry. I didn't mean to yell. It's just that he's ready for a nap and we have to get started. Today might be our only chance to go through all the stuff."

Colleen continued rocking the baby, a watchful eye trained on Kate as though forming an assessment.

"Well? What's wrong?" Kate asked when Colleen didn't respond.

"I'm not used to seeing you like this. All philosophical, truth-seeking. You get like that when you're melancholy or..."

"Or what?"

Colleen sat straighter, shifting Benjamin to her other arm and tugged at his T-shirt as though stalling for time.

"What were you about to say?" Kate demanded.

"Well. It crossed my mind. I should have asked sooner, if I was a better, more insightful friend."

Kate's hands bracketed her hips. "Now you're making me angry. Next to my sisters, you're my best friend. Just spit it out."

"I'm wondering if all this anxiety you're feeling about Eric is really postpartum. You know, baby blues."

"Yeah, I know what postpartum means. And no, this isn't baby blues, although I will admit that some of my craziness stems from not sleeping. But I think my not sleeping is directly related to the stress of Eric not being here."

Whatever fueled Eric's change of heart had to be more than realizing he's a family man. Kate sensed him running from something or someone. She wouldn't rest until she found out what. She sucked in a deep breath. "I'm worried about him. It's not because I'm depressed. I can't explain it, but I think he's in some sort of danger."

"Yesterday you thought he was living a double life. Today he's in imminent danger. Do you understand how erratic you sound? Maybe not to me, but to other people?"

"I have a nearly month-old baby and his father might as well be on the other side of the world. I can't reach him. He doesn't respond to my texts." Kate realized her voice rose from conversational friendly to rock-concert loud. "I'm sorry. I didn't mean to yell, again. It's just that everyone is dismissing me. Discounting my concerns. They're valid. There is something wrong. I sense it. Eric might overcome the threat without me butting in, but I'm still panicked at the possibilities."

"The threat! Kate, you're going off the deep end. The man is working. What's threatening about importing textiles?"

"That's just it. Wherever Eric is, I don't think he's working for Adele and Ben. Too much doesn't hold together. I get conflicting stories from him; even his parents can't keep the story straight."

Silence filled the room.

Dangling from a thin strand of possibility, Colleen was her only hope to expose Eric's whereabouts. Realizing she might find solace in the unearthed truth, Kate couldn't let Colleen believe her concerns were driven by postpartum depression. She stepped closer and touched her friend's hand.

"Don't you understand, I have to find out. I can't continue living in limbo-land; one of us present in our marriage and the other treading on distant soil. You're the only one I trust to help me; the only one who can track down a missing person."

"Eric's not missing."

"He's not here and he's not reachable with any regularity. He might as well be missing." Kate coughed as though the words caught in her throat.

Benjamin stirred, and Colleen patted his back. "I think he's ready for bed."

Kate motioned for her friend to follow her.

"You want me to do it?" Colleen sounded slightly freaked out.

"Shhh! You're terrific. Lay him on his back. Here's his binkie."

Benjamin happily accepted his pacifier and closed his eyes. "There. You did it," Kate commented in a hushed tone. She secured the blanket around her son before they snuck out of the room together.

Colleen stopped Kate partway down the hallway and put her hands on her friend's shoulders. "I understand your concern and I'm hoping that Eric contacts you soon to calm your fears. I believe you're worried but I also believe there's nothing to worry about. So, while we're waiting for Eric to check in, let's look through the boxes you've found. Maybe there's something in there that offers a rational explanation to his mysterious actions. If nothing else, in the meantime, it will keep your mind off the what-ifs."

Kate's heart slowed to a normal rate, feeling the tiniest bit guilty for not revealing her recent conversation with Eric.

It doesn't matter if Colleen thinks I'm overreacting, as long as she helps me find some answers.

***

Kate slid open the wardrobe door and stepped back.

"Here we are," she said to Colleen. "The history of Eric, starting with his fifteenth birthday."

The women stared at a short stack of boxes before Colleen asked: "What about the other fourteen years?"

"Not represented here or in anything else I found."

Colleen put her hands on her hips. "Are you sure? I've met Adele. She'd have containers of photos and baby books and videotapes of his first steps. She'd keep his loose teeth and those corny kindergarten graduation diplomas. Have you asked her?"

"I'm planning to, but I think she'll give me the runaround, like she does whenever I mention Eric's childhood. She clams up like a Venus flytrap after a bug lands on its leaves."

"That's a creepy visual." Colleen grimaced.

Kate lifted a carton marked "Eric" from the stack and placed it on the bed. "I know. Everything about this is weird. Just another reason why I'm so suspicious and puzzled. You'd say obsessed and paranoid."

"Stop! I made one comment about baby blues. I never said I'm driving you to the psych ward."

"Thank God. I wouldn't be much help with our investigation from a padded room!"

"So glad you haven't lost your sense of humor." Colleen chuckled and pulled another box from the wardrobe, moved it to the far corner of the room and unfolded the flaps. "There's only these boxes?"

"And the metal box I told you about with the old photos."

A perplexed look swept across Colleen's face.

"What? What are you thinking?"

"Not sure yet. One thing I've learned the hard way is not to jump to conclusions."

"But something caught your eye. I can tell."

"Maybe. Before I add another theory to your already-growing pile, let's dig into these first," Colleen pointed around the room. "Then I'll take a closer look at the contents of that metal security box. Funny that it wasn't locked. Or did you find a key for it?"

"The key was taped inside the lid, but the box was unlocked. Not too secure, unless the only goal was to keep those documents safe from fire."

Colleen nodded, concern bunching her eyebrows, as though part of her process in assessing information.

Kate waited for her detective pal to add some breakthrough revelation, an epiphany of reasoned deduction based on what she'd observed so far. Surely Colleen, with her criminology background, would have an intuitive grasp of the situation. If she did, she wasn't sharing her discovery.

Instead, Colleen turned back to her open box and continued removing the contents.

An hour later, mementos of a teenage boy growing up cluttered the room, but they were no closer to the answers she desperately needed. After pawing through the memorabilia, Colleen arrived at the same conclusion Kate drew: Eric Wiley enjoyed an average adolescence, complete with braces, high school crushes, and a letterman's jacket.

Kate rose from the carpet where she had been sitting cross-legged and stretched. "I'm going to check on Bennie," she said, even though she could see him clearly in the monitor she'd brought into the room earlier.

She needed a moment alone to reevaluate her actions. Perhaps she should let go of this wild goose chase and release Colleen from going through the motions only to mollify her anxieties.

Eric was coming home. He said so late last night. Enough digging through yesterday. Time to start building tomorrow. When Bennie woke, she'd suggest they all go to the park and enjoy the sunshiny day.

"Gotta tell you, that pimply-faced boy matured nicely. What a handsome hunk of a man," Colleen said, pointing to a yearbook photo as soon as Kate returned.

"What are you looking at?"

"Homecoming king Eric."

"There are photos of him as junior prom king somewhere around here. He was homecoming king, too. Ugh!"

Kate grabbed the book. The homecoming queen smiled from the page, but Kate's eyes tracked the eighteen-year-old boy with a crown standing alongside her. The man Kate knew as her husband.

"He rarely talks about high school or college for that matter," she said, paging through his yearbook. "He once mentioned something about being in student government. Wonder what else he did senior year."

"From that stack of letters, looks like he spent a lot of time applying to colleges." Colleen pushed herself to stand.

"I'm gonna take a break Do you want me to bring you something to drink on my way back?" she asked.

"Naw. I have my water bottle." Kate dropped into the spot Colleen had cleared on the floor and began sifting through memories of Eric's senior year. Satisfied there wasn't anything new in those pages, she put the volume down.

A folded newspaper clipping stuck out from the back of the book, almost like a bookmark. She opened the page to see a group shot of the junior ROTC. She wasn't sure what the letters stood for, but she was pretty certain it had something to do with the military.

Kate scanned the faces until she found the one that made her heart skip a beat. As though a spotlight had been dropped on the boy standing in the middle of the third row, she blinked at a scowling Eric sandwiched between fellow members.

She unfolded the clipping and read the photo caption:

Student Commanding Officer Eric Wiley receives training from junior ROTC instructor, retired master sergeant Billy Butler.

"You look like you just saw a ghost," Colleen said, returning to the room. "What are you reading?"

"What does ROTC stand for?"

"Reserve Officers' Training Corps. Why?"

Kate handed the news clipping to Colleen. "Apparently Eric was a recruit in high school."

"So?"

"He never mentioned it to me."

"Maybe the subject never came up," Colleen said. "In college, I was in the Army ROTC for a while. I thought I wanted to serve in the military. Going in as an officer is a good move, especially when you're a woman."

"You joined the Army?"

"No."

"What happened?"

"I met Trace. He had other plans for our future. I dropped out toward the end of my freshman year and I applied to the Pittsburgh Police Academy. You pretty much know how the rest of that romance turned out."

Colleen returned the clipping to Kate. "Trace hated me as a cop. Hell, what would have happened if I had become a commissioned officer? Probably never would have married me."

"You might have been better off." Kate regretted her assessment as soon as she voiced the words.

"Stupid things women do when they're in love." Colleen leaned against a chest of drawers and sighed hard. "I would have done anything for that man and I thought he felt the same. I'll never be that vulnerable again."

"At least Trace knew the truth about your goals and aspirations."

"Yeah. And he made me change them."

Kate frowned. "This is another secret Eric kept from me."

"Don't jump to conclusions. The ROTC is a great way to pay for college. For women like me, the program instilled confidence and self-reliance. Maybe if I had hung in there a bit longer, I would have had the courage to stand up to Trace. To make my own decisions."

"But you didn't keep any secrets from him."

"I should have. Right after he proposed, he pressured me into quitting. Said if I really wanted to make the world a better place I should start closer to home. Applying to the police academy was our compromise. As a cop, I couldn't be deployed to a foreign country."

Kind of like where Eric is right now.

"And then he reneged on that bargain, too." Colleen's eyes fired angrily, recalling the betrayal. She caught herself and smiled, infusing a lighter tone into her cadence. "But hey, Eric finished his stint long before he met you. Probably doesn't even think about it."

Kate wasn't so sure. She sensed that Eric's career training involved more than determining thread counts and shipping logistics. She'd assumed his degree was in finance or business management, but as she stared at this photo of him in uniform, she realized during their three years of marriage, they had never discussed his higher education.

"Where did Eric go to college?" Colleen asked.

"I don't know. Somewhere back east, maybe."

"You never talked about it?" Colleen asked, incredulous.

"When we were dating, he mentioned changing majors and I assumed that it had something to do with the family business." Kate folded the clipping, returned it between the pages and placed the open yearbook on her lap

"Adele and Ben's company?"

"Yeah. Like maybe he wanted to be an astronaut, but they pressured him into settling for a business management degree," Kate said.

"Well, from reading all this, it looks like Eric wanted to be a soldier, not a business owner."

Kate considered Colleen's words. "Now that I think about it, he wanted to know everything about my college years, but when I asked about his, he changed the subject."

"When he calls, ask him about what we found. Where he went to college and why he signed up for the ROTC. You'll probably learn that his best friend joined, and he followed along. Nothing more sinister than that."

Kate ran her tongue back and forth across her lips, moistening the surface. She pulled a tube of lip balm from her pocket, opened the cap and dragged the salve over her lips. "I feel like a sponge left out in the sun, all cracked and dry. All the moisture is being sucked out of me. Piece by piece, life is being drained from my body."

"I thought we were talking about Eric and his military background," Colleen remarked, obviously perplexed at Kate's sudden change in focus.

"Yes, we still are. It's just that I'm exhausted. It's taking every ounce of my energy to keep searching for the truth." Kate retrieved the yearbook from her lap, slammed it shut and tossed the book across the room. "Why can't he come home and be a regular husband like everyone else's?" Tears took over, pushing forth in gushes like a levee break.

"Hey. Hey." Colleen squatted to where Kate sat and wrapped her arms around her friend's shoulders. "There is no such thing as a regular husband. Or a regular wife, for that matter. Just ask Trace," she joked. "When do you expect Eric to call?"

"He didn't say."

"When was the last time you spoke to him?"

"Last night, around ten-thirty."

"What?" Colleen stood. "You talked to him and didn't tell me?"

"I was afraid you wouldn't help me figure all this out," Kate confessed, waving her arm in a sweeping motion across the room. "No matter what he says, I still need some answers."

"Of course you do. But Kate, Eric is your best source to explain all this."

Kate held Colleen's stare for a full second before standing. "For some reason, he won't give me straight answers. He skirts around everything I ask, or he hurries off the call. I think that if he didn't miss Benjamin, I wouldn't hear from him at all."

Colleen shook her head. "You don't really believe that, do you?"

"I'm not sure what to believe. All I'm certain of is that I can't continue the way things are. I have to make sense of what's happening. And I'll do that, with or without your help."

"Listen, how about we pack all this stuff up and then develop a list of questions. Sorta help you organize your thoughts," Colleen suggested. "I'll bet once we write everything down, your suspicions won't seem so ominous and sinister. Just some miscommunication."

"No!" Kate slapped her hand against the wall. "I want to finish going through the boxes. There are clues here, some connection that makes sense. We haven't even gotten to the strongbox yet. Please don't abandon me now th—"

A familiar wail emitted through the speaker and interrupted their conversation. Kate turned toward the monitor screen and witnessed Benjamin's tiny body shifting in his cradle. Time was up.

"Sounds like our investigation will have to wait until after lunch," Colleen retorted. "Let's take a break. You feed the baby and we'll get back at it later this afternoon."

Kate swiped at new tears gathering in her eyes, her heartbeat pounding in her ears. "Okay. I'm sorry I lost my cool, but I know something is wrong. Maybe the answers aren't in this room, but I have to start somewhere."

"I'll go down this road as far as you want to travel and follow the clues to where they lead. I won't desert you. But I want you to know that I think you're making much more out of a few unrelated facts than is healthy or rational."

Kate nodded. "Maybe so, but I won't rest until I learn what's really going on and that my husband is not in any danger."

Chapter Twenty-Five

Kate scooted into a cross-legged position on the guest bedroom floor, relieved that Colleen stayed through lunch and appeared eager to plow through the boxes.

Earlier, they walked to a nearby sandwich shop and enjoyed an impromptu picnic in the neighborhood park. They purposely didn't discuss Eric or his whereabouts. Bennie fell asleep on the way back and Kate, worried he'd awaken, left him buckled inside his stroller, peacefully snoozing away in the master bedroom, in full view of the monitor camera.

Kate picked up the stack of black and white photos nestled inside the strongbox and marveled again at the family resemblance. Could the Wileys and the Khorys be related somehow? She reconsidered her earlier hunch that Leah and Adele were sisters, in spite of the fact that their maiden names were different.

Who were Simon Erol Khory and Leah Haddan?

"This woman reminds me of Adele," Kate said, holding up a snapshot for Colleen to see. "I think she might be Leah, the one named in the marriage certificate."

"Did you compare that photo with her passport picture?" Colleen asked, hunkering down in a corner of the room and displaying a renewed interest in the project at hand.

"I didn't think to do that," Kate said, quickly pawing through the box and retrieving two blue-covered passports. She held the photo alongside the one inside the pages and turned them for Colleen to view. "What do you think?"

"Very possible. What are the dates on the pictures?"

"They're taken about five years apart. The passport photo is newer."

"And who might Leah be?"

"I have no idea, but Eric clearly hid this box from me for a reason."

Colleen stretched her arms overhead and sighed. "You're not starting that again. Just because Eric didn't give you a guided tour of this room, doesn't mean he deceived you. He lived here first, right? He's probably holding stuff for his mom or someone else who doesn't want to pay for a storage unit."

"Maybe," Kate murmured, not totally convinced of Colleen's latest rationalization.

"Before he married you, Eric was a bachelor, with all this empty space. I can almost hear how the request went down." Colleen rolled her eyes.

"You're much better at giving him the benefit of the doubt. Still, no one keeps stuff from people they don't know."

"True, but if his mom asked…"

"Doesn't matter. I want to know who Leah is. And Simon."

"Judging by the age of this stuff, Eric probably did a favor for his mom or dad. You need to ask him or Adele. Whichever one you get ahold of first."

"I have a funny feeling that storing these boxes amounts to more than doing a favor for a family friend," Kate surmised. "Don't give me the evil eye. I will ask Eric about this. But I want to have a better handle on what 'this' is before I formulate my questionnaire."

"Oh, you're funny. All of a sudden Kate turns comedienne."

"You always said my sense of humor is my best asset."

"Because that's the only sense you have. You lost your common sense weeks ago."

"Now who's trying their hand at stand-up?" Kate waited for Colleen to stop laughing. "Seriously, who are these people and what do they mean to Eric?"

"He probably never met them. Anyway, we've spent enough time trying to unmask the identities of Leah and Simon. Give me their passports. I have a pal who can run a trace. Find out a bit more about them."

Kate handed Colleen the booklets and closed the lid of the metal box. "Okay. I guess we've done enough for one day."

Colleen pointed to a legal tablet laying alongside Kate. "How's that list coming?"

"I'm up to fourteen," she responded, referring to her growing list of questions. She pushed herself to stand and grabbed the metal box. "You want to review my work and add anything?"

Colleen waved her hands back and forth. "Oh no, not me. I'm sure you're covering every possibility."

"Except the one you won't share. What were you thinking earlier when you said I shouldn't jump to conclusions?"

"I'm still not sure. I had an odd flutter in my stomach when you were talking about the security box. When I was a detective working a case, right before I figured something out, or a missing piece fell in my lap, I'd get this unsettling, queasy feeling. That same jolt passed through my gut when you mentioned the box."

"The security box gave you the jitters?"

"Yeah, it doesn't match with everything else in the closet. You know the children's song: *one of these things isn't like the others.*"

"Are we talking children's TV shows now?"

"Exactly. Imagine three red balls and one white one. What doesn't fit?"

"The white ball."

"Yes. That's what we have here: a lot of cardboard boxes and a single metal one. Just stuck out like a sore thumb, but it's probably nothing."

Kate sighed. "We're getting nowhere."

"Sometimes nowhere is a cool place to be."

"Well, thank you, Colleen McCool!" Kate grabbed the metal box and moved toward the closet.

"Where exactly did you find that box anyway?"

"I almost didn't," Kate said. "I was giving up on my search for finding an outfit in Eric's old clothes. I was so tired, I laid flat on my back on the carpet. From that angle, I saw the metal on the box glint, maybe from the recessed lighting. Anyway, it was burrowed in the side corner of that top shelf. I would have missed it if I wasn't looking up."

Colleen stood for a moment, scrutinizing the contents of the closet. "It was stored in a different place than the other boxes?"

"But that could be because it's so much smaller."

"Perhaps, but that's another reason it's different. These boxes might have been moved into this room willy-nilly to make space for your stuff. But the strongbox was probably here before Eric knew you. Someone purposefully placed it on that top shelf, out of view."

"You make it sound so mysterious."

"Isn't that why I'm here? To come up with alternative shadowy scenarios."

"Well, yes," Kate said, now on her tiptoes, placing the metal box on the high shelf.

"Wait a second," Colleen shouted. A moment later she returned with a stepstool. After setting it inside the closet, she climbed the two steps. "Hand me that," she directed, pointing at the metal box. "Is this where you saw it?"

"Yes, but a little farther back. Only the edge was visible."

Colleen pushed the box deeper on to the shelf, but it resisted. "Something's in the way," she said, feeling around, but unable to see what was in the darkened corner. She shoved the box harder and heard a click.

"What the... Look at this," Colleen said in awe, pushing open a hidden panel on the side wall revealing another room.

Kate's mouth dropped open. "What. The. Hell."

Chapter Twenty-Six

Kate's pulse pounded in her ear as she and Colleen silently took in the narrow chamber. Large enough to accommodate built-in shelving, several banks of drawers, a wall safe and a hutch displaying a wide variety of guns.

The exposed space reminded Kate of a skinny walk-in closet. As far as she could tell, the only accessories missing in this set-up were an extravagant jewelry chest and shoe storage roomy enough to hold hundreds of pairs.

"What are you thinking?" Colleen asked.

Kate blew dust off a shelf and set the baby monitor down. "I'm thinking, how the hell did I not know about...about all of this." Her hands waved around frantically, the shock of finding a secret room in her home still fresh.

Colleen crossed her arms and scanned the windowless space. Her astonished expression matched the disbelief swirling inside of Kate.

"Where exactly is this, anyway? I mean, in relationship to the rest of the house? And...and, how did I never find it before now?"

"Because you never had a reason to search for it."

"I'm an architect, for Chrissake! I'm supposed to know about structures," Kate said, still glancing around the space.

"Eric owned this house before he met you, right? It was already full of furniture and stuff before you ever set foot inside."

"Yeah. We moved here temporarily until we figured out where we wanted to live. He said it made more sense because it's bigger than my condo. He was right. We would have outgrown that place the day we brought Bennie home." Kate continued surveying the area, her heartbeat spiking with each step. "Colleen, what the hell is this? It reminds me of a bunker or some clandestine operations center you'd see in a cheap spy thriller."

"What's on this side of the house?" Colleen asked, pointing to where the wall safe and shelving were attached.

"The garage, I think."

"We'll check the dimensions later, but if I had to guess, I'd say this is a panic room constructed between the garage and this extra bedroom. There was no change to the house's original footprint. For all we know, all of your neighbors might have one. Could be one of those options you can select on track homes. You know, upgrade the granite, add a fourth bedroom or select a panic room."

"A panic room? Why would he need a panic room?" Kate asked, her voice a spiraling frenzy.

"Calm down."

"Seriously? The best advice you have for me right now is to be calm? My husband has a hidden room with guns, and safes and God knows what else. The last thing I can be right now is calm."

"I meant, it's not that unusual. Folks build them for lots of reasons. They call them safe rooms. Doesn't mean Eric's up to no good."

Kate studied Colleen and appreciated her friend trying to put a lighter perspective on something that defied explanation. "It might when you keep it a secret from your wife. Why didn't he tell me about this?"

"Could be lots of reasons," Colleen added, tempering her vague reply.

And none of them good, Kate thought, reflecting on her own experiences. "I've designed a few for executives in office structures. Mostly as escape-hatches from disgruntled employees. I never knew anyone who installed one in their home. For the record, I'm not upset that it exists, at least not yet, anyway."

"Then what's sending you into a panic? No pun intended."

Despite the craziness of the situation, Kate half-grinned at Colleen. "I'm mad that Eric never told me about the room and why he needs it. We've lived here for two years and I don't even know what's in my own home. What's next? I'll stumble upon a moonshine distillery in an underground crawl space. Damn, I can't believe any of this."

Kate tugged a few drawer handles, but none opened. "I wondered why he kept delaying our hunt for a larger home, but I stopped nagging him about it. I figured he was worried about taking on a huge mortgage. I hoped that we'd move before the baby was born, but Eric never had time to look at the houses across town I'd found. Or even talk to the realtor. Now I know why. He couldn't leave command central."

Colleen furrowed her brow. "This is hardly command central, at least not like any I've ever worked at. There's nowhere to sit, no computer screens to monitor. I don't see any sort of communications linkup. This is more like storage central, and judging by the thickness of the dust, not used very often."

"Just a place to keep ammunition and paraphernalia he didn't want me to know about," Kate mocked. "I've heard of man caves, but this blows that way out of the water. Do you think it's possible the house was like this when he bought it?"

"I'd like to say yes, but if you want my guess—Eric had it constructed, or built it himself. The garage has probably been altered to mask this space. Very exacting work. Not something any contractor would or could do. He must know people."

"Holy crap. I've been dropped into an alternate universe like a seedy late-night sci-fi movie. The world I operated in, believed in, doesn't exist."

"Don't be silly. Your world is still intact. That baby will be crying in a few minutes for his dinner. Life doesn't get any more real than that."

"Yes." Kate glanced at the screen to see Benjamin still fast asleep. "But I'm married to someone who requires a panic room and decides to keep that a secret from me. In my world, we're a happily married couple, raising a newborn son. Then this," Kate flapped her arms in frustration. "There are two very different realities for Eric, I play a part in one of them. What's going on in the other galaxy he lives in?"

Colleen stepped toward the wall safe and eyed the front of the mechanism.

"You're freaked out about this, too. I can tell by the look on your face. That's not your run-of-the-mill home wall safe is it?"

"Well, no. It's a bit more industrial than a typical family requires. I recognize the manufacturer's name, though. This might be built to resemble a more extravagant version than a family wall safe." Colleen placed her hand on the panel next to the safe. It beeped but remained closed.

"What was that?" Kate asked, a mixture of disbelief and fear churning in her stomach.

"A biometric fingerprint recognition lock."

"A biometric what?"

"Exactly. Electronic safes offer this locking option, but this safe looks maybe twenty years old or more. I didn't think they were available in the consumer marketplace until the last five years or so."

"New technology?" Kate asked.

"Not for the government," Colleen supplied. "Been around awhile for military and government purposes. Everything gets invented first by the government, don't you know."

"Yeah. The microwave, GPS. I've heard." Kate stared into space. "Are you saying that somehow the feds are involved? This thing gets crazier and crazier."

Colleen patted Kate's hand. "We may be overreacting. Eric probably has a reasonable explanation for this."

"I'm sure he will." Kate rolled her eyes. "Should I be more worried about why he didn't tell me, or about what the necessity of a room like this means?"

"Good question, and one you'll ask your husband the next time he calls."

"Damn right." Kate pounded the flat of her hand against the only empty wall space, surprised at the solidness of the contact. "This room is built like a fortress. I think it's soundproof, too."

Colleen huffed.

"I'm not sounding silly anymore, huh? This proves it. Something weird is going on. Even a former police detective—one who's not in the throes of baby blues, of course—can't deny this anymore."

"Sheesh. I already apologized for that comment. Boy, can you carry a grudge. But yes, this is a bit off the beaten path. I'm curious at the very least. Still, it may be nothing. So, don't go flying off the handle, terrified that something sinister is going on."

"Too late for that," Kate scoffed. "Normal families don't have safe rooms. Normal husbands can be reached during the workday. Normal—"

Colleen raised her hands in surrender. "I get it. Still, there are a hundred explanations for this. We could drive ourselves nuts creating worst-case scenarios. There are better ways to spend our time."

"Like going through all the stuff in here. Take a look." Kate pointed. "The drawers are locked, but maybe those safety chests stacked in the corner are open, like the first one we found."

"No such luck," Colleen said, struggling to open a lid. "I wonder if the one we rummaged through was left unlocked because Eric was getting something out of it."

"Or putting something in, and didn't have time to secure it back in the room," Kate finished Colleen's thought. "And what about these?"

Kate gestured to the five cardboard boxes piled neatly against the back wall. Each carton clearly marked EROL and designated by age. Birth to two years; three to five years; six to nine years; elementary school; junior high.

"Who's Erol? The guy in the photo?"

"Maybe, but these don't look that old." Kate examined the handwriting. It wasn't Adele's, but she thought it resembled the script on the back of the photos she'd examined earlier.

"I'm getting a little claustrophobic in here. Let's move some of these into the bedroom and go through them," Colleen said, passing a cardboard carton to Kate. "We can kill some time until Eric calls, or you call him."

Kate took the box, toted it through the narrow opening and dropped it onto the comforter topping the bed. A few seconds later, Colleen added a second.

An uneasiness mushroomed in Kate's gut. Would Eric be angry when he found out that she and Colleen pawed through his property,

"Is what we're doing wrong?" she asked, troubled that she had no right digging through her husband's belongings, items he had obviously hidden. "All of this is prior to me becoming his wife; well before he even knew me."

"We are on shaky ground as far as marriages go. Still, this is your home and you could make the case that we stumbled on to the concealed storeroom. He'll ask why you didn't talk to him first before plowing through everything. He might be mad that you involved me."

Kate pointed to the labels on the boxes. "We don't know who Erol is. We could be scrutinizing possessions that have nothing to do with Eric and what's going on."

"True. I'm willing to stop if you want." Colleen sounded like a practiced detective calming a rattled victim after enduring a crime.

Kate huffed a guarded sigh of relief. That got her off the hook, but was that the right choice? Would Eric provide any meaningful answers or just perform his usual symphony of misdirection? No, she had to keep pushing.

"What was Simon's middle name? Wasn't it Erol?" Kate asked, hurrying to retrieve the passports and photos she had reviewed earlier.

"That sounds right. Let's knock off for now," Colleen prodded as Kate dug through the original security box. "I can still run a check on Leah and Simon Khory. Maybe find out where they sell that type of biometric wall safe. By then, Eric will have called and straightened all this out. Let me do some legwork and you relax with Benjamin."

"I will, but look at this first. Simon Erol Khory," she pointed to the name on an old passport. "And compare the handwriting. It looks a lot like the scrawl on the boxes. I'm no expert, but several of the letters are formed the same way. See?" Kate asked, holding the photo next to one of the boxes and tracing the letters. "Look at the Ts and the Es. I'll bet they were written by the same hand."

"Could be, but I still don't know what any of this means."

"You'll figure it out. I know you will," Kate said, feeling euphoric that she had uncovered clues; clues that might get her closer to understanding her husband and his whereabouts.

Colleen tapped a finger to her lips and Kate waited as her friend pondered the situation unfolding before them.

"What ages did you say were missing from Eric's childhood?"

"Everything before middle..." Kate stopped. "No, it can't be. These boxes are for someone named Erol, not Eric."

"Eric and Erol sound very similar to my ear."

Kate ripped the tape off the box labeled "Birth to Two." She removed the usual baby mementos mothers collected for their infants, including a threadbare baby blanket, several children's fairytale books, a christening gown and a *Memories of Baby* journal. Kate tossed everything aside except the journal and pored over the contents.

Taped inside the cover was a light blue hospital ID bracelet. The imprinting had faded a bit, but Kate could still read the baby's name, weight, and length. And date of birth.

"What are you staring at?" Colleen asked. "You've turned white as a sheet."

Kate swallowed, taking a moment to process the information in front of her.

Mother's name: Leah Khory. Baby Boy Khory born: July 12. The same day as Eric.

"Kate, what is it?" Colleen asked again.

"Eric and Erol might be the same person."

"What?" Colleen grabbed the book from Kate and her eyes widened.

"Whoever Erol is," Kate finally said, "he and Eric have the same birthday."

"Maybe they're twins?"

"A twin brother he never told me about? Can't be. This boy's last name is Khory, not Wiley."

Colleen agreed. "All the more reason to talk with Eric. Could be a cousin, maybe who was born on the same day. Unusual, but not impossible."

"You're quite the princess of possibilities, aren't you?"

"Just saying. It could happen. But…"

"But what?"

"Even I'm having a tough time selling that one." Colleen handed the book back to Kate. "There is a connection between these two boys. I'm not able to come up with a plausible explanation, except that they are one and the same. Eric's not adopted, is he?"

"Adopted? No way," Kate exclaimed. "At least I don't think so. But with all the secrets he's been keeping from me, I wouldn't be surprised to hear that one."

"Doesn't make any sense, though. Why would he keep that from you?"

"Beats me. Maybe he thought I would react weirdly. Nah. That can't be true. Adele and Benjamin hover over the baby. Bennie is their grandchild. I'm sure of it. Benjamin Simon is definitely…"

"Benjamin Simon?"

"Yeah. Eric picked it to honor some distant uncle."

"Well, there's your answer. Simon Khory is a relative. Erol is his son. It's all making sense. Sorta."

Kate nodded, not fully embracing Colleen's theory. Pieces were falling into place, but the answers she desperately sought weren't accompanying them, at least not in the ways she had hoped.

"Will you still run those background checks on Simon and Leah? I want to believe all of this is an innocent coincidence."

"Me too." Colleen puffed a breath. "Me too."

Kate's hearing perked up when Bennie's whimpers radiated from the monitor speaker.

"Time to pack up," Colleen said.

"No! Leave everything where it is. When I talk to Eric, I want to be specific with my questions. Seeing all this will help."

"Okay. Can't believe we didn't pick up on the Simon connection sooner."

Kate closed the door to the extra bedroom.

Sometimes the obvious was the hardest to recognize.

Chapter Twenty-Seven

"Way to go, Wiley."

Eric recognized the gruff voice and the approaching, methodic clomp of dress wingtips clicking against the patio pavers. Ralph stopped and stood next to Eric, watching the ambulance drive away.

No doubt he's here to bust my balls for what happened to Trish.

Eric grounded his stance, preparing for the justified chewing out Ralph would unleash. Eric didn't blame him. In fact, he deserved whatever reaming Ralph intended to deliver. He and Trish should have never gone to an unsecured public place after their interrogation went awry. They knew better.

"What were you thinking?"

Eric didn't respond. He shifted his gaze to the space where Trish had crumpled in pain waiting for help to arrive. Minutes before, the medics had loaded her into a military ambulance, and sped off toward the compound. But not until after she downed her vodka Collins, complaining the entire time of the apparent cherry shortage at this crummy establishment.

She had handed her glass to Eric as the attendants wheeled her by him. "Get to work," she cajoled, before turning her full attention to the handsome emergency technician monitoring her blood pressure.

Eric breathed a momentary sigh of relief, grateful that a cursory examination revealed Trish's wounds appeared to be superficial.

Her earlier words swirled in his mind. "*...you can't quit. You gotta find out who put a bullet in me.*"

Those haunting words added guilt to the blame and shame mounting inside his chest. Eric rubbed his forehead, erasing from his mind the realization that they had been easy targets for the approaching gunman. Committing such a rookie mistake further convinced him that his long-overdue decision to leave was the right one.

"Can you explain what in the high hell is going on?" Ralph's question rebounded off the brick wall, sounding more like a command, and snapped Eric back into the present.

"I'm not sure. Some dude jumped out of a van across the street." Struggling to maintain an even and reasoned tone, Eric pointed to the liquor store in the distance. "Made a beeline toward where Trish and I sat. I spotted the gun in his hand, and yelled for everyone to hit the deck."

"Yeah, not fast enough. Trish got shot. How do you explain that?"

"I can't. There's a lot about these past few hours that defy explanation." Eric turned to face Ralph. "Like who knew where Trish and I were going. That knowledge pool is very shallow, wouldn't you say?"

"You accusing me of setting you up? I always thought you were a cocky SOB—but now I know you're a certifiable bastard." Ralph poked Eric in the chest as his voice rose. "The last thing I'd want to see is Trish hurt. You, I don't give a good damn about."

"You think they were after me, and Trish got caught in the crosshairs?"

"Don't know what to make of this cluster. All I know is, you've been sloppy, even if this situation was unintentional. Mistakes like these are deadly, so I'm expediting my recommendation for you to be taken off this team."

Eric puffed his chest defiantly. "Thought you already did that."

"Cocky crap gets you nowhere. This time it got one of our own wounded."

"Yeah, I know," Eric confessed, the full weight of Trish's injury bearing down on him like a tractor-trailer on the I-19 heading out of Phoenix. All he could do was move out of the way and let the truck rush through. But he couldn't let Ralph boot him off the case, not yet, anyway.

"Come here. I want to talk with you," Eric said, knowing the risk he was prepared to take could blow up in his face like everything he touched these days. Still, he motioned Ralph to follow him to a dark corner inside the restaurant. The stagnant, fried-oil smell still permeated the air. Eric didn't care. He had to take a gamble on this guy he'd worked with for years. He had to take a chance on someone. Ralph was right. Eric's cocky attitude was getting him nowhere. He needed help and Ralph might be the fellow to provide it.

"What is it, Wiley? I have to get back to my desk and fill out a butt-load of paperwork on this little boondoggle you call an innocent after-hours drink with a friend."

"Tell me straight," Eric insisted. "Do you believe I had anything to do with what happened to Trish tonight?"

Ralph hesitated. "Well, er, no, I guess…"

"Or Maher being poisoned?"

"I don't know for sure, but my gut tells me no. You don't have the brains to pull off that precise of an operation."

"I'll take the vote of confidence without the sarcastic slap," Eric said.

"What are you getting at?" Ralph asked, his thinning patience apparently reaching its limit.

"Before this shootout—"

"What shootout? You never even lifted your gun from its holster."

"Okay," Eric sucked in a frustrated breath. "Before the ambush occurred, I was telling Trish my plan to resign tomorrow. You were working to get me removed anyway.

After the debacle with Maher, I had nothing left in the tank. I was done."

"I know the feeling," Ralph said, impatiently. "Get to the point."

"We need someone working externally, someone undercover, watching stuff happen from the outside."

Ralph erupted in a dismissive chuckle. "You want to be the outside guy? I don't think—"

"Just hear me out. If you decide I'm shoveling crap, then I'll leave without a whimper. But if what I'm proposing makes sense, then you have to give me a chance at ending this."

"And what does 'ending this' look like in the world of Special Agent Eric Wiley?"

Eric smiled, detecting for the first time in Ralph's demeanor a tiny bit of genuine interest or curiosity. That was the crack in the door he needed to reveal his hastily conceived plan and get Ralph on his side.

"Well, I was thinking—"

"I'll listen, but not here. I have to tie up some loose ends with the restaurant manager right now. Be in the office trailer in an hour."

"I'll be there," Eric said, fighting the urge to send a fist pump in the air. Anmar X thought he had him beat. *Not yet, you rat bastard.*

"And, Wiley."

"Yes."

"Wipe that syrupy grin off your face. I only said I'd listen."

"Yes, sir. I understand. I'll be waiting in the trailer," Eric said to his team leader's retreating back. At this point, listening was all he needed. Ralph wanted this murdering gunrunner as much as Eric did. Neither man could allow the last several years to end with nothing to show except weekly reports that amounted to little more than tracking of a ghost.

Ralph would be game for pretty much anything Eric had in mind, especially if he could claim plausible deniability. And

Eric's plan gave him that in spades. He sauntered through the exit and walked toward the parking lot, a satisfied joy flaring in his gut. He couldn't put his finger on it, but for the first time in a long, long while, Eric believed he held the upper hand. The winds of chance finally were shifting in his favor.

No more waiting for a sign or a tip to roll their way. Eric would make his own clues, follow his own leads, but not under the scrutiny of the agency. He would change the game, change the rules…and change the outcome.

Anmar X had no idea what was heading his way.

***

With sunrise barely thirty minutes ago, the night's horrific events stretched unendingly behind as Eric entered the office trailer. The bottomless quiet played a stark contrast to the adrenaline rush pulsing inside his body. Earlier last night, a few insults were hurled in his direction, but Eric would rather listen to his teammates' yells instead of Trish getting injured.

On the drive back to the compound, Eric could barely contain the surging excitement at casting off the constraints of the CIA. Faced with a brazen attempt on his life, the loss of confidence from his superiors and a fellow agent shot, he knew that going rogue was his only hope of uncovering the hostile powers hidden in the bowels of the Agency.

Not wasting another minute doing things by the book, he thought. Starting now, there were no rules, protocols or procedures. Capturing Anmar X. That's what mattered.

He took out his phone and scrolled through the photos, stopping at the shots he just took after parking the car in the compound's lot. More proof that inside forces operated against him. Before he officially became a defrocked agent, he'd stop by the hospital to check on Trish. Then he'd walk through the gates and not look back.

Come on, Ralph. Get here so we can get this over.

Eric moved to his desk and opened each drawer. Knowing that the military police would examine everything he removed from the facility, he gathered only his personal effects, and there wasn't much. Just two snapshots, one of Kate on their wedding day and the other of him holding Bennie with Kate looking on. He set them on the blotter and retrieved the engraved pen clipped to a file folder on the desktop. He'd nearly forgotten the pen Benjamin had given him the day he joined the CIA.

"Sort of a graduation gift," his adoptive father had said while shaking Eric's hand after watching him take the oath. "Keep this with you for a bit of good luck." And Eric had. The pen was always with him, no matter where he had been stationed, except for today.

He scanned the group of papers inside the folder, killing time waiting for Ralph. But it didn't matter. Everything he needed to move forward was emblazoned on his brain, not in these files and reports that led to nowhere.

What was he missing? The questions circled his mind like clothes stuck in the spin cycle. A ceaseless loop, no beginning, no ending, no solution.

On many occasions, Eric and Ben had discussed the case. They speculated about possibilities, and role-played a variety of outcomes. But the information, Ben would point out, consistently lead to Anmar X's highly developed circle of weapons smugglers as his protection. A circle Eric nor any of his fellow agents could uncover, much less infiltrate.

Always at the twelfth hour, Anmar managed to slip away. Never leaving behind a photograph or a surveillance video to aid the CIA in unmasking him. The meager descriptions, on the rare occasion when they could be obtained, could have been of any man of Arab descent, now approaching his mid-fifties. How had he avoided being photographed? As far as Eric could tell, Anmar X was little more than an apparition.

Eric and Ben had volleyed theories back and forth, but the sought-after key never presented itself. Their conversations always ended with Ben urging Eric to quit the service and enjoy his life. Ben had upped the pressure when Eric married Kate. He and Adele took their campaign to new heights as soon as Kate became pregnant.

Sitting in this tomb-like silence, Eric scratched his head, grinning at the absurdity of his life. Whoever was pulling strings in this melodrama messed up big time. He would be on a plane to the states, had Anmar's henchmen backed off. Eric wouldn't abandon his team now, not until he tracked those guys down.

There had to be video footage of them from the restaurant security cameras. The Indulge Me Grill would be his first stop. He'd pull off a photo of the shooter and the driver from their surveillance cameras, and maybe one of the getaway van, now probably abandoned.

He peeked out of the trailer door. Still no Ralph. He dialed Kate.

"Hello."

Eric's heart leaped at the sound of her voice. "Hi, honey. Hope I didn't wake you. I know it's early."

"Eric. Thank God. You're not calling to say you're delayed again, are you?"

"No. No. I'm calling because I miss you."

"Then you're still coming home tonight?"

"Yes. Of course."

"Good. Listen, I have so much to tell you and ask you about," Kate said, breathless enthusiasm coating her voice.

"Me too, sweetheart. How's Bennie?"

"He's asleep, hopefully for another hour."

"Who do I hear in the background?"

"Monica's here with Bodie and Bella. They brought breakfast," Kate said. "The same egg and cheese burritos I used to bring to their house."

"Wish I was there to have some. Give Bella a kiss from me and tell Bode-man that Uncle Eric will be home soon to throw the baseball around."

"I will, but first I need to talk to you. Wait a second, I want to go where I have some privacy."

Eric listened as Kate changed rooms. He heard a door click shut and then she continued. "I found some boxes in the spare bedroom."

"Boxes? What kind of boxes? The ones I moved after we were married?"

"Yes, but there's more. I didn't have anything comfortable to wear, so I looked through your clothes to see if you had an old pair of sweats I could borrow until I got to the store. Your folks were coming to watch Bennie so I could go shopping."

"You were going to wear my castoffs? Honey, there had to be something nicer around the house."

"Stop interrupting," Kate snapped. "Why I was going through the boxes isn't important. While I was in there, I found cartons of stuff from when you were in middle school and high school."

"Strolling down old memory lane, huh?"

"Will you be serious for a minute!"

"Sorry. I didn't mean to—"

"Why are there no mementos of you when you were a baby or a toddler?" Kate asked, obviously losing her patience.

"I don't know," Eric replied, worried about why Kate was asking about his childhood. "They're probably in Mom and Dad's spare room."

"They're coming over later, so I'll ask, but your mom is always fuzzy when I talk about you as a baby."

"Fuzzy?" Eric answered, knowing full well why Adele's responses were vague, sometimes bordering on lies. Perhaps Eric should have told Kate about his family history while they were dating. At least before Benjamin arrived. She had a right to know who she married and parented a son with.

"She doesn't have any cute stories to share, no photos of you as an infant. That kind of stuff," Kate continued.

"How do you know that?"

"Because I've been asking her ever since I got pregnant and especially after Bennie was born. I wanted to see what you looked like and compare old photos of you to our son."

Eric understood Kate's curiosity. She wanted to know more about her child's father, bask in the "he's-got-your-nose-and-my-upper-lip" kind of speculation families routinely participated in.

She had innocently opened a door Eric had bolted shut. Their conversation careened in a direction he wasn't ready to travel. They would have this talk someday, but not today. He couldn't go into the horrific details of his parents' deaths over the phone. That was a discussion that should take place in person.

"I don't have a lot of time," he blurted, hoping to end the call and refocus his mind on the task at hand. "I just wanted to hear your voice and tell you I love you."

"What are you rushing off the phone for?" Kate's question dripped with attitude. "Seriously, Eric, we *have* to talk. Now! There's something weird going on here. Along with the school mementos, I found a strongbox with official-looking documents for a couple named Simon and Leah Khory."

"Simon and Leah who?" Eric's stomach tightened at the mention of his parents.

"Cor-ee. I think that's how you pronounce it. There are photos too. She looks a lot like your mother."

Eric combed his fingers through his hair, stalling for time. Finally, he responded. "Kate, baby. I can't help with this right now. I've got to get back to work."

"Well not before I tell you this. Colleen and I found a doorway to a hidden chamber in the back of the closet. She called it a panic room."

Eric's chest tightened. "What! What in the world are you talking about? What kind of panic room?"

"I don't know, but inside there were guns and a safe and...boxes filled with mementos of a little boy named Erol Khory. Eric, his birthday is the same as yours."

Chapter Twenty-Eight

Kate held her breath, not sure how Eric would respond to her mining their home for clues about his past and turning up mysterious, seemingly unrelated pieces of family history. Some of the information she dismissed as irrelevant, some might be coincidental. Her suspicions had been confirmed, though. There was a lot he had hidden from her. A lot she needed to know.

"Well?" she asked, pushing the point. She wouldn't let him dismiss her concerns and sideline their conversation for another day. "Who is Erol Khory?"

"Ah... I mean."

"Just what do you mean?" Kate's pulse spiked as she pressured Eric for a reasonable explanation.

"Kate." A rap came at the door and Monica entered. Four-year-old Bella trailed behind, cradling her dolly the same way Monica held the baby. "Benjamin is munching around his old auntie, but my milk store closed many years ago." A smile graced the corners of her big sister's eyes. "Sorry to interrupt, but a nursing baby won't wait."

"What's going on?" Eric asked.

"Your son is hungry. I have to go, but promise me that we'll talk about this. Soon!"

"Not sure there's much to talk about. A secret room with guns and safes. Sounds to me like you've watched one too many spy movies."

"Don't," Kate said flatly.

"Don't what?"

"Dismiss me like I'm some raving loon. I can send you photos if you like."

"Truly, Kate I have no clue what you're talking about. My folks lived in that house before I bought it from them. If there's some secret chamber as you say, it was built before my family owned the place."

"Or your parents constructed the room."

"Now you're really going off the deep end. I can hear Bennie crying."

"What does all of this mean?" she screamed into the phone, no longer maintaining her cool or shielding her sister from the mounting anxiety building inside.

"I'll take Bennie back into the living room," Monica volunteered. "You finish up with Eric. Come along, Bella. You can help me keep your cousin entertained until Aunt Kate is done with her conversation."

"Can I still burp him? Bodie got to do it last time," Bella chirped.

"It's your turn." Monica, holding the infant in the crook of her arm, directed Bella out of the room with her free hand. She turned to Kate and mouthed, *is everything all right?*

Kate nodded dismissively. "I'll be there in a minute."

Monica closed the door, helping to muffle the baby's cries. Still Benjamin's yelps invaded Kate's ears. She had about two minutes before they crescendoed into hysterical shrieks.

"I have to go. What time can you call back?"

"I'm not sure."

She gulped a batch of air and blew out slowly. "I can't. No, I won't live like this. Tell me when I can expect your call."

"I'm not sure. Things have gone sideways here," Eric confessed, a weightiness shadowed his speech.

"Well, I passed sideways a long time ago." Kate's voice and anxiety twisted higher.

"Can't this wait until tonight?" Eric asked.

"No, it can't. I can't wait that long."

"Sweetheart, you're overreacting."

Kate flushed with anger. "This is like a really bad spy movie and I'm caught in the vortex of your choices. Give me a time to expect your call or I'll call you."

"How's three hours?"

"Great, and be ready to tell me the truth."

"I have the answers you're after, Kate." Eric paused. "But I'd rather tell you in person."

"That would be great, but I can't count on you coming home when you say you will. You can't stall any longer. I want to know what's going on. I'll be waiting for your call." She clicked off, hoping she had made the right choice. Her only choice—demanding the truth—empowered her a bit.

She'd wait for Colleen's research, but she didn't need an official report to confirm her suspicions. In her heart, she knew Erol and Eric were the same person. Eric would eventually confess that fact.

Her deeper anguish came to the realization that he had kept this serious secret from her. She spent a few moments imagining why.

Every guess frightened her more.

***

Eric jumped at the sound of a door slamming. Lost in the discoveries Kate had shared moments ago, he hadn't heard Ralph enter.

"This is one royal screwup." Ralph kicked a chair, sending it crashing into a filing cabinet near Eric. "One massive, friggin' cluster–"

"And how are you involved?" Eric asked.

"In your colossal mess? I don't know, Wiley." Ralph raised his eyebrows. "I have a few minutes. Why don't you tell me?"

Eric held up his phone. Ralph glanced at the screen and then at Eric. "What's this?"

"A photo of the license plate from the getaway van that drove the gunman."

"Nice work. How'd you manage to take such a close-up picture while being shot at?" Ralph asked.

"That picture isn't from the restaurant. I took it a few minutes ago when I walked through the compound parking lot on my way here. Looks like the same van you picked Trish and me up in from the airport."

"Let me see that again," Ralph grabbed the phone. "Can't tell nothing from this picture."

"Scroll left. There are more photos. Trust me, Ralph it's the same van. YBC-45-56. That's the same plate number I turned in to you at the scene of the shooting."

Baffled at what he was seeing, Ralph checked his notes.

"What I'm wondering is, why were the occupants of an agency van firing guns at two of your agents?"

"Are you saying I had something to do with Trish getting shot?"

"I'm not sure what to think, but I don't believe in coincidences."

Ralph dragged his hands up and down his face and released a long sigh. "I don't believe in coincidences, either," he said finally. "We rented that van. Anyone in this facility could have access to the keys. Anyone here could be the traitor."

"Like I said, it has to be someone on the inside. Kick me out of the agency. At least on paper. That's the only way I can uncover the leaker."

Ralph laughed, not a hearty, happy laugh. His haunting chuckle oozed irreverent and dismissive. "Good old Eric Wiley riding in to save the day by going under deep cover.

Just like his daddy. Well, excuse me all to hell if I don't buy a ticket to that freak show."

Eric closed the space between them. "I know you never liked me being shoved down your throat. I'm not sure asking to be assigned to this team was the right thing. But at the time, all I could see... Well, requesting this assignment was something I had to do. I can't go into all the reasons."

"No, of course not. Ben Wiley pulls some strings and the rest of us are supposed to snap to. Your assignment leapfrogged you over some very talented agents, and delayed their promotions."

"I never realized—"

"Of course you didn't. The only channel you watch is Eric TV. Hey, look. I never held it against you, because you did your job well, at least in the beginning. I've been around long enough to know how the game is played, politics in everything. But now, Trish has been shot. Maher is recovering from being poisoned while you watched. Don't matter who your daddy is anymore. It's time for you to slink away, tail between your legs. Go back to wherever it is you call home."

"Ralph, listen, please."

"Can't. Gotta wipe my hands clean of your mess and get back to finishing this mission. But thanks for the tip on the license plate. Just might mean something."

"I don't blame you for resenting me. I would too if I were in your shoes. You have to know that all I want is to resolve this case."

"If I ever doubted your conviction, you would have never unpacked your duffel," Ralph barked. "But now—"

"Hear me out."

Peddis turned a chair around and straddled the seat. "If that will make you leave, then I'm listening. He glanced at his watch. "Five minutes. Not a second more."

"That's all the time I need," Eric claimed, pulling a chair near to where Ralph had settled.

187

Eric quickly outlined the facts as best he could recap. Ralph grudgingly interspersed a snort of assent or a grunt of skepticism to the summary. Occasionally, he rewarded Eric with a nod of agreement, enough encouragement to keep Eric pleading his case.

"No matter what approach we took, every clue dried up and disintegrated like fall leaves in November. One way or another, our surveillance continued to be disrupted. To the brass, we look like sloppy investigators, too dumb to gather the intelligence, fill in the missing pieces and capture this guy. This time *they* screwed up and left a loose end. The van. Let me follow up."

Ralph released a loud huff of agreement, a signal to Eric that his plan might have a chance.

"This BS has been going on, no matter what team worked this case," Eric hastily continued. "You know all this firsthand. You inherited this espionage cluster. The only constant has been shoddy detective work, derailed by a crooked agent—"

"And your dad, Benjamin."

"Huh?" Eric asked, thoroughly confused.

"You said the only constant in this probe has been a string of bungling task force teams never able to follow the investigation to its conclusion, right?"

"Yeah. So?"

"There's one other consistent factor you forgot to mention—your dad. He's been involved with tracking down weapons smugglers from the beginning. Even after Langley enforced his mandatory retirement, he kept his hand in. One way or another, Ben played behind-the-scenes, advising, second-guessing or offering tips."

"I didn't realize that." Eric had believed that Ben retired on his own, eager to take on the role of entrepreneur. He seemed satisfied to negotiate deals and rake in money as their store chain grew. He had told Eric about how much he loved talking to the green agents, the new guys, as an occasional training session speaker. Ralph's assertion about Ben still ramrodding the Anmar X case, especially after Eric had been assigned to the team, left an uneasiness in his chest.

Ralph snorted. "I do believe that's how we were rewarded with you."

"Ben was very close to the couple Anmar X killed."

"I know. Simon Khory was his partner. He's taken this case very personally. Not a good quality for a spook."

"It's bothered him that justice still remains unfulfilled," Eric defended, not sure why he felt the need to. "That's another reason why I want to try something off the track. I want to put this investigation to rest so Ben can let go and move on with his life."

Ralph shifted in his seat, as though evaluating Eric's words and deliberating the percentage of truth contained in his plea.

"Someone on the inside is altering, losing, falsifying or intentionally misplacing evidence." Eric blustered ahead with his theory before Ralph could hand down a decision, ending all hope. "There can't be any other explanation for why every tip we follow winds up at a dead end. If they think I've been dismissed, they'll let their guard down. Maybe we'll catch a break. Things sure as hell aren't panning out now. What do we have to lose?"

Ralph remained silent, sizing up Eric as though he were a used car salesman, hawking a junker with low mileage and plenty of tread on the tires.

Eric pushed on. "I can flush out the traitors, catch them in the act. And put this horrible chapter in the CIA's history to rest. Don't you want to see Anmar X pay for what he did?"

Eric's chest released with that final question. The decision now rested with Ralph. Either way, he had done all one man could do to bring justice to his parents' memory and pride back to the CIA. With a clear conscience, he would return to Kate, confess everything and begin to rebuild their lives. That promise he intended to keep.

"All right. I'll play this charade, but only for forty-eight hours."

Eric started to protest, but Ralph's voice grew louder. "You're an active agent with all the rights, responsibilities and protections that role entitles you to—for two more days. As far as anyone around here knows, I've fired your ass and sent you packing. May God be with you because you're going to need some divine intervention."

Ralph reached into his bottom desk drawer and palmed a small package. "Here. Open this after you leave. That's how we'll communicate. Check in every three hours. Your hotel room is still available, but don't plan on staying there for very long."

Eric accepted the small box containing a burner phone with Ralph's number pre-programmed, a small amount of cash and a fake passport. These would be his lifelines until this situation played out.

"I'm cutting you loose in forty-eight hours," Ralph repeated. "As for act one of your little drama beginning, pack up your crap and get the hell out of here."

Eric tucked the package under his arm, gathered the few personal items he had stored in the trailer desk and left.

What now? Eric leaned his body weight against the closed door seconds later. *Where do I start?* With his sole focus on getting Ralph's approval for his scheme, he hadn't actually outlined a strategy, even a vague one.

A fleeting thought of calling Ben for help passed quickly through his mind. He had always been Eric's go-to person, no matter what the quandary, personal or professional. Ben Wiley was forever ready with the right answers, but Eric couldn't push that button. At least not yet. Too many catastrophes had occurred in the past several hours, heightening an uneasy feeling swelling inside. An invisible tug cautioned him to keep his plans quiet and not contact the man who aided him as more than a mentor, for most of his life.

Eric patted the souvenir pen from Ben tucked inside his shirt pocket, secured his few personal belongings and headed across the grounds toward the hospital complex. He plodded as though he were traversing into unknown, dark jungles on an African safari. The foreignness of being on his own, coupled with the weight of the recent disasters, enveloped him like a leaden shroud.

Once inside the hospital, he located Trish's floor and headed to her room. He pushed open the squeaky, swinging door and held his breath. Trish rested under snow-white sheets, nearly as pale as her skin.

"Hey, sleepy head. Don't you know how to duck?" Eric grinned.

Trish waved him closer. "You talkin' about this little thing?" she pointed to her shoulder. "Just means I get some R&R on Uncle Sugar's dime. Probably bump up my pension a few thousand."

There's that sass I rely on. Eric released a tense breath, thankful the assassin's bullet hadn't compromised Trish's quirky personality, too.

"How ya feeling?" he asked, dropping his belongings on a chair before standing next to the bed.

"I'm fine. It's you I'm really worried about."

"Me?"

"Yeah, you crazy fool." Trish snorted. "If you weren't protecting me, you'd have gone all macho on those guys. You'd be dead or worse."

Eric nodded, wondering what fate was worse than death. Never seeing his wife and son again qualified.

Trish had saved his butt too many times to count. "I'll be forever indebted to you. So are Kate and Bennie. I'll give them your regards when I get home."

"Home?" Trish pushed against the mattress to sit up. "You're not deserting, are you?"

"Don't think they call it desertion when your boss kicks you out the door."

"Ralph fired you? I don't believe it. He thinks you're really close to—"

"Close to what? Doesn't matter. I'm heading home as soon as I book a flight," Eric said, louder than necessary in case that elusive mole also hung out in hospital corridors. The sooner the quisling knew Eric was dismissed, the sooner he'd let down his guard.

"You don't need to yell. I'm right here," Trish growled. "People across the hall can hear you, for cripes sake. Look Eric, I know you feel bad about all this." She waved her hand in a circle, as though lassoing the day's events. "What happened tells me we're getting close. We made someone nervous. You need to backtrack and figure out what triggered the shooter." Trish grinned wide. "No pun intended."

"Naw, I'm done."

"This isn't the time for you to bail."

"I'm not bailing. I'm fired. Don't you get it?"

"Right. Peddis is terminating you, right when things are getting interesting. I don't believe that for a second."

"Believe it. You taking a bullet was the final straw."

"He can't fire you that fast. Let me talk to him."

"Trish. Let it go. I wanted to quit anyway. That's what I was talking to you about when the slaphappy shooter showed up. This really is for the best."

Trish laid her head on her pillow and searched Eric's face as though a clue would appear. "You're not kidding, are you? I never thought I'd see the day when you'd give up on any case, much less this one."

"I have no choice."

"What will your dad say? I'll bet he has a fit."

"I haven't told him yet, but I'm pretty sure he'll be glad. We're both ready to accept the fact that things don't always work out."

"What a crock of crap. Take your pity party somewhere else, Wiley. That is if you're still Eric Wiley. 'Cause the Eric Wiley I know would never give up like this."

"Time to get real, Trish. I have a wife and a son. I could get used to a nine-to-five existence, wheeling and dealing with textile mills and manufacturers. That's what Kate thinks I'm doing when I'm away, not chasing down the scum of the earth. It would be nice not lying to my wife the way I've done since we met."

"You hate this...deception," Trish said, apparently searching for the right word. "I always wondered how you kept things straight. You're not the kinda guy to say one thing and do another. That's what this job makes you do."

"Trish."

"Let me finish." She sighed. "I knew you'd eventually return to your family and the business. Just thought it would be after we completed this. I get it, though. Sometimes things get too hard and you question your reasons for staying the course."

"Maybe we've both passed the tipping point," Eric said.

"For a minor scrape like this, they'll send me stateside for recovery. Maybe I'll put in for a desk job, find me a nice guy and settle down like you."

"Might be for the best." Eric planted a quick kiss on her forehead. "I'm gonna go now, but I'll keep in touch."

"Sure you will," Trish said, punching her pillow. "Have a nice life, Wiley."

"Don't be like that. This really is for the best. Chasing Anmar X burned out my dad and now me. Can't let this go on forever," Eric repeated, working harder to convince himself more than Trish.

She nodded. "It's funny. This case has been passed down through the years. According to every agent assigned to this detail, apprehending these smugglers meant a lot to Ben. He was the original agent and the only person to have actually seen Anmar X."

"I know. He made tracking down his friends' murderer his life's passion," Eric volunteered.

"I didn't realize he knew the Khorys. Did he work with Simon?"

"They were in the same unit back in the day, tracing a gun-smuggling ring headed by Anmar X." Eric continued, "That was nearly twenty years ago and we're no closer to capturing him."

"Someone came after us, Eric. We're getting close," Trish declared, her eyes filled with serious emotion replacing her usual teasing twinkle.

Too close, Eric thought. "I gotta go, Trish, and I will stay in touch."

"I know you will." Trish extended her uninjured arm in mock surrender. "Give Kate a hug from me and tell Bennie his auntie Trish loves him."

Eric nodded and turned to leave.

"It's still weird, though," Trish added as Eric reached for the door handle. "All we have to go on is a sketch artist's composite portrait based on a description your dad provided two decades ago. As far as I know, Ben Wiley is the only living person to have seen Anmar X–ever."

Chapter Twenty-Nine

"Baby Ben sleeping again, Auntie Kate?" Bella's tiny voice welcomed Kate into the family room where she, Monica and Bodie waited, watching TV.

"He is, precious girl. And thank you for helping him to get that big burp out this morning."

Bella blushed and hugged her doll Lacey tighter. "It was stinky."

Monica and Kate laughed.

"Then you shouldn't have put your face in front of his mouth," Bodie scolded, taking a moment to turn his gaze away from the sitcom playing on the screen.

"Mommy Monica!" Bella cried out to her adoptive mother.

"Stop, you two. You'll wake up the baby." Monica pushed up from the couch and gathered the paper plates dotted with traces of breakfast burritos. "We need to get going," she said, turning toward Kate. "Tomorrow's a school day for these two, plus God only knows what Brady, Brian and Burke have been doing while I've been gone."

"Dad's home," Bodie volunteered. "Besides, Brady's all grown up. That's what he keeps telling me."

"Brady's not as grown up as he thinks," Monica declared, moving toward the kitchen.

Kate picked up the empty glasses and followed. "Thank you for spending the morning with me."

"Anything we can do before we leave?" Monica asked as Kate searched for an open spot to squeeze a few more things into the already overfilled dishwasher.

"No. You've done so much already." Kate reached for her sister's hand. "I love you being here and helping me with Bennie. Sometimes I feel so alone and unqualified to be anyone's mother."

"We all feel that way, no matter how many children you have or how old they are."

"It's so different when you're the mommy, not the fill-in auntie."

"True that." Monica smiled. "You are doing a fabulous job. Everything about your son is perfect. Mom would be very proud."

A tear teetered in the corner of Kate's eye. Bridget Jameson would have loved Bennie, her ninth grandchild, as much as she would have surely treasured all of her grandbabies. She visualized her mother's serene smile now and the image filled her with warmth as though Bridget arrived for a visit.

Kate swiped an errant tear. "Mom was always proud of me. Her encouragement fueled me to accomplish anything, or at least try."

"Like the time you went around the neighborhood selling handmade birthday cards. Most little girls sold cookies."

"Don't laugh. I sold a few to Mrs. Lawson and that nice lady down the street, what was her name?"

"Maggie?"

"Yeah, but I never called her Maggie. Mom would have sent me to my room if I didn't refer to all the adults as Mr. and Mrs."

"We didn't have much money," Monica recalled, "but Mom made sure we were courteous and respectful, especially to adults. Said good manners were free. Being raised properly meant a lot to her."

"Somehow Mom saw the talents inside each of us. She encouraged my drawing, even though, at ten, I didn't know my skills would be better suited to designing buildings than illustrating heartfelt greetings."

"I loved your cards. I still have some inside my hope chest."

Kate smiled. "I know now that any success I've had is largely because she nurtured my self-esteem. She was behind me, no matter what. I hope I can instill that sense of confidence in Benjamin."

"You will. You're his best fan already."

"It's scary out there on your own," Kate said.

Monica encircled Kate with her arms and held her for several minutes. "You are never alone. Need I go through the rundown of people who love you?"

Kate tugged away. "I know."

"I don't want to pry, but it sounded like you and Eric were arguing on the phone earlier," Monica said.

Kate shrugged. "Seems like that's all we do anymore. Sometimes I feel so overwhelmed. He's always traveling…"

"But he's coming tonight."

"Yes, and he promised to cut back on the sales trips," Kate forced a smile.

"Sunny skies are ahead. In fact, there's so much *son*-shine in your life, I think I'm getting burned. Get it? *Son*-shine."

Kate widened her eyes and huffed.

"Laugh at my corny jokes, for Pete's sake," Monica admonished.

"Am I interrupting?" Kate turned to see Colleen standing in the doorway.

"Bodie let me in. I have some information I wanted to share with you right away. Didn't want to tell you over the phone."

"Sounds important," Monica said, sending a. perplexed look to Colleen and then to Kate. "Maybe I should leave."

Kate moved toward the kitchen table. "No, I want you to hear this, too, and tell me your thoughts." She pointed to the chair next to her before turning to Colleen. "What did you find out?"

Her friend opened the cover of her notebook and turned several pages. "Not sure how to string these beads together."

"What beads?"

"Sorry, I mean bits of information. Guess I'll cut to the chase, and we can backpedal from there."

A swarm of fluttering butterflies invaded Kate's stomach, causing her throat to tighten. From the stern look on Colleen's face, what she would reveal wouldn't be good or comforting news.

"Simon Erol Khory was a CIA agent. Covert, from what I can tell. Part of the clandestine arm of the agency."

Kate leaned forward. "What do you mean, was?"

"Some twenty years ago, he, along with his wife, Leah was murdered."

"How? Where?"

"Not sure. Some speculation about the deaths being related to the job, but we can't confirm that yet. My contact attempted to dig further, but was frozen out of the system. Denied access, was the term he used."

"Who is this friend?" Kate asked.

"I can't tell you. He's someone doing me a favor, off the record, for old times' sake," Colleen confided.

"Can't he check other databases, news clippings? There has to be more information available about them besides the fact that they're dead."

"I'm sure there is, but the public records, as far as we can tell, have been scrubbed," Colleen said. "You need a higher level of clearance to access whatever information remains with the agency."

Kate glowered, but remained silent as Colleen continued.

"Before my friend hit the roadblock on the system, he learned something else. Leah and Simon parented one son, Erol, but there is no record of him since their death."

"Except for the stuff we uncovered in that secret room. None of that is dated more recently than when he was thirteen or fourteen. The age he would have been when his parents were murdered," Kate added, a quiver of dread vibrating in her chest. "All of this coincides with the timeline of the boxes we found. And…how Eric's life seemed to start around that same age."

"What are you talking about?" Monica exclaimed. "CIA? Murder? A missing child? A secret room?"

Kate shifted her gaze to her sister, whose face glowed in disbelief.

"Here's the short version," Kate responded. "We think Eric isn't who he claims to be. He's someone named Erol Khory."

"What? Why?"

"Two of the many questions we've been asking ourselves the past few days," Colleen recapped. "Kate needs to ask her husband for answers. And soon."

Monica shifted toward Kate. "You and Colleen are worrying me. The way you make this sound, Eric might be involved in something dangerous. Why else wouldn't he tell you his true identity?"

"So far all we have is supposition," Colleen hurried to add. "No real proof of anything sinister. Just a lot of inconsistencies that, frankly, have the tiny hairs on the back of my neck standing at attention."

"Exactly my point," Monica pressed, returning her stare to Kate. "Pack a bag, grab Bennie and come stay with me."

"I'm not in danger." Kate hoped she infused enough calm into her voice to convince Monica. "I'm not afraid for my safety. I just want to know what's going on. Eric probably has a reasonable explanation for all this. He alluded to the fact that another family lived here before he did."

"That may be," Monica said. "Stay with me and call Eric from my house."

Kate smiled. "I want to be in my home, with my son. Colleen is here with me. If anything gets weird, I'll come over. I promise."

Monica glanced at Colleen before looking at Kate. "You know best. I'm heading out, but I'll call in the morning. Okay?"

Kate accepted her kiss, wondering what changes would have occurred by the time Monica phoned tomorrow. If Eric kept his word, she'd talk to him in less than two hours and he would be home tonight. Then he'd straighten out this entire misunderstanding.

She prayed that his responses would satisfy the growing tension nesting in her soul and jeopardizing her faith in him.

***

On the drive to the hotel, Eric glanced at his watch, realizing he hadn't slept in more than twenty-four hours. There wasn't time to recoup all of that missed shut-eye, but maybe he could grab a quick power nap at the hotel before pursuing his next step—whatever that would be.

Events of yesterday didn't offer him the luxury of concocting an elaborate strategy to smoke out Anmar X. Eric would have to hit fast and hard, his only hope being the snitch or snitches bought his story about being fired.

Still, he worried more about stalling Kate long enough to wrap up things here. Knowing his wife well, she would be waiting, phone in hand. If she didn't hear his voice on time, she'd be calling him.

He needed a plausible explanation, one that kept her believing in him, until he could get home, confess his past and the reasons for his deception. He couldn't lose her love. That was too high a price to pay for this last-ditch effort to capture a gunrunning murderer.

Trish's words rang in Eric's ears.

Ben Wiley is the only living person to have seen Anmar X—ever.

In this day of technological everything—surveillance cameras, facial recognition, speech identification software—how could that still be true? Someone, somewhere must have seen him recently, spoken to him, bought him a cup of coffee. Was he in the Middle East or had he relocated to Central America? How had he aged? Hell, that composite sketch had been updated at least four times, as far as Eric knew, to reflect what Anmar X might look like now. Assuming they ever knew what he really looked like, to begin with.

Eric entered the hotel and made his way up to his room. The moment he stepped through the door, he turned on the lights and spilled his body on to the bed like a rupturing sack of potatoes. He turned on the phone Ralph gave him, setting the alarm for forty-five minutes. A nap would re-energize his spirit and his mind.

Eric kicked off his shoes, laid back on the pillow, and closed his eyes, willing sleep to overtake him. Slumber wasn't accommodating his wishes. Unable to turn off his thoughts, he replayed scenes from the past few years over in his mind.

In each vignette, a common thread appeared. The lack of any other crimes directly attributed to Anmar X, even though his name was always bantered about in brainstorming meetings. It seemed to Eric that Ben and some of the senior agents kept the legend alive. Whenever a random bombing occurred, or a shipment of weapons went missing, one of the "old dogs" as they were called, would throw Anmar X's name into the pot of possibilities. Many of those cases were solved. None were ever traced to Anmar X.

Sleep finally overtook Eric, but only for a brief moment. His burner phone chimed. Ralph, not the alarm, interrupted his slumber.

"Hello," Eric answered.

"Letting you know Maher is out of critical condition," Ralph said. "He's being transferred tomorrow before noon. Not sure where. I think your timeline just got shortened."

Eric rubbed his eyes, surprised that Ralph disconnected before he could respond.

Maher getting transferred? Who was behind that move?

The mountain of questions enveloping Eric continued to grow, pressing against him like a lead apron. No time for sleep. He needed answers.

He picked up his personal phone and dialed his wife, hoping Colleen would be visiting. The former cop would be a Godsend in keeping Kate calm and handling the home front if Eric's suspicions proved to be true.

Chapter Thirty

Kate and Colleen sat at the kitchen table, a pot of tea and the metal security box between them. Colleen shuffled through the pages of her notebook, as though drawing conclusions from the information she had uncovered.

Kate knew her attempts were in vain. If anything, Colleen's investigation left them with more questions. CIA. Murder. A missing child. A secret room. How did any of that fit together?

Both women jumped at the vibration from Kate's phone. "It's Eric," Kate frantically announced, nearly dropping the cell.

"Hello."

"Katie. Baby. Got a minute?" Eric said.

Kate swallowed hard, recognizing the same heaviness in his voice from earlier.

"Of course, I have a minute," she said, hopeful he was finally ready to talk.

"Is Colleen with you?"

"Yes. Why?"

"I have to tell you some things that you might not want to hear, and I want someone there with you since I can't be. At least for the time being."

"You're scaring me." Kate's throat tightened as though protecting her from breathing in something foul and poisonous.

"I don't mean to. Is Monica still there?"

"No, only Colleen." Kate paused. "Monica and the kids left about a half-hour ago."

Eric huffed out a relieved sigh. "Where are you in the house?"

"In the kitchen."

"Good. Put the phone on speaker. I want both of you to hear this and then I need for you to do something for me."

Kate did as Eric requested and waved to Colleen to move her chair closer. The serious tone of Eric's voice sent a spike of fear through Kate. He was about to reveal something she needed to know, but wasn't certain she was prepared to handle.

"Hi, Eric," Colleen said.

"Can you hear me?"

"We both can," Kate replied, an edge of terror outlining her response.

As Kate listened to Eric confess to his double life, she vacillated between relief and despair. Maybe she was better off not knowing the entire truth. Still, she wondered what kind of man was she really married to? Could she ever trust him again?

In between revelations about tracking down drug and weapons smugglers, bombings and other covert actions, Eric directed a few words to comfort Kate.

"Please try to understand," he said. "Being orphaned the way I was, I had to search for answers. Even though I was a kid when they died, I felt responsible in some ways for what happened to my parents. I was wrong to not realize that my actions caused you to question my love. I apologize for my insensitive stupidity."

Kate sent a glance to Colleen as though requesting her opinion, only to receive a vague shoulder shrug in return.

"It's clear that I've spent too many years chasing the wrong man," Eric continued. "Based on everything I've learned during the past twenty-four hours, I wonder if Anmar X ever existed."

"I don't know what to think," Kate said. "This is too much for me to absorb in one sitting. I mean, are we married? Who are you? Eric or Erol? Adele and Ben aren't really Bennie's grandparents?"

"Of course they are. Legally, I'm their son. And legally, Eric Wiley is your husband." He remained quiet for a moment before adding, "We're married, Kate, and I hope you don't want that to change."

A wave of emotion clouded Kate's eyes, but there wasn't time to get emotional. Eric was in trouble and needed her help. She sat straighter, as though a steel spike fortified her spine. "We'll talk about this when you come home. What does all this mean now? What do you need us to do?"

"Can you go into the hidden room and tell me what you see?"

"What are you looking for?" Colleen asked.

"That's just it. I'm not sure. Simon, my real dad, took me in there a few weeks before his death. I haven't gone in since. In fact, when Adele gave me Mom and Dad's strongbox, I purposely set it on the shelf inside the closet, not wanting to enter that secret space again."

"Simon and Leah were the original owners of this house?" Kate asked as she and Colleen made their way down the hall to the guest room.

"Yes. That's the house I grew up in," Eric replied.

Kate sighed. "That explains a lot."

***

Eric waited as Kate and Colleen walked to the other side of the house. He held little hope that the room would provide any major revelations, still he couldn't move on without fully flushing out every clue.

The shuffling of feet, followed by the sound of doors opening and closing, seeped through the telephone line.

"We're inside," Kate said. "Where should we start?"

"I have no idea," Eric said. "I'm trying to view everything with fresh eyes. If you'll tell me what you see, maybe I can figure out what to do next."

Eric reached for a hotel notepad and pulled his pen from his shirt pocket, ready to record Kate's observations. He listened intently to her words, increasingly aware she described a space he had long forgotten.

"Here's something odd," Colleen interjected. "There's a biometric fingerprint recognition safe."

A flicker of familiarity lit inside Eric. He recalled the safe and the day his father placed his hand on the screen after securing several documents inside. "Does the safe have a manufacturer's name?" he asked scribbling as he listened. "Damn."

"What?" Kate asked, panic rising in her word.

"Pen ran out of ink," he complained. "Let me see if I can find another one around here."

"Shake it or tap it against the desk," Kate suggested. "Sometimes there's dry ink clogging the tip."

Eric banged the fountain pen against the desk, hoping Kate's trick would get the ink flowing. Instead, the barrel cracked, and the insides spilled out. A string of cursing followed.

"Run out of paper now?" Kate joked.

"No. No. Everything is okay." Eric left the pen on the desk and headed to the bathroom and closed the door.

"Katie, honey…" He lowered his voice to where it was barely above a whisper.

"Yes," Kate said, "I can hardly hear you now. We must have a bad connection. Can you speak up?"

"Listen carefully," Eric continued, not increasing the volume of his voice. "I want you to get Bennie and leave the house right now. Go somewhere safe and call me at this number from a landline, not your cell phone. Understand?"

"Eric. What's happened? What's wrong?" Kate asked, a renewed anxiety infusing her reply.

Eric read the numbers from the burner phone and waited for Kate to repeat them.

"Eric, you're scaring me. What's happened? Are we in danger?"

"This is just a precaution. Do what I ask and call me as soon as you're away from the house. I have to go now."

"Eric!" Kate's voice cracked with worry.

"Everything is going to be fine. Leave the house. Don't say anything to anyone. Promise me."

"Yes, but—"

"I'll explain soon. Just leave now. And remember, I love you."

Eric disconnected and returned to the hotel bedroom, pretending to still be talking to Kate. "Okay, sweetheart. Call me back after you're done. I'm going to catch some sleep. Love you, too."

Eric's pulse pounded in his ear and his hands shook as he set the phone down and stared at the insides of the gift Ben had made such a big deal out of presenting him with. The pen that held a microscopic tracking device and audio recorder. No wonder Eric's team could never catch the bad guys. Ben knew his every move, every word and practically every thought.

Until now.

Eric couldn't simply disconnect the fiber-thin wire, and sever Ben's means of eavesdropping. He had to continue the ruse. At least for the time being. He placed the pen on the desk, shoved his belongings into his bag, and headed back to the compound. He had to get home in less than an hour. That didn't leave much time to convince Ralph into letting him take a military flight.

That would be a tough sell, but that wasn't the sequence of events tormenting Eric. As he ran through the darkened night toward the compound, he struggled with the real possibility that he'd unscrambled the mystery too late.

If he didn't act quickly, he may lose this chance to capture his adoptive father and finally bring his parents' killer to justice.

Chapter Thirty-One

Kate sat immobile, processing the urgency of Eric's words.

Get Bennie and leave the house right now.

The man never panicked, no matter the danger. She had witnessed his levelheaded behavior firsthand the day he rescued her from an ex-boyfriend holding her at knifepoint. She should have realized then that Eric wasn't the ordinary guy he pretended to be.

"We need to get out of here," Kate mumbled. Her heart pounded as she and Colleen raced to the bedroom.

"You grab Bennie, and I'll grab his diaper bag," Colleen said, a calm in her voice that Kate appreciated.

"Okay, good. The bag is by the bed." She lifted a sleeping Bennie from his bassinet. Startled, he began wailing. "It's okay, baby," Kate soothed as she hustled them toward the living room and placed Bennie inside his carrier-car seat. Still crying, the infant squirmed as she clicked the harness in place.

"What else do we need?" Colleen asked.

"That's it. If we're missing something, we'll buy it." Kate searched the dish in the entry table where she usually dropped her keys. "Crap. Can you stay with the baby for a second? Must have left my car keys in the bedroom."

"Happy to." Colleen dropped the diaper bag on to the floor and sat next to Bennie who, exhausted from his crying, had dozed off.

Adrenaline pumping through her veins, Kate rushed into her bedroom, mentally scolding herself for considering that Eric was a criminal. His career, serving his country, was an honorable one. His quest to capture his parents' killers rose to a higher level than any goal she had ever set in her life.

Unable to find her keys, she turned when she heard a squeal and a thump echoed down the hall.

"Everything okay?" she hollered, shaking the bed covers and then shuffling the items on the nightstand around in search of the keys. When Colleen didn't respond, Kate hurried toward the bedroom door. "Colleen? Is everything all…"

"Hi, Kate. Looking for these?" Ben stood in the hallway, dangling her keychain between his thumb and forefinger.

"D—Dad? What are you doing here?" A nervous worry spread through her veins and she immediately ached to be in the same room as her child. "I need to get Bennie."

Adele stepped from behind her husband, holding the baby. "Don't worry. I have him."

"Mom, hi. I didn't expect you two until later."

Ben moved closer. "You've been digging around the house, sticking your nose into places you shouldn't."

"I don't kn-know what you're ta-talking about," Kate stammered, trying to push past him and out of the room.

"Of course you do, honey," Adele answered, swaying from side to side, keeping a sleepy Benjamin content.

Kate extended her arms. "Give me my baby and my keys. I was just on my way out."

"You're not going anywhere." Ben pushed Kate down the hall.

"Give me Bennie!" she insisted, as he latched onto her upper arm and forcibly escorted her away from Adele and to the living room. "What are you doing? Why—"

Kate gasped.

Her hands flew to her mouth.

Colleen, eyes wide, panic tinging her features, stared straight ahead, her wrists and ankles bound to a dining room chair that was shoved against the wall. Her friend grumbled around the red gag rammed into her mouth.

Kate whirled around. "What the hell is going on?" she yelled at Ben, who towered over her.

"Sit down and be quiet!" he ordered, but Kate remained standing.

"What are you…" She gulped back the question. Terror invaded her, like a spilled glass of curdled milk, spreading bitterness and dread across her insides.

"Don't worry. No one's going to get hurt. As soon as I talk to Eric, we'll settle everything and go back to life as we know it." Ben grinned, but his smile wasn't comforting. His implied threat struck a menacing chord that vibrated through Kate's spine. She, Bennie and Colleen were bargaining chips in whatever scheme he wanted Eric to comply with.

"You and Nancy Drew here," Ben continued, pointing to Colleen, "got yourselves involved in something you shouldn't have. But it's okay. We can still fix things. As long as my son plays along."

"Plays along with what?" Kate screeched. "Give me Bennie and get out of my house."

"Weren't you listening?" Ben asked.

"No one will get hurt." Adele stepped next to her husband. "There's been enough pain and misery. Kate, dear, just be patient. All of this will be straightened out and then we can continue as a family."

Kate stared at the woman she once knew and loved as her mother-in-law. *Are you crazy?* she wanted to shout. Instead, she reached for Bennie, squirming in Adele's arms. "He's getting hungry. I need to feed him."

Adele pulled back and turned toward the kitchen. "Don't worry. I'll fix a bottle. You do as Ben says." With those words she was gone, taking Benjamin and any sliver of hope Kate held of escape with her.

"Give me my son!" Kate implored, swinging her fists at Ben's chest. "And untie Colleen. This is sheer lunacy."

"Perhaps, but until I get a handle on this situation, you will sit quietly and wait." Ben seized Kate's wrist with more force than necessary and dragged her to the couch. "Sit. Otherwise, I'll secure you in the same fashion as your police friend."

The wild look in his eyes cemented any doubt in Kate's mind that her father-in-law meant every hostile word, every unspoken threat.

She sat, biding her time. Eric would be expecting her call. What would he do if she didn't phone? What could he do? He was across the border in another country.

Too far away to help.

***

Eric's boots crunched against the gravel as he jogged to the trailer. Ralph had to still be there. Though the flight from El Paso to Phoenix took about an hour, no flights were scheduled until six o'clock that evening.

And even if there was an earlier flight, Eric would still need to make the thirty-minute drive from Juarez to El Paso International before he could board a plane. He couldn't wait that long to get home. He needed military transportation. Eric knew what Ben was capable of doing.

A wave of fear washed over him at the thought of anything happening to his wife and baby. He couldn't lose his family. Not again. He had to be certain she was secure before he could confront Ben and demand the truth.

Eric yanked open the trailer door and froze.

"What the—"

"No time for rhetorical questions," a voice echoed behind him.

Eric spun on his heels to face Ralph. "Where is everything? The computers? The surveillance? The com linkup?" All equipment and furniture had been stripped from the trailer as though no one had ever used the space.

"This was never a field command post. I wanted you to think it was."

"You were playing me?" Eric's heart slammed against his chest. He took a step back, unsure of who to trust now. "You can take all of this and shove it up your ass."

"Calm down. We had to work behind your back but listen. We've been investigating Ben for a while. We couldn't take a chance that he'd get to you. That's why you were on the outside."

Eric paced back and forth, stopping occasionally to assess Ralph's nonverbals. Was he telling the truth? A nervous tension shot through Eric's brain, as though a carnival strongman swung a sledgehammer to ring the bell. "How long have you been surveilling him? I'm mean, when did your little operation begin? When I joined the team?" Eric asked, curious as to how he was set up by Ben and now by Ralph.

"Not quite that far back." Ralph put his hand on Eric's shoulder.

"Doesn't matter. I don't have the time right now to care. I need your help," Eric pleaded.

"I know," Ralph answered. "Ben wasn't the only one monitoring your calls. I heard everything you said to Kate. There's an aircraft ready for us to board," Ralph said, directing Eric out the door.

"He used me," Eric said, as they trotted toward the airstrip. "He killed my parents and he used me to keep his cover-up intact. Damn him. Give me the whole story. I have to know."

"I'll tell you what I can when we get to the plane."

A short while later, Eric sat next to Ralph in the requisitioned twelve-seat private plane. Half of the seats were filled with undercover agents Eric had never met before.

"Buckle up. We'll be on the ground in about fifty minutes," the pilot said, and headed to the cockpit.

Ralph leaned back. "Hopefully we can fly in under Ben's radar; otherwise, things may get complicated."

"He's a very smart guy," Eric said. "He knows how to manipulate people. Don't fool yourself into thinking we're going to catch him off guard. We won't."

"He is really good at what he does, but he's not invincible," Ralph retorted.

"When did the agency first suspect Ben?" Eric asked, surprised that the thought hadn't ever crossed his mind until a few hours ago.

"As best we can figure, Ben's been running a weapons-smuggling operation since before you were born. Over the years, the agency had set him up in a dozen or so businesses that served as fronts for CIA stings. He used selling textiles as a believable cover to travel from the US into Mexico and the Middle East. The CIA willingly complied with his story because it got us into places we wouldn't normally have covert access to."

Eric listened as Ralph recapped how Ben and Adele built their enterprises. All the wealth and success surrounding him, from his teen years through college and now, had been amassed on the cold bodies of his parents and others.

The truth cascaded down on him like an avalanche. Ben had invented Anmar X to throw suspicion away from himself. There were lots of missing pieces, but if any part of Eric's conjecture was true, Kate could be in danger. Her innocently digging around the hidden room threatened her safety.

"Ben wasn't supposed to get wealthy off the fake businesses," Ralph continued, "but somehow he did. He turned those deals into illicit gun arrangements with Mexico, Lebanon, Libya. Pretty much any government with ready cash."

"And that's what cost my parents their lives?"

"Afraid so. Don't get me wrong, during his tenure as an agent, Ben Wiley made some decent busts, got a lot of bad guys off the streets, and all the while, he lined his pockets selling guns to rebel governments."

"Why did he kill my parents?"

"That's a bit trickier." Ralph paused. "From what we can piece together, while Simon and Ben were partners, Simon discovered Ben's illegal undertakings. At the time, there were sources claiming Simon was about to turn him in when he was murdered. We could never prove that."

"And my mother. She didn't work for the agency."

"Must have figured Simon told her what was going on. He couldn't run the risk of her talking. You, on the other hand, were too young to be a threat, but he adopted you just in case. That way, he had total control."

"Well, his shitty plan worked." Eric rubbed his hands down his face. He should be exhausted, but adrenaline pumped through his veins, keeping him jumpy and on edge. "Ben guided every decision I made. Where I went to college, what jobs I should take when I joined the agency. Hell, he even pushed my marrying Kate. He thought she could keep me home."

"Pretty brilliant, when you think about it. He couldn't get you to stop the investigation, so he watched you. Eric, you were feeding him intelligence without knowing it."

"All this time, I didn't have a clue. Not until Trish mentioned that no one other than Ben had actually seen Anmar X. That's when I started questioning the past twenty years of my life."

"We've been asking those questions, too. Now, thanks to your honesty and diligence, we have proof."

Eric chortled. *Honesty and diligence.* Two characteristics he inherited from his real parents. Certainly not Ben and Adele. They were anything but honest, orchestrating lies and falsehoods as the foundation of his life.

"The man built a smokescreen and kept us all too busy to wonder why no one had ever seen the guy." Eric shook his head, incredulous at the reality striking him. He sought the facts and now, face-to-face with the truth, its repercussions unsettled him.

Ralph offered Eric a soda can, popped the top on his own and took a swig. "Ben is smooth. In his prime, he was one of the best operatives the agency ever employed."

"He really tricked me with the pen. So simple, I didn't see it coming."

"Don't feel bad. We've had a slate of professionals on this for years. He deceived all of us. Guess we didn't want to believe that one of our own went bad. He's not the first and he sure as hell won't be the last."

Eric knew there had been a few cases of agents going bad and fewer cases proven. The proof was hard to come by in an organization of spies skilled at making unpleasant things disappear.

"We've been tracking his movements for years, but he always stayed a step ahead, no matter what maneuver we made. In fact, for a while, I thought you were his mole."

Eric winced at this newest betrayal dropped on his chest like a hot iron, searing his pride and his soul. "For five years, I've busted my balls on this task force and the entire time, my fellow agents thought I was a traitor."

"For what it's worth, Trish never bought my idea. Even from her hospital bed, she was still throwing out theories on why we never collected any actionable intel on Anmar X."

"When will she be released to fly home?"

"Tomorrow," Ralph said.

"But the rest of you thought I was working with Ben?"

"You know the mantra: Don't assume anything," Ralph reminded.

"That's the biggest bunch of BS I've ever—"

"Might be, but we had to know for sure. There was only one way to find out. That's why we tracked you. When we heard Kate mention the secret room, we realized you were sitting on the evidence we needed. And we better get to it before Ben has a chance to destroy it."

"So, the only reason Ben and Adele adopted me was to find this evidence?"

"It would seem so." Ralph finished his drink, crushed the can and tossed it into a nearby container. "No flight attendant coming by to collect our trash."

Eric leaned back, stunned that his life had been one lie after another. The love he once felt for Ben and Adele washed away, like a flash flood forcing itself down the river. One thing hadn't changed, though; Eric's commitment to making his parents' killers pay. He was closer than ever to achieving that goal.

He unfolded a sheet of paper and reached for a pen. "So, what's our plan."

Ralph nodded and motioned for the others to join them.

Chapter Thirty-Two

Eric looked out the airplane window to see a blanket of twinkling lights. The city of Phoenix sprawled below. Satisfied that their strategy to capture Ben would work, he reached for his burner phone and eyed the screen. Still no contact from Kate.

Maybe it's taking her longer to find a hotel.

Eric wanted to believe she, Bennie and Colleen were simply delayed in reaching their destination. That nothing bad had happened to them. As the minutes dragged, a fierce panic spreading through his veins conflicted with those hopes.

"Why haven't we landed yet?" he asked, itching to get this attack underway. Their plan to surprise Ben and Adele at their home freshly cemented in his mind, Eric mulled over the layout of Ben's house. The team's best chance was to invade from the far side, over the neighbor's fence. Still, Eric knew Ben would be ready for them.

"We should have touched down by now," Ralph agreed, unfastening his seat belt. He lumbered toward the cockpit. After a brief exchange with the pilot, he returned.

"Another five. There was a priority hold on the airspace but it's clearing soon." Ralph resumed his place next to Eric.

"Priority hold, my ass," Eric said, every nerve pulsing with fear at the realization that his family was in danger. His adoptive father had the upper hand. "Ben knows we're coming. He has Kate and the baby. He's telling us to get prepared for his style of negotiation."

"Nothing to negotiate," Ralph said. "We got him dead-bang. This case is open and shut."

Legally, that was true, but as Ralph had cautioned earlier, "don't assume anything." Eric suspected Ben wouldn't surrender without a fight. Ben never did anything the easy way.

Eric remembered how the man he then called Uncle Ben had treated him after Simon and Leah's deaths, vowing to take care of everything.

Even in his shocked state, Eric recalled the madman-like fervor Ben used while combing through his parents' personal possessions before moving Eric to live with him and Adele. He had been looking for something. His consoling words and assurances had erased the urgency of Simon's earlier directive.

The shock of his parents' deaths and the kindness of Adele and Ben combined to dim Eric's memory of the safe, and the hidden room. The fact was, he wanted to forget but now he realized that secret chamber, and what it contained, held the root of all his troubles. Soon it would be a panacea of truth.

***

Ben handed Kate her cell phone. "Call your husband and tell him to come home now. That you're worried about him."

"What?" Kate asked, fighting a new wave of nausea sweeping through her. The familiar gag-reflex crawling up her throat had surfaced earlier, when Eric told her of the brutal way he had lost his family. Now facing a man who would stop at nothing to get what he wanted, the volatile bile returned.

"Are you hard of hearing? Tell Eric you need him. I don't care what reason you give. And you better be convincing, or you and your yoga pal will regret your mistake."

Kate forced herself to swallow. "I have no way to reach him."

Ben stood, towering over her. "Things were going along so nicely and now you have to start lying to me. Kate, darling, I've heard everything you two said to each other. I've been monitoring Eric since I arranged for him to join the agency."

A glimmer of understanding ignited the recesses of Kate's mind and sent her thoughts tumbling. If Eric's life was a masquerade, then Adele and Ben's must be, too. She folded her hands in her lap, hoping to repress their shaking. She had to think clearly, but with her son in Adele's control, panic leached into every nerve.

"Why are you doing this? Why do you want to hurt us?" she screamed, swiping at her tears, but they fell faster. Were Eric's suspicions that he'd been chasing after the wrong man coming to fruition?

Could Ben and Adele have murdered his parents?

No. No. That can't be right. But no other explanation for Ben's aggressive behavior seemed plausible. The retired CIA agent standing before her was somehow involved in assassinating Eric's parents.

An icy shudder roiled down her spine as she glanced at her friend, afraid of what Ben had in mind for them. She rubbed her sweaty palms down her thighs, feverishly thinking of what she could do. She had to figure out a way to get her, Colleen and Bennie out of there.

"Still don't get it, do you?" Ben roared, obviously frustrated at Kate's attempts to delay.

"Stop yelling at her," Adele said returning from the kitchen, Benjamin held in one arm and a bottle in the other. She glanced at the baby and then to Kate. "She'll do what you want."

Kate swallowed hard at Adele's veiled coercion and attempted to control the unstoppable shaking that permeated her body. Bennie's grandmother was using him as leverage. Her precious child had been co-opted as the means to an end. But what were Ben and Adele after?

"I know he gave you the number to his burner phone. Dial. Now!" Ben barked out the command, ignoring Adele.

"Then you must know that the number is on a piece of paper in my purse," Kate said, mustering more confidence than she possessed. Maybe she could stall for time, but why? No cavalry would be riding to their rescue. Eric was hours away and even if he were here, her worry for his safety would be greater than risking Ben's wrath.

"Get your purse and sit back down," Ben snapped.

With shaky hands, Kate did as he instructed, keeping her eyes on her child the entire time. "Adele, please let me hold him," she pleaded, a pain deeper than any she had known mushroomed inside.

"As soon as Ben gets what he wants, I'll give you what you want." Adele's voice held no compassion, no inflection, as though it was programmed.

Kate didn't believe her assurances. She sliced her gaze to Colleen. *What can we do? How can we get out of here?*

Colleen, shoulders sunken in defeat, shrugged. This wasn't the first time her friend had witnessed heartless evil. Kate searched the room for a way out, mentally apologizing for inviting Colleen into this unknown misery. *I'm sorry.*

"What do you want?" Kate finally asked, afraid of the answer.

"Just what's coming to me. Eric—or should I say, Erol—knows. Dial the damn phone."

Kate listened as the number connected.

"Oh, thank God," Eric answered on the first ring.

"Eric. Your dad is scaring me. He's tied Colleen up and—"

"Erol. It's Ben."

***

Eric froze. Hearing Ben's voice coming through Kate's cell sent a chilling surge through his heart. With his worst fears unfolding, he knew he had failed. Miserably. And now Kate and Bennie would pay the price if he didn't get to them soon.

He gripped the phone tighter, cutting off circulation to his fingers. "Where is Kate? Wh-what have you done to my wife?" he asked, trying to remain calm but unable to keep the tremble from his voice.

"Calm down, son. Kate, little Bennie, and Colleen are with me and Mom. Everyone is just fine. Are you on your way home?"

"You know I am," Eric said, a vile disgust rising in his throat. "If you hurt my wife or son, I swear—"

"Don't swear. Cussing was never your strong suit. Just listen. I want Simon's papers. And after listening to you and Kate chat earlier, we all know where they are. Give me everything in your safe and Adele and I will be on our way."

"What are you talking about?" Eric said.

"Don't go playing dumb with me, boy!"

"We can talk about anything you want, once you let Kate, Colleen, and the baby go. You can take me as your prisoner."

"I don't want any damn prisoners! I want my bank account numbers and any evidence Simon gathered to turn me in."

"What bank account numbers?" Eric asked, confused, frantically searching his mind to remember if he had ever seen any bank statements or paperwork. "Please, let me talk to Kate."

"You should be landing about now. I've lifted the airspace restriction. A fifteen-minute ride from the airport to your house. Come alone. And tell that pencil-pushing Peddis to back the hell off. That is, unless he wants someone to get hurt."

"Ben, you can't get away."

"Don't worry about what I can and can't do. Just get your ass home to your family." Ben disconnected.

Eric immediately redialed, but the call rang unanswered.

"What's up?" Ralph asked.

"He has my wife!" Eric yelled, yanking on his seatbelt. He had to get out of there. He had to get off of that plane and get to his family.

"Whoa. Wait. Calm down," Ralph consoled, placing a firm hand on Eric's arm to keep him in place. "Tell me what's going on."

Eric sucked in a deep inhale and glanced out the small window of the plane as he released the breath slowly. He had to keep it together, if not for himself, for Kate and Bennie. If he lost it now, he'd be no good to them.

He recounted his conversation with Ben and shared his demands with Ralph. As he talked with the team leader, a memory flooded to the forefront of his mind. He thought about the day his birth father, Simon, asked him to align his fingers onto four sensor pads on the biometric safe's front panel. Eric had asked if they were the only family in the neighborhood to have a hidden room. Simon never answered that question, detouring his son's curiosity with a lecture about whorls, loops and arches.

"Your fingerprints don't change as you get older," Simon had said. "They increase in size, but your unique pattern remains the same. Isn't that interesting."

After verifying that the safe opened only with Eric's fingerprint pattern, Simon double-checked the several manila envelopes he had placed inside and clicked the door shut. "Don't be frightened," he had said, locking the chamber. "If anything happens to me, I want you to take those envelopes to the authorities."

Understanding that his fingerprints would solve the mystery and give Ben what he sought for two decades, Eric weighed his options. If Eric had to give into Ben's coercion, he had to do it alone. He wouldn't endanger Kate and his infant son. His overriding goal–bringing Anmar X to justice– dissipated like smoke up a chimney.

Eric could only guess how many other lives had been lost and how much blood money had been traded for illicit guns.

He couldn't allow his family, or anyone else's to be added to the tally.

Chapter Thirty-Three

Eric secured an audio tracker inside his waistband and slipped his jacket on. Twenty minutes had passed while the team agreed to a revised plan. He was already five minutes late, making the chances of getting the drop on Ben improbable. Still, he directed the driver of the unmarked car that had been waiting for them at the airport to let him out a half a block away from his home.

Reluctantly, Ralph and the rest of the agents would be stationed nearby, awaiting Eric's signal for them to close in.

Eric checked the bullets in his gun before returning it to its holster. He buttoned his jacket and crept toward the house. Hoping to get a glimpse of Kate through their living room picture window without being detected, he pressed his back flat against a neighbor's siding. He could make out silhouettes of movement, but someone—he guessed Ben—had closed the shades, making it impossible to tell where Kate, or anyone, sat.

Best to enter through the back.

Eric shifted his weight and turned toward the gate, but halted when the front door swung open.

"Put your hands up!" Ben's voice blared across the street. Eric spied a small pistol in his hand.

He complied with the order, his arms raised above his head, and slowly ambled toward the home he had grown up in.

Ben, wild-eyed as though sleep had evaded him for days, filled the doorway. The gun pointed at Eric sent an eerie dread pulsating through him. Ben was on the edge. It wouldn't take much to push him over.

Eric couldn't let that happen.

"Please. I'll give you anything you want, just let Kate leave with Bennie. I promise. I won't try anything."

"No one is going anywhere yet. And what you do next will decide everyone's fate," Ben snarled. "Get your ass in here." Once Eric stepped inside the entry, Ben glanced left, then right down the street, the entire time his gun trained on Eric.

"I'm alone," Eric said. "Just the way you wanted."

"Good." Ben shoved him. "Get moving."

Eric took measured strides into the living room. Once the site of joyful Christmas mornings and birthday parties, now replaced with a hostage scene.

He made a move to go to Kate, but he was stopped.

"Stay where you are," Ben commanded.

"Are you okay?" Eric asked Kate, his heart pounding so loud in his ears, he thought everyone could hear. His gaze took in every inch of his wife. She looked unharmed, but he wouldn't put anything past Ben.

She nodded, her eyes glassy with tears.

Eric assessed the rest of the area, alarmed to see Colleen tied to a chair by the far wall, wedged against a beverage cart. Finally, his gaze landed on Adele, the woman he called Mom. She held his son, her arms clasped solidly around his little body as though secured with bolts.

His attention went back to Kate. "Are you sure you're okay?"

"Enough already!" Ben growled. "There will be time for a loving reunion as soon as old Erol here finishes his end of the bargain."

"What the f—" Eric started to say. "I'm not here to negotiate with you. I'm here to apprehend you."

Ben laughed before patting Eric down. "In case you haven't noticed, I have the gun. And now I have yours, too," he said, lifting Eric's revolver from his holster. "I always wondered why you never got ahead in your career, but now I see it clearly. You miss important, obvious clues." Ben shoved him again. "Let's take a walk to this secret room I've overheard so much about."

"My father built it as a safeguard against you," Eric accused.

"How can you treat us like this?" Kate shrieked. "Who are you, really?"

Eric turned toward Kate, her screams sending a helplessness vibrating through his senses. He had failed to protect her. And Bennie.

"Love to catch you up on the backstory, but we don't have time," Adele snapped. "I want you to know that after what happened, Ben and I took good care of Erol."

"And we would have continued doing so if he could have left well enough alone. But he didn't and here we are," Ben interrupted. "So much for old home week. Adele, put Bennie in his crib and keep an eye on them while Eric gets me those papers. My guess is, Peddis is cooking up some half-baked rescue, so we don't have a lot of time. Lead the way, son."

***

Adele, cradling a crying Bennie in her left arm, shifted enough for Kate to see the gun resting alongside her right thigh. In spite of Ben's instructions, she hadn't put the baby in the crib.

Kate's heart constricted as though gripped inside a vise. Every passing second tightened her jaws, accelerating her pulse and the throbbing behind her eyes.

"He wants to sleep, and he can't the way you're holding him. Let me put him down," Kate beseeched.

A half-cocked grin spread across Adele's face. "From the whiffs I'm getting, Bennie's not crying to go to sleep. He soiled his pants."

"I'll change him and put him in his bed. He's not a part of this, Adele. Please…please don't hurt my baby."

Adele sighed. "We never meant to hurt you and I'd never harm this little boy. Just be patient. Once Ben gets what we came for, we'll be on our way."

Kate knew if Eric saw a viable chance to rescue them, he would. He needed an opening, a diversion, a way to distract Ben for even a couple of seconds. She weighed her options. If she made a run for Adele, she and Colleen might be shot. In the scuffle, Bennie could be hurt or worse.

She had to do something, but what?

She glanced at Colleen, who seemed to be swaying from side-to-side. If she could create enough momentum to topple over the wine glasses and bottles on the bar cart, perhaps Kate could disarm Adele in the confusion when everything crashed to the floor.

Kate stood, her protective mother's instinct taking over. "Give me my baby, Adele."

"Can't do it. Sit down," Adele bit the words. "This will be over soon."

She took a step closer and Adele reached for the gun. "I said sit down!"

Kate stopped, positioning her body to obscure Adele's view of Colleen. Harnessed, Colleen could provide little aid to overtake the older woman, but if Kate understood Colleen's nonverbals, she'd give Kate the split second she needed to wrestle the gun away from Adele and reclaim her son.

Kate heard the squeak of Colleen's chair.

"Were you in this from the start?" Kate asked. "Why would you agree to be a part of this?" she added quickly, hoping to draw Adele into a conversation.

"All the reasons don't matter anymore," she said. "It's enough for you to know that we never meant for things to go this far. Leah and I were best friends. Closer than sisters."

Until you killed her.

"Then how could you go along with what happened?" Kate asked, incredulous at Adele's version of the facts.

"Some of this was her fault," Adele said.

Preoccupied with a crying baby and sharing her personal story, Adele didn't pay attention to Colleen rocking back and forth. "They introduced me to Ben. Simon didn't know his partner as well as he thought. By the time we met, he was already deep into the weapons trade, using his position at the CIA as leverage for the next deal. The rest came easy."

Without turning, Kate sensed Colleen's efforts to topple the chair intensified. She spoke louder. "Easy? What's easy about betraying your best friend?"

Rocking the wailing baby, Adele waited to respond, as though deciding how to frame her story in the best possible light. "I fell in love with Ben and the lifestyle he provided. I thought Simon and Leah were into the same thing. But they weren't. If only Simon would have looked the other way." She frowned. "Some people don't know how to ignore a few shortcomings."

"How could you let this happen? You're not a ruthless killer."

Adele snickered. "You don't know me very well." She lifted the gun. "Sit down!" she yelled, her voice reaching a shrieking timbre.

Kate pressed on. "How could you let him kill your friends and make Eric an orphan? How did you face Eric all these years knowing the truth?"

She waited for Adele to respond. Inching closer, Kate yelled, "How can you sleep at night?"

***

"Well I'll be a damn fool," Ben said, his cavalier attitude returning. "That son of a gun wedged a panic room between the bedroom and the garage. Brilliant. Adele and I tore this house apart, and the only thing we found was a metal box with some of their old photos and passports. The ones I gave you. Guess I'm not the gifted detective I thought I was. Oh well. I'll get over that. Open the safe."

"I can't let you get away with this."

Ben stepped closer, his gun steady on Eric. "You have no choice. Open the damn safe."

Eric held his ground. "What you want isn't in there. I moved it years ago."

"Nice bluff. Did you even remember this room existed?"

Eric remained silent.

"Yeah, I didn't think so." Ben sneered. "Either way, open it up and let me see what's inside."

With Ben's gun directed at his head, Eric placed his fingers on the sensor pads and waited for the safe to open. Instead of hearing a series of locks releasing, a loud thud followed the sound of glass shattering rang out from the living room.

"What the hell was that?" Ben yelled. "Keep your hands where I can see them. You better hope your wife didn't do anything stupid."

With Ben's revolver pressed against his back, Eric staggered toward the living room, afraid of what he would find.

Relief washed over him to see Kate holding baby Benjamin in one arm and brandishing Adele's weapon with her other hand. Adele, crumpled on the ground, sat motionlessly.

"What the hell happened?" Ben snapped. "I leave for a minute and—"

"They distracted me," Adele said.

Eric looked to where Colleen lay sideways on the floor. Still secured to the chair, she appeared unharmed. Shards from broken bottles decorated the floor around her like an explosion of glass confetti.

"Put your gun down, Ben or I'll shoot your wife," Kate said, no mercy or compassion to her command.

Ben laughed. "Our lovely architect knows how to fire a gun? This I gotta see."

Under Kate's watchful eye from the far side of the room, Adele nudged toward Ben. "Don't move," Kate yelled. "I swear to God I will shoot you."

Ben released another ruthless laugh. "But not before I kill Eric...and the ba—"

"Hell, no!" Eric yelled. With his back still to Ben, he pummeled the heel of his shoe into the man's kneecap. Ignoring his howl of pain, Eric spun, sweeping the other leg, sending Ben and his gun crashing to the floor.

Kate, still holding Adele at bay, kicked the revolver out of Ben's reach.

Eric grabbed the gun in Kate's hand and aimed it at Ben. "You're done! Your days of hurting others are over!"

He motioned to Adele to join her husband, face down on the floor, before he spoke the words he'd waited so many years to utter.

"Suspects are contained. I repeat. The suspects are contained." A well of relief flooded through Eric. "Ralph, I got him. I finally got the son of a bitch."

Epilogue

Three months later

Kate straightened the satin bow tie under her son's chin and secured the white booties on to his feet. "How did you find such a perfect outfit?" she asked Julie, taking in the cherubic vision of her son on his baptismal day.

"Fairy godmothers are magical; don't you know that?" Julie answered.

"Of course she does," Monica added, squeezing in between the two of them. "She's a godmother, too. But Kate is more than simply magical, she's charmed."

"If by charmed you mean lucky, I have to agree." Kate lifted the four-month-old from the changing table, his eyes heavy with sleep and handed him to Julie. "Erol and I are so blessed that you and Trevor will be his godparents."

"We're honored." Julie planted a kiss on the baby's cheek.

"Let's get little Bennie...I mean, Simon Erol to the church," Monica said. "Sorry. I got used to calling him Bennie."

"No need to apologize. I slip sometimes, too. But he is truly Simon. What a hassle changing his name on his birth certificate, but we agreed that our son would be the namesake of a real hero. Simon Senior died protecting his son and our country."

Erol stepped into the small space. "So true."

"Looks like we're ready to go." Julie carried the baby from the room. Monica followed, sending a broad smile to Kate as she exited.

Erol walked toward his wife and placed his arms around her. She leaned into his embrace and they remained entwined for several minutes.

Awaiting Ben's and Adele's trials had put a strain on their lives. Kate and Erol had already accepted the fact that most of their assets would be seized by the US government, including the chain of discount stores. The only property that remained legally theirs was this home, complete with a panic room. Simon and Leah had purchased the house before their death and left it to Erol in their recently discovered will.

She and Erol had spent many nights discussing his parents' bravery and the multitude of deceptions by the Wileys. Kate had encouraged him to continue his career with the CIA, but Erol wasn't so sure. His motivation for criminal justice no longer existed.

As for her job, Kate had accepted Harry's offer to work from home part-time for the next six months while they followed Ben and Adele's case and awaited the outcome. She and Eric, satisfied that their testimony for the feds would result in convictions, were in no rush to go back to their all-consuming professions.

For now, they would delight in their rekindled romance and explore their new role as parents. The future held plenty of time to decide on career choices.

"Leah's a great name, too," Erol said, finally breaking the silence. "How does Leah Katherine sound?"

"Wonderful and way too soon," Kate joked. "Not ready to start planning a little sister."

"But not too soon to practice," he answered, pulling Kate deeper into his arms.

She melted into his embrace, soaking in the peacefulness enveloping her. After weeks of anxiety, doubt and turmoil, she welcomed the tranquil security only her husband could bestow.

"Practice does make perfect," she said, tilting her head back awaiting his kiss. Their lips touched with renewed trust, hope and love.

In his own way, Erol had kept every promise.

*

If you enjoyed this story by
Claire Yezbak Fadden, consider leaving a review on any online book site, review site, or social media outlet.

Excerpt from

A Corner of Her Heart
(Monica & Brad's story)

Copyright © 2016 Claire Yezbak Fadden

Monica Morgan spied her husband, Brad, chatting with his boss, Greg Baylor, BayRock Tech's owner and CEO. In moments, Greg would announce Brad's promotion to president. Catching Brad's eye, Monica winked. He smiled and lifted his glass as she sipped from her champagne flute, soaking in the festive atmosphere.

Am I really here in this beautiful place? An oversized chandelier glistened in the soft light of the Phoenix Grand Ballroom, and a harpist played gently in the background while she made small talk with Greg's wife, Margaret.

Monica could hardly believe this day had finally come. The endless weeks Brad spent out of the state, away from her and their sons finally paid off. This was their night to celebrate.

"Have you met?" Margaret said to a young woman hurrying past their table, interrupting Monica's blissful thoughts. "Monica, this is Samantha Stewart. She works in our New Mexico location."

Monica placed her glass on the table. "Nice to meet you." It was as if the room instantly turned quiet when she accepted the perfectly manicured hand extended in greeting. She swallowed hard, struck by how the young woman's hazel eyes contrasted against her curly, chestnut-colored hair. This woman had never changed a dirty diaper or scooped nacho cheese sauce at a little league snack bar. Suddenly the slinky black dress Monica had slithered into ninety minutes ago, tightened in unflattering ways.

"Pleased to meet you," Samantha said, diverting her gaze to where Brad stood.

There was something about this woman. Something ...

Her name seemed familiar. Could she be the co-worker Brad referred to as Sam? He never mentioned she was a woman.

Monica suddenly knew why.

"She's about to become a bride," Margaret remarked. "Show her the ring, Samantha."

"It's lovely." Monica studied the solitaire diamond resting on the woman's finger. "When is the wedding?"

"In a few months," Samantha replied, her gaze searching the room.

"Congratulations. So you work with Brad?" Monica glanced at her husband. He stared back. Was that panic in his eyes?

"Yes, I do. Please excuse me," Samantha said quickly. "I need to find Jeff, my fiancé. The program is about to start."

"Of course." Monica smiled weakly and reached for her champagne flute.

Calm down. Brad would never cheat. There was a reason why he hadn't mentioned that Sam was a beautiful, young woman.

Monica raised the glass to her lips, but the flute slipped through her fingers, spilling into her lap.

"Oh dearie." Margaret leapt into action, patting Monica's lap with her napkin.

Before Monica could form her next thought, Brad was at her side. "Are you okay?" He placed the empty glass on the table.

"I'm fine. Let me go to the ladies' room to dry off," Monica said in a rush, her throat feeling as if someone had their hands wrapped around her neck. "I'll be right back."

Instead, she headed toward the parking garage, pausing long enough to yank off her stiletto sandals. She ignored the ache caused by the wire-like straps that had cut into her ankles.

"Monica, wait up." Brad trailed several feet behind, pleading for her to slow down.

She lengthened her gait, ignoring the garage's uneven pebbled floor poking the soles of her bare feet. *Why did I even purchase the stupid shoes?* she thought, now angry at her plan to accentuate her legs. Brad's eyes had popped when she first arrived, pleased at her sexy appearance. Now Monica wondered if other reasons had caused his surprised expression.

She should have worn sneakers. Sneakers were stable. High heels made you wobbly. That's how she felt—wobbly.

Monica's chest heaved, her breaths coming in short spurts as she kept up her rapid pace. She had wanted to look special for Brad. But who was she kidding? Sexy wasn't the look for a mother of four. Samantha made that obvious. Samantha Stewart. The person her husband had been referring to as "Sam" for the last four years. Her heart ached as she swiped at the tears streaming down her cheeks.

"Monica, for God's sake, stop!" Brad yelled.

She heard him gasping for air, getting closer. She scurried between the parked cars, her pulse pounding in her ears. She couldn't talk to him right now. Maybe never.

"Monica." His hand clasped her arm just as she reached their car.

Jerking out of his grasp, she dug in her purse for her keys. When she looked up, she hardly recognized Brad's face. Lines of tension creased his forehead, his mouth taut, as though awaiting a prison sentence.

"Some surprise, huh, Brad?"

Brad grabbed Monica by her shoulders and pulled her to face him. "Baby, what is going on?"

"You know what's going on. So don't play stupid. Let go of me."

"Not until you tell me what's wrong. What are you running from?"

"Not what. Who."

"I don't understand." Brad shifted his stance. He understood.

"I'm running from Sa-Samantha." The name caught in Monica's throat. "You call her Sam. I call her your mistress!"

"It's not what you think."

Tears filled Monica's eyes. *That's what they all say.* "Just get away from me!" she ground out.

Brad stepped closer and reached for her arm.

Pulling back, Monica swung her hand across his face, her palm stinging. "I said, get away!"

*

Get your copy of A Corner of Her Heart
today from any online retailer!

Join Claire's Mailing List

To get sneak peeks of upcoming stories
and to hear about giveaways Claire is sponsoring,
visit www.clairefadden.com.

Author Biography

When she's not playing with her grandchildren, Pennsylvania native Claire Yezbak Fadden is writing contemporary women's fiction. Her books feature strong women who overcome life's challenges, always putting their families first. She loves butterflies, ladybugs and holds a special affinity for carousel horses – quite possibly the result of watching "Mary Poppins" 13 times as a young girl.

The mother of three lives in Orange County, California with her husband, Nick and three spoiled dogs, Bandit, Jersey Girl and Bowie. Claire's work as an award-winning journalist, humor columnist and editor has appeared in 100 publications across the United States, Canada and Australia. Follow her @claireflaire, email her at claire@clairefadden.com or visit her at clairefadden.com.

Other Books by Claire Yezbak Fadden

A Corner of Her Heart
Maybe This Time
Ribbon of Light (coming summer 2018)

www.ingramcontent.com/pod-product-compliance
Lightning Source LLC
Chambersburg PA
CBHW061617170626
46811CB00001B/449